A Better Place

A BETTER PLACE

A Better Place

ALAN BEATON

COLUMBINE PRESS
Toronto 1998

This book is a work of fiction. The characters are fictitious,
as are the plot and events of the story. Any references to
actual persons and places are made only to set the story
in the context of its time and any further resemblance to real
persons, living or dead, is purely coincidental.

Cover photo: T.E. Zsolt
Design: Fortunato Aglialoro,
Falcom Design & Communications Inc.

Canadian Cataloguing in Publication Data

Beaton, Alan, 1958-
  A better place

ISBN 0-9683153-0-5

I. Title.

PS8553.E276B47 1998   C813'.54   C98-930936-3
PR9199.3.B32B47 1998

Printed in Canada

Distributed in Canada by
Hushion House
36 North Line Road
Toronto, ON M4B 3E2

The author wishes to acknowledge and thank those who offered encouragement, suggestions and practical help as the book was written. Particularly Tom Zsolt and Lynne Brown who were there from beginning to end.

Chapter One
CHAPTER ONE

O N A QUIET MONDAY MORNING in the spring of 1972, a haggard-looking Jesuit priest entered his home classroom. While the old man's tranquil entrances were never enough to bring the class to order, the hush that came over the room when the whiskey-torn cleric immediately announced, "Ed Flanagan is dead!" was deafening.

That room, which only seconds before had been abuzz with the mindless banter of adolescent boys, suddenly seemed to freeze. The old man's surprising announcement hit the assembled class with such impact that for a split second it was as though the world had actually stopped.

I had been listening intently as Ernie Fleming explained to me how he had persuaded Karen Corrigan to remove her sweater the previous Saturday night... "Yeah, I was sort of running my hands along the outside when all of a sudden she sits up, pulls her arms over her head, and two seconds later I'm looking at the two biggest..."

While on the outside I may have been nodding somewhat knowingly to Ernie's story, inside I was dying. I didn't know her all that well, but I had adored Karen Corrigan since the first moment I'd laid eyes on her. In every way that a fourteen-year-old can imagine, Karen was simply beautiful.

So the thought of her naked upper torso was the last thing I needed to deal with as I prepared myself for class that morning. Yet think about it I did. And even the fact that I was fairly certain Ernie was lying about the whole encounter did nothing to lessen my fascination with his story.

Whether it was true or not, just the idea of Ernie gleefully slobbering all over this treasured ground was at the time so incomprehensibly erotic, it was impossible to think about anything else. So I hung on his every word. At least I did until I started to feel that my enthusiasm for his story was beginning to show.

In an attempt to dampen my growing sense of excitement I clumsily placed a textbook on my lap and began focusing on some of the less racy conversations circulating throughout the room.

All around me the room was filled with the routine chatter of a typical Monday morning. Brian Sullivan was yammering on about some movie. Dave Ardil had taken his old man's car out for a joy ride. Mark Clarke had gotten drunk and thrown up in John Mulroy's basement - which was the only unusual news of the day. Usually it was John who threw up in Mark's basement.

Mark and John's shift in venue aside, all the stories making the rounds that morning were pretty standard fare. I'd heard them all before in one form or another. So had everyone else in the room. Yet focusing on them for a moment (along with the textbook I continued to press firmly into my lap) did lead my thoughts away from Karen Corrigan, and move them to less dangerous ground.

My crisis at least partially abated, I had turned my attention back to Ernie's story by the time Father Brisebois entered the room, but only to consider it from a personal point of view.

It was depressing to think of pug-faced Ernie Fleming enjoying the glories of second base, while I, John Rankin, or Hannibal as my friends call me, had never even kissed a girl.

The fact that I had never kissed a girl was easily my most closely guarded secret in 1972, and in order to maintain it I tried to appear unimpressed with Ernie's tale. Which I'm sure I did. Although I must admit that when he told me how Karen reached back around herself to unhook her own bra, I did have to drop another textbook on my lap.

Father Brisebois' announcement was so shocking that at first it didn't seem to have any meaning at all. Ed Flanagan is dead... Ed Flanagan is dead... What did he mean Ed Flanagan is dead?

"Father... Father, what are you saying, that Ed is really dead?" Paul Brown shot from the back of the room.

"How?" cried another

"Are you sure?"

"Why?"

As the room's silence quickly retreated in the face of a free-for-all of loud and panicked questions, Father Denis Brisebois, S. J., stood quietly at the front of the class, his diminutive body almost totally hidden by the oversized workstation that served as his desk.

Home room that year, while serving as a standard classroom for us, was actually a science lab for the school's older grades. Brisebois' desk spanned half the room and was elevated about eight inches above the floor. The purpose of this elevation was so that everyone could see the various experiments that would be conducted on the desk throughout the course of a day.

The effect of this elevation, in the case of our ninth grade French class, was to obstruct each student's view of our under-sized teacher. When the old man sat down, and due to his advanced years he sat down often, all we could see was his tiny head bouncing back and forth on his unseen shoulders. From our lowered seats, he appeared to be only a head, like some novelty item one might see bobbing around in the rear window of an automobile.

"Father, Ed was just here on Friday, he can't be dead," Mike McTeague cried out as tears began to flow down his acne covered face.

Watching as the old man prepared to address the many questions at hand, it seemed as though much of the class was sneaking peeks at me. As if the fact that Ed sat directly behind me had granted me some special insight into his death. However, soon after I started to return the vacant gaze of the boy sitting beside me, it became clear that it was not me garnering so much attention. It was Ed's empty desk.

Realizing this, I half turned around to look for myself. The desk was definitely empty.

Father Brisebois was an old skeleton of a man, obviously well beyond his teaching years. He was not simply a priest. He was a Jesuit priest, an important distinction in the church's hierarchy of pious standing. These were learned and scholarly men. Their training went well beyond the imprecision of theology. Their calling also demanded a thorough understanding of the secular world's intellectual agenda, including mathematics, the sciences, history and languages. It took no less than twelve years to become a Jesuit. It took no less than twelve years to become infallible.

The old Padre appeared quite shaken by the gravity of his early morning announcement and was ignoring the many questions we were firing his way. The fact that Brisebois was over the hill was not all that unusual at St Ignatius Loyola Secondary School, or any other Separate high school operating in Toronto. In those days Separate high schools received no government money for the bulk of their students. Consequently they were under constant financial pressure. So in order to alleviate some of its ongoing fiscal problems, each school kept a couple of old priests around to teach the less crucial subjects to some of the earlier grades. This arrangement kept these old guys amongst their own, as well as giving them something useful to do. At the same time, they cost the school no more than room and board and a small allowance.

In the case of Father Denis Brisebois, it was plain to see that the school had sent this guy to the well once too often. His build seemed frail, even set against his undersized head, while his face was so distorted by the ravages of alcohol, he seemed to be only a very cruel caricature of what he once might have been.

His nickname within the student body was "old piss tank". And while it was a name generally used only by the school's older and more cynical students, even the kindest of young men at St Ignatius realized that if Denis Brisebois had shown the same devotion to his faith as he had obviously shown to Jack Daniels, he would have been beatified long ago.

Even the man's robe was beyond salvage. This once proud and imposing garment, the very symbol of Brisebois' vocation, was so constantly covered in chalk, dandruff, and body sweat that it had become a desecration unto itself. It was amazingly dirty, and a standing insult to at least three of the five senses.

4

As Father Brisebois' self-imposed silence dragged on, it was becoming clear to all of us that no detailed explanation into the passing of Ed Flanagan would be forthcoming any time soon. The old man seemed to be the most lost soul in the room. His ancient lips were speckled with dry white saliva and pressed out slightly from his old carnival face. He stood rigidly, bowed at the waist, staring blankly into space - an old, used-up man with nothing left to say.

Finally, after ignoring us for what seemed like several minutes, Brisebois lurched forward and began walking towards the tearful Mike McTeague.

It was strange to see Mike crying. The whole class was stunned by the news about Ed, but it was only Mike who was openly sobbing. Which was odd because it never seemed he and Ed were all that close. Yet there was Mike, bawling like a baby. Perhaps he and Ed were better friends than I had thought? Or perhaps Mike was thinking about a past experience with death. Mike's mother had died earlier that year. Maybe a past experience with death caused one's tears to flow more easily?

Mike McTeague notwithstanding, I dare say not a single student in the room had ever seriously contemplated the notion of death or dying, in the first person. We all knew death was bad, but that was about all we knew. It was numbing to move so quickly from talk of joy rides and bra straps to suddenly confronting the grim reaper's dark handiwork. The news had come at us too quickly. Its immediate acceptance and comprehension was impossible. It would take a detailed explanation into the hows, whens, and whys of Ed's untimely passing before most of us could have any emotional response to it.

In a perfect world, the delicate task of coddling a room full of young teenagers at such a moment of crisis would be entrusted to a wise and respected authority figure. But alas, even at that age most of us realized the world was not a perfect place. And as Father Brisebois pulled up in front of Mike McTeague, it became clear that we would be receiving our guidance on this matter from old Father Piss Tank.

Upon reaching Mike McTeague's desk, Father Brisebois placed his yellowed left hand on Mike's shoulder, and gently squeezed as an offer of reassurance. Standing solemnly in the room's perfect silence Brisebois purposefully steadied himself, before reaching his free hand into the robe from hell and retrieving a handkerchief.

McTeague's reaction to this move must have been one of horror. I mean, nobody honestly believed Brisebois had washed or changed his clothes in all the years he'd been at the school; so one could only imagine what ancient crustaceans and carbuncles might be clinging to that hankie. Of course, given the crustaceans and carbuncles that had grown on McTeague's face since first semester, it was difficult to tell who would be getting the worse end of the deal.

In any case, as it turned out, our collective concern about the handkerchief was quite unfounded. The cloth in question was in fact both clean and perfectly folded. The letters D.S.B. were stylishly etched in blue calligraphy and set in the cloth's top right corner. The handkerchief appeared so white, set against the old man's badly discoloured hand, it seemed to have something of a hallowed quality about it. Not bad at all, considering most would have given odds that Father Denis Steven Brisebois would not have so much as a piece of Kleenex in his pocket that would be less than two years old.

Mike McTeague, having buried his richly contoured face into the palms of his hands, turned away from Father Brisebois' charitable offering, leaving the handkerchief unclaimed, resting patiently in its owner's shaky hand.

As young Mr McTeague became more despondent, his sobs deepened. Tears began pouring out through his fingers, running down the backs of his hands until they soaked into the sleeves of his school blazer. A blazer no different than the one we all wore that day. A blazer no different than the one Ed Flanagan would be buried in.

After concluding there was nothing more he could do for McTeague, the old priest carefully placed his handkerchief on Mike's desk and gave his quivering shoulder one final squeeze before continuing down the row, toward the back of the room. Circling around, Brisebois turned up the next aisle and began walking back to his desk. His left hand was clenched in a fist as it rested passively on his hip, while his right hand gently rubbed his bright red cheeks.

After reaching the front of the class the old cleric slowly turned to face us, and as he did he leaned against the front of his over-sized desk and to the astonishment of all, Brisebois then seemed to ascend to the top of the desk.

This was amazing. Given his small stature and advanced years, no one would have believed Brisebois could have gotten on top of that desk with a step-ladder, let alone slide up there with the deftness of a circus cat. It was also amazing because nobody had ever seen the old man up there before. It was so un-him. Yet, there he was - perched up high, calm and poised, like it was the most natural place in the world for him to be.

"Fellas, it seems as though our friend Ed picked up a virus on the weekend and tragically - it killed him... We don't know all the details, but apparently he complained of a headache yesterday afternoon, and by the time he got to the hospital, whatever it was had shut down his central nervous system. He left us early this morning... The doctors don't think he could have transmitted the virus to anybody at the school. However if your parents are concerned, Ed died at North Central Hospital and your family doctor can call there for further details... I'm terribly sorry to have to tell you this. It never should have happened to such a young man, but it did. I don't know why."

As the old man spoke, his words rang out with an unfamiliar clarity. In stark contrast to my first impression, Father Brisebois was remarkably in control of himself. The poise and purpose of his words was unmistakable. This was most unlike his normal bumbling, foot-in-the-mouth delivery, to which we had all grown accustomed. Today he was sharp, focused and to the point.

"It seems so unreal when something like this comes at you from out of nowhere. In Canada, the death of a young boy is such an aberration... it shakes you to the very core. It's just not an outcome we can rationalize... here, at home."

At this point Father Brisebois took a long pause. He seemed to know what he wanted to say but was reluctant to say it. Then in a very hushed tone he carried on.

"As you may or may not know, I spent thirty years of my life in the most forsaken corners of this world trying to make a difference in the lives of our most unfortunate... In Africa we fed the masses till the last crumb had turned to dust, then watched them die anyway... die in agony and despair, bloated and dehydrated, a sea of flies ensuring their death not be marked with even a moment of peace... It was the same in India... and Central America as well... men, women and children – all with good souls – dying, dying and dying... in the most unbearable ways imaginable. And so often all we could do was watch... I tell you all of this because I want you to understand that things like this do happen in this world. They happen every day... and are happening somewhere right now... We sit here in our cozy corner of the earth, and while we see these countries and the horrific plight of their people, it all seems too far removed for us to comprehend the extent of their anguish... and we become desensitized to their suffering... I must confess that even living in the middle of one of these man-made hells it was sometimes impossible to feel the full extent of the suffering."

Listening to Brisebois speak, it was difficult to understand where he was coming from in this heartfelt address. The information he was relating to us was news to everyone in the room and while it fully captured our attention it was tough to figure out how any of it related to Ed. Yet we listened to his every word, stunned and red-eyed, our young minds straining for greater comprehension.

"Eventually, surrounded by widespread and endless misery... even while your faith tells you not to, your head eventually starts to accept death as inevitable. As if the inevitability of a poor person's death... should somehow make it easier for them to bear... To have accepted human suffering as inevitable brought an element of doubt to my work, and I often fortified my resolve to carry on in a manner most unworthy of a priest. I drank, I drank heavily. I'm sure the scars I carry as a result of this are apparent to all of you... I can assure you they are a great source of shame to me."

Stopping for a moment as if to reflect on this, Brisebois took on the look of a man who had perhaps said too much already. But if this was the case he pondered it only briefly before removing his thick glasses and turning his thoughts back to the assembled class.

"It is with further shame I tell you that even as I worked eighteen hours a day to aid the sick and destitute of this world, I took considerable comfort in the knowledge that my time in these tragic locales was only temporary. No matter how long I stayed in any given spot, part of what got me through it was the knowledge that one day I could leave all of the misery behind me... And I sometimes felt like a coward for finding comfort in the thought that one day, I would abandon my flock... As time grows shorter for me, it is my greatest fear that in my selfish desire to escape to the comfort of Canada, I had, in my heart of hearts, undermined my life's work and betrayed the very people I had been sent to comfort... Yet I also understand that as a man I had done my best."

This was really getting confusing. What was he talking about - his life's work? Wasn't he a French teacher? No student in the school had ever known Brisebois as anything other than a failed cleric and damn poor French teacher. Could he really have spent thirty years working in hell? Thirty years as a front line missionary, was this possible? Did old Brisebois really have such a life prior to his recurring role as the resident freak of St Ignatius? How come nobody knew this about the old fossil?

"My desire to return to Canada was a selfish one, but not one based on fears of my own mortality - for in the years I spent away, I witnessed too much courage in the face of death to ever fear my own passing... My wish to return home was based simply on my desire to live life one more time as the Creator had intended... Free of the endless maladies that plague so much of this world... Free to accept health and happiness as a given... Free to accept opportunity without a second thought... Free to pursue higher achievement for no other reason than the satisfaction of having done so... Is this not the reality of life in our nation? Is this not the essence of what we as Canadians expect in our life? Is this not the implied promise to all fine Christian gentlemen?... Then one day the phone rings, and suddenly you realize that all the potential and promise that comes with being fourteen, and all the opportunity we accept without a second thought, and in fact the very life that God gives you, can end in a moment... without notice... and without recourse. How can this possibly be so, is this not simply too unfair for us to accept?... Yet, fair or not, accept it we must. Because you see fellas, while your youth, the great affluence of our society, and the individual wealth of your families, have skewed most of life's variables in your favour, as we have seen here today, none of these factors can completely immunize you from this... this most improbable of all outcomes."

As Brisebois spoke, the sound of teenage sniffling grew more and more prominent. Yet in spite of all the emotional distress filtering through the room, at no point did I look around to acknowledge any of it. Both Brisebois' words, and the cryptic silence through which they filtered, had so fully captured my attention that I couldn't seem to take my eyes off him.

"From the moment you pass from your mother, you are in *the game.* And whether you are from Toronto or Calcutta, whether you are young or old, whether you are rich or poor - it's the same game, and you are in it. And for all of the blessings that we so routinely accept, sometimes life will play no favours... I'm not sure if what I am saying makes any sense to you at this point in your lives. I know you sit in this room day after day certain that high school will never end. And that it all seems like some sort of ghastly internment that you must endure while you wait for your life to begin... But I assure you, one day you'll look back and realize that the years you spent at St Ignatius passed in the blink of an eye. And when you do, if you remember only one thing from your grade nine French class, let it be this... Your life has already begun. It is happening right now. It started the moment you were born and will continue on without interruption or time-out... until it ends. God did not give you life at a fixed point in time fifteen years ago... for life is not a one-time gift. The Lord gives you life every second of every day. It is an ongoing miracle... a gift from the Creator... to all of us."

Pausing for a moment as a distraught Ricky Chisholm tried to snort out a question, Brisebois calmly waited until Ricky's words became indistinguishable from his sobs, before attempting to lower the room's rapidly rising temperature.

"I see that many of you are getting more upset as we talk about this, and that is okay. But please, do not be afraid. We must never embrace life out of fear of losing it. We must embrace it for the joy it offers to others, and the hope that it creates in all of us. And gentlemen, never underestimate the value of hope.

"Hope will allow you to rise to any occasion, and go beyond the limits of anything you thought possible. And no matter what happens in your life... you will always have hope."

The word "hope" was still hanging in the air, as Ken Reid began shouting out from the back of the room.

"But Father, what does this have to do with Ed? I mean Ed's gone... Why? How can he just all of a sudden be gone. I don't understand...?"

Ken was the biggest and toughest guy in the class. But for the moment, he seemed anything but. Tears the size of golf balls were flowing freely down each of his cheeks, while his face, which twitched uncontrollably as he spoke, had turned a shade of red I had never seen before. He was not a pretty sight.

Father Brisebois, unshaken by Ken's startling appearance, calmly began to address his concerns.

"There are no answers regarding the whys of this matter, Ken. At least there are none that I am aware of. If you have faith, and you should, you can take comfort in the notion that Ed is now in a better place.

"I can also tell you that time, time itself has a miraculous healing quality about it... and will one day afford you a greater perspective of Ed's passing.

"However, neither time nor faith will ever answer why this happened. We are only human. We aren't meant to understand things that go beyond our limits of reason."

Listening carefully, it was surprising to see a priest, especially an old Jesuit priest, put himself on the same level as his students. I had never seen such a thing before. With a situation like death before him, a situation that cried out for some sort of religious clarification, Brisebois was telling us that he didn't understand what had happened to Ed Flanagan any better than the rest of us.

"As to the question, how can Ed just simply be gone? Well, let me tell you... When I was nine years old my twin brother died of pneumonia. That was seventy-two years ago. His name was Marcel... and I still miss him.

"The remains of my brother have been resting peacefully on the shores of New Brunswick for over seven decades, and still not one day has passed that I have not missed my brother Marcel. I speak with him daily, now it seems more than ever. I can visualize him very clearly... yet only as a young boy. While I see him as a boy, we converse as old men, and of course only in French.

"During all times of crisis in my life and sometimes just for the pleasure of being with him again, I have sought the company of my brother Marcel."

After mentioning his brother Father Brisebois' words became almost playful as he paused to offer his students an unsolicited suggestion.

"Now perhaps it would be best if we keep this bit of information about my relationship with my dead brother amongst ourselves. For I do not offer you these thoughts to add to the popular notion within the student body that I, old père Frenchie, or old Father Piss Tank as some might prefer, am a raving lunatic."

Then just as quickly as his words had become playful, they once again began to resonate with the same soothing tones as before.

"I offer these thoughts to you because I want you to understand something. Marcel Brisebois was a living, breathing, human being... and he was very important to those who knew him.

"The place in my life I hold for him is not reflective of a feeble mind... for I have visited his gravesite many times and am painfully aware that my brother is dead and buried.

"But I still hold a place within myself for him because the bond between us was not severed simply because Marcel died. His death could never break that bond. Cause you see fellas... his death did not nullify his existence.

"No matter the decades that have passed since his departure, Marcel Jacques Brisebois will always be my brother. His importance to me... shall never diminish.

"And the same is true of Ed Flanagan. Ed is still a very important person and, like my own brother, his death has not nullified his existence. This untimely ending to his life will not lessen the contributions he made to those who knew him.

"Yes it's true that Ed is no longer with us... but to my way of thinking one cannot simply say that he is gone... poof... gone... no longer relevant... gone... no longer significant... just gone... No, I do not believe this to be true.

"It is only in matters of science that it is not possible for something to exist, and not exist, at the same time. In matters of life and death, this fundamental principle of physics is not quite so clear. For while your friend Ed has surely left this earth, part of him... in ways you may not yet understand, will always remain with you."

Stopping for a few moments, Father Brisebois scanned the

room in order to make eye contact with each of his students. And it was only after he had assured himself that everybody was starting to settle down, that he began to wrap up his morning address.

"Tomorrow, we will have a service in the chapel to send Ed off, and for those of you who may not yet see the ongoing importance of Ed's time here, I believe you will see it tomorrow when you meet his family. It is in Ed's family that you will see how he will always be with us.

"In the meantime we will have to carry on about our day. No other classes will be held in this room this morning, so please feel free to take as much time as you need before moving on to your next class.

"If anybody needs me I'll be in my office all day. Talk to each other… be there for each other… and let's all be there for Ed's family tomorrow."

And with those final words, the Reverend Denis Stephen Brisebois placed his glasses back on his head, slipped down from his desk, and calmly ambled out of the room.

Watching the old man slip through the door, I resisted the impulse to call out to him after realizing I had no idea what I wanted to say. But soon after Brisebois was gone, I found myself wishing that someone had said something to stop him.

All of a sudden, so much of what the old man had said became difficult to understand. It was like the whole thing had come at us from a dream sequence. It had to have been a dream. None of this could really have happened. Ed Flanagan couldn't be dead. And that crumpled shell of humanity I had just seen hobbling out of the room certainly could not have been Brisebois.

What in the hell was going on here?

If that was Old Father Piss Tank, how did he get to be so smart all of a sudden? Father Piss Tank?… Old Père Frenchie. Geez, he even knew his nicknames. How in the hell could he have known about his nicknames? The man was deaf, dumb, and blind. So how could he have known what others called him? And how could he have known so much about what we were feeling, when half the time he didn't even know our names?

Looking around, I could see that while most of the major blubbering had subsided, I was not the only student in the room who was uncertain as to what we were supposed to do next.

Confusion reigned, though it was quiet confusion.

There was a bit of shuffling going on in the back of the class. It was almost inaudible at first. Metal chairs quietly sliding away from desks, followed by deferential tiptoeing, as a small handful of boys started to move towards the room's only exit. But most of us just sat there, still not quite ready to, as Father Brisebois put it, "carry on about our day".

I'm not sure how long I sat there contemplating what the old man had said, but I do know that it wasn't until one of my classmates said something to me that I looked up and noticed the room was half empty.

"You really looked like you were gonna lose it there. You okay... Hannibal, you okay?"

Looking up, I saw a red-eyed Norm Poole leaning over my desk. "You okay?"

"Me, ah sure,... yeah, I'm fine." I answered, surprised to hear I had looked on the verge of "losing it".

"Good, good,... how 'bout that Brisebois, I wouldn't have thought he'd know enough to come in out of the rain... Who 'da figured, uh? I'll see you outside," Norm responded, as he gave me a reassuring pat on the back before joining the line of boys exiting the room.

Watching him leave, I couldn't help but notice how dishevelled most of my classmates were as they began to disappear through the doorway. Never before had I seen such a universal violation of school standards. There were a couple of guys who wouldn't keep their ties in the strangulating position the school demanded, and were prepared to pay the price for their impertinence. The penalty for this crime was referred to as a JUG, a euphemism for Justice Under God, a ridiculous way of saying detention. But such cases were rare.

The dress code at St Ignatius was strictly enforced on all students while on school grounds and while in transit to or from the school. Enforcement was the key to compliance and one very rarely saw the code violated.

However, in the matter of the young men filing out of room 32 that day, the dress code violations were both flagrant and numerous. A wide array of dispirited shirt tails dangled lifelessly beneath the jacket lines of several blazers. A number of the barber-striped ties that accessorized the uniform were pulled down and twisted to the side, revealing unfastened top buttons on almost all the offenders. Dean Edwards and Paul Indos, renegades that they were, had actually removed their ties altogether.

In the great scheme of things, a dress code violation may not seem like much. But seeing my classmates leave the room in such disarray did serve as a further reminder that this was no ordinary day.

As the doorway began to clear, I found myself sitting alone in the classroom. In its empty state there was no evidence of what had taken place that morning, and just for a moment I allowed myself to be fooled into thinking that maybe none of it had happened. But, as I began to rise, not quite ready to leave the safety of my denial, my attention was inexplicably drawn to Mike McTeague's desk - and there it was, the handkerchief of the Reverend Denis Stephen Brisebois, S.J. This was no dream.

Father Brisebois, the drunk, the laughing stock. Wasn't it just last week he conjugated the verb "to be" in Latin? It was never a given that the old man could successfully conjugate any verb in French without some prompting from one of the smarter kids. But to actually conjugate a verb in the wrong language, this was something new, even for him. Yet there he was... "to be"...

> sum
> es
> est
> sumus
> estis
> sunt

When Mark Flynn respectfully pointed out that perhaps

> je suis
> tu es
> il est
> nous sommes
> vous êtes
> ils sont

would be more appropriate, he did so over a torrent of laughter from the rest of the class. The old man had simply waved his hands frantically in a futile attempt to halt the laughter, not seeming to grasp the nature of his linguistic error.

Ed Flanagan had laughed too, as hard as any one.

Was that really last week? Could that really have been Brisebois? Or was that the real Brisebois we met today? The man who knew so much about *the game*.

Picking up the pristine cloth, I studied it carefully and found that it was even nicer up close. Unfolding it, I ran my index finger across the blue embossed letters, D. S. B., as Normie Poole's words replayed in my head… "old Brisebois, who'da figured?"

Still studying the handkerchief, I couldn't tell why I was so impressed by the old man's address. It wasn't as if I could agree with, or fully understand much of what Brisebois had said. I had never previously contemplated what might constitute the nullification of one's existence. I was unable to quantify the value of something as intangible as hope. And I wasn't sure I could see the difference between Ed Flanagan no longer being here, and his being gone – "poof" – just simply gone. But I was willing to accept Father Brisebois' view of such notions on faith. Not just for the substance of his explanations, but also for the manner in which he delivered them.

For it seemed as though he had reached out to us with everything he had. He had not only risen to a level we had not seen before, he had raised us with him.

Refolding the handkerchief, I never had such a feeling in my life that God was watching me. A thought that actually scared me more than comforted me.

Stepping over two aisles, I gingerly placed Brisebois' handkerchief on Ed Flanagan's desk, before quietly turning towards the door. I'm not sure why I dropped the handkerchief on Ed's desk. I guess I thought maybe he was watching me as well.

The rest of that day I recall as being remarkably uneventful. Out in the hall most of the kids seemed to have regained their composure, even Mike McTeague and Ken Reid. Although Ken's head was still an extraordinary shade of red.

The remainder of our classes were spent listening to the rest of our teachers offer their personal regrets about Ed and, to an irritating degree, flog their own views of life and death. So much so that by fifth period everybody had heard quite enough about Ed Flanagan. No disrespect was intended in this attitude. It was just simply impossible to hear about Ed over and over again. We were Ed Flanaganed out, in just three hours.

By a small twist of fate, the teacher of our final class, history, was absent that day. As was the custom at St Ignatius, the school rector and roving supply teacher, Father Mancini, filled in. We were all aware that for this day we would be spared any further scholarly demands, but we were not prepared for Father Mancini's decision to leave us on our own, "for quiet reflection on the day's events." To be left unsupervised at St Ig's, this was unheard of.

And upon the moment of Mancini's solemn departure, the room instantly burst into the same raucous atmosphere as had prevailed in classroom 32 early that morning. Loud conversations regarding after-school plans, and scenarios for the coming weekend, broke out the second we were left on our own. There was the usual bitching about life at St Igs, and life in general for that matter. And I could even hear Ernie Fleming telling Andrew Zsolt about his date with Karen Corrigan. In its afternoon telling, Ernie boasted about how easily he had unhooked Karen's bra. (Which confirmed what I already suspected – Ernie's story was a lie.)

Regardless of what conversation any student was engaged in during the day's final period, conspicuously absent from our collective consciousness was the late Ed Flanagan. Not once, during our forty minutes of "quiet reflection", was Ed's name even mentioned. That day, which had started out like no other in our lives, was ending so remarkably like any other, it was tough to believe it was the same day.

Even that evening, as I discussed the day's news with my parents, we covered it during an episode of *Hogan's Heroes*. My parents were doing their best to show parental concern, but not so much that we actually turned off the television. And so Ed's passing was rehashed much the same way as the rest of the day's events - during commercials as well as the show's less critical moments. (I think it was the one in which Sergeant Schultz sells out the Third Reich for a handful of chocolate bars.)

As the day concluded, it was in the comfort of my bed that I made one final attempt to bring some sense to the day's events.

And I could not decide whether Ed's quick exit from our thoughts was indicative of a callous disregard for the sanctity of life, or if in fact it was testimony to the resilience of the human spirit - evidence of our great courage to carry on in the face of tragedy.

So many questions, so few answers. I knew that many hours of contemplation into the mysteries of life would be required before any sleep would come my way that night. And I was determined not to rest until the answers were clear.

However, in spite of my best intentions, long before I was able to solve any of the mysteries associated with life and death, my thoughts began drifting. For the previous few years almost all of my bedtime contemplations had been geared towards solving another kind of mystery. And as it turned out, this night was to be no different. And as I rocked myself to sleep the same way I did every night, my thoughts were both peaceful and sublime, for all of my thoughts were with the lovely Miss Corrigan... Karen Corrigan.

The next day, as promised, there was a service for Ed. At eleven o'clock sharp, Father Brisebois and the entire class assembled in the school chapel, along with Ed's parents, and his three younger brothers. It was a quiet scene, although the mood among the students was not quite as sombre as it had been the day before.

Ed's family sat in the front row, all huddled closely together. Mrs Flanagan and her remaining sons were crying, while Mr Flanagan tried to give comfort by extending his long arms around all of them.

Cecil Flanagan was a giant of a man and, to his wife and sons that were now clinging so closely to him, he was determined to be the rock his frightened family needed. At this moment of profound crisis, Mr Flanagan refused to bend to the agony of the moment.

Even as he hugged and patted his despondent family, not once throughout the entire service did his facial expression demonstratively change.

Yet, in spite of his best efforts, there were almost imperceptible flickers of anguish that did somehow escape his hardened exterior. They were tempered and brief, but were enough to expose the full depth of his sorrow.

It was a kind of sadness that neither I, nor any of my classmates could fully understand, but it spoke volumes to each of us about what was in the heart of this horribly wounded man.

Cecil Flanagan had surely loved his first born child.

Brisebois was right, Ed Flanagan would not soon be forgotten.

No one really listened that closely to Father Mancini's combination of sermon and eulogy. Those of us not held spellbound by the sight of Ed's family had become too preoccupied with his coffin to listen to anything Mancini had to say.

The chapel at St Igs was so small that the large box had to be wedged between the altar and the front pew. We were almost standing on top of poor Ed, or at least on top of his coffin. I, for one, hadn't expected to see a coffin at all. I don't know why. It's not like I had been expecting them to prop Ed up in his old desk and wheel him into the room. (Not that such a showing would have been any worse than the sight of that shiny brown box). When you've never been to a funeral, the coffin is such an eerie presence. It was awful to think that Ed was lying in there.

Once Mancini had finished tying Ed's death to God's grand design, or some such nonsense as that (Mancini knew why Ed was dead, he was dead because God wanted him dead - how comforting), Ed, his family, Father Brisebois, and the six classmates chosen to walk Ed that final mile, trundled out of the chapel and off to the graveyard.

And that, as they say, was that.

The following morning, Wednesday at 9:03, Father Brisebois made his usual mummified entrance into classroom 32 where, from behind his enormous desk, he carried on with his passionless mutilation of the ninth grade French curriculum. There were no reassuring looks, or words, as a preamble to the day's lesson. And no acknowledgement of what had happened just two days earlier. The old man simply walked over to the blackboard and for the umpteenth time that year, butchered the verb "to have"...

j'ai
tu as
il as
nous ai
vous as
ils as

Nobody wanted to ridicule Brisebois as before, but as Mark Flynn patiently corrected the old man not everyone was able to hold back their laughter.

Only forty-eight hours after being told one of our classmates had died, life was moving on. Amid the laughter Ed's desk was still empty. It just wasn't noticeably empty.

Less than a week later Ken Reid, perhaps in an attempt to help fade the image of his own performance that day, began referring to Ed Flanagan as "Dead Flanagan". It was a little skit he and Charlie Gorman would play out for small segments of the class.

"Hey Charlie, you remember Dead... oh, I mean Ed Flanagan, don't you?"

"Sure, I do Kenny... Dead... I mean Ed, was a good friend of mine."

Everybody howled with laughter, myself included, the first time I heard it. And Ken and Charlie continued their little drama on through the end of the school year.

By the time school broke for summer that year, Ed Flanagan was just a distant memory. He was, contrary to Father Brisebois' argument, gone, just simply gone. To us, he was anyway. The events of that apocalyptic Monday morning were never really mentioned again, and eventually faded from memory, much like the old man who had taken command.

Father Brisebois continued to roam the halls of St Ignatius, once again ignoring the snide wisecracks that shadowed his every move. And while I looked for it often, never once in his muddled gaze did I ever see a trace of recognition, or a hint of acknowledgement, confirming that we had shared anything special that day.

The old man died that very summer. He went in his sleep one night at a seminary in New Brunswick. I remember being saddened by the news, but took heart in the fact that at least he was in New Brunswick - where he could be with Marcel.

Given that I only knew Denis Stephen Brisebois for one hour of his life, I really don't know why his death mattered to me at all. But it did. It mattered a lot.

And for some reason, contrary to my former belief that the day Ed Flanagan died had passed like any other, as time moved on I came to realize that not only the event itself but also the old priest, and every student present that spring morning, had made an indelible impression on my life. It just took me a couple of decades to figure out why.

Chapter Two

CHAPTER TWO

*A*H, LIFE IN THE BIG CITY. *It was a humid Friday afternoon in late June. A dark Lexus 400 purred up Toronto's Don Valley Parkway en route to a suburban eatery, the car's driver eager to arrive at his destination. For it was Patio Time, the highlight of yet another uneventful week.*

It was a beautiful early summer's day. The city had finally reached full bloom and the picturesque riches of the Don River ravine fanned out proudly against an impressive blue sky. Though no doubt most commuters sped by oblivious to the roadside kaleidoscope.

The road travelled, much like life itself in 1993, offered no great ride. The Parkway was a twisting "freeway", running parallel to the city's Don River. It was marked with unexpected undulations and phantom dips. The road seemed to be graded more for drainage than drivability, and the lack of a continuous emergency lane, along with a scarcity of exits, and steep roadside embankments, combined to create a true feeling of confinement.

Of course none of the road's design or asphalt inconsistencies posed any problem for the sophisticated Lexus ECU engine. Its Formula One styled, computer monitored, double wishbone riding design, taxed the driving skills of its operator no further than the ability to drive a straight line. And with the soothing offerings of Don Henley flowing through its seven strategically placed speakers, patiently lamenting the end of our collective innocence, the Lexus deftly rolled on down the highway.

Sunk deeply into the soft leather of his perfectly contoured seat, Hannibal Rankin absorbed the insulation and protection of his $70,000 cruising machine. God, he loved that car. Almost every time he drove it, he had to marvel at its genius. And even the knowledge that he would probably have to surrender it back to the dealer within the next thirty days (sixty tops) did nothing to lessen the satisfaction he felt each time he took the wheel.

Pressing down on the accelerator, as he struggled to relight the cigarette he had butted out only moments before, Hannibal pondered the peculiarity of his mood. He had been feeling strange all day and it bothered him that he couldn't figure out why. These were troubled times for him to be sure, but overall it had been a reasonably uneventful day, and even week for that matter, so it was tough to comprehend why he should be feeling so uneasy today.

Sliding over towards a far-off exit ramp, Hannibal audibly sighed above the refrain blasting from the car's stereo. Biting down as the burnt foulness of tobacco clawed its way down his parched throat, he cursed himself, and the cigarette, before lowering his window and tossing it away (after forcing down one final drag). Never again, he thought as he watched the wilted butt tumble and somersault helplessly down the moving roadway behind him. Never again.

* * *

Pulling off the Parkway, and proceeding west towards the Genuine Deli, I began surfing the FM dial in search of distraction, when my eyes locked onto the car's analog clock and discovered the first settling aspect of my day. The time was 3:55. At least I was on schedule. And as I continued searching for an acceptable station, the flashing 3 5 5 of the clock brought me back to a moment, exactly three weeks earlier, when Jack Mac-Donald called me at home to ask, "What time is it, cousin?"

The question was one he'd asked a thousand times before, and was completely rhetorical. It had nothing to do with time as measured by either a clock or a calendar. It did however have a lot to do with having a drink. And when cousin Jack called on a sunny Friday afternoon the time was always the same. It was Patio Time.

This would be the fourth Friday in succession I had met Jack at the Genuine Deli, and on two of those occasions we had been joined by our mutual friend Bruce Thatcher.

As people who were self-employed, Jack and I were both free to begin these weekly gatherings anytime we wanted, but it was at my request that we held off until at least 4:00. (I held the line at 4:00 because I feared that going to a bar any earlier might further confirm my growing suspicion that I was actually more unemployed than self-employed). While Bruce, being a dedicated company man, would not arrive until sometime closer to 5:30 or 6:00, if he were free to show up at all.

Once gathered, the three of us would usually do a little reminiscing before putting our own spin on the various news and sporting events of the day. While these weekly meetings were for the most part routine and unexciting, given the abundance of time the current recession had freed up in my previously busy schedule, Patio Time was now the most anticipated part of my week.

Outdoor bars were a relatively new phenomenon in this city on the lake. Sometime in the early eighties a cash flow crisis convinced the municipal politicians who manage Toronto the Good that the purity of its citizens would not be compromised if they were extended the right to consume an alcoholic beverage at a place of business not enclosed by four walls and a roof. This remarkable breakthrough in bureaucratic thinking led to the issuance of several hundred patio-bar licenses, and up they sprang into the city's landscape.

A new frontier had been created. Outdoor summer havens, from where one could take on some sun while openly quaffing a cold one, were now ours to discover. And nobody recognized the appeal of such a place more than Jack.

Aside from being my cousin, Jack had also been my closest friend for my entire life. We had grown up together in the city's Beaches district, in a neighbourhood where he was the local hero. And while I'm sure that such heroes can be found in any neighbourhood where children exist, you'd never convince me that any of them could have held a candle to Jack MacDonald.

He was the kid that every other kid wanted to be. Even in my earliest memories Jack was always a step ahead of the pack and, though three years my senior, my cousin was always very careful to include me in almost everything he did. He took me everywhere he went, whether I was invited or not, and over time became not only my unquestioned mentor, but also the man who named me.

In 1957 my parents requested of our parish priest that he christen me John Michael Rankin. In 1966, after watching me win a Cub Scout "chicken fight" against a much larger boy, Jack renamed me Hannibal. A name he knew from his continuously inebriated father's weekly countdown of history's greatest military strategists. (While the only battle my uncle Alexander ever actually fought was trying to remember where he left the Scotch, a brief stint in the US military had somehow caused him to believe that he was a man who might easily be mistaken for General Douglas MacArthur.)

There was never anything so spectacular about my victory over Fatty Roachford that it should have warranted the assignment of a lifelong nickname. All I had done was sidestep a fast-charging, slow-thinking, pituitary case and allow his own momentum to send him toppling to the floor. Not exactly the kind of physical confrontation from which legends are born.

However, as fate would have it, Fatty and I were the last match of the evening and therefore the entire encounter had played out in front of the roomful of senior Scouts who were entering the gymnasium to replace us.

My besting of the largest boy in our troop had been witnessed by every big shot in my neighbourhood, including the biggest shot of all, cousin Jack.

It was on the way home that night Jack started calling me Hannibal. And while I didn't know it at the time, it was at that very moment my popular cousin rendered my given name obsolete. (To this day, even people who know me reasonably well are still caught off guard when someone calls me John.) It's not a bad nickname – at least it wasn't until a bunch of bastards in Hollywood made a movie called *The Silence of the Lambs*. After that I started getting the same look people named Adolf must get after being introduced.

Throughout most of the 1980's Jack was a broker for a downtown investment firm. It was a simple job. Buy low – sell high, make sure the clients make a little money. And his uncanny ability to attract people had made him the golden boy of Flynn and Gunn Investments. People simply liked Jack, and as such they practically lined up to have him handle their affairs.

In 1989 a client of his by the name of Michael Kilroy offered Jack the opportunity to manage, and one day own, the publishing company that had been Kilroy's life's work. And Jack, ready for a new challenge, accepted the man's offer and became the President of Good Word Publishing Inc., a small firm that catered to the religious community.

It was a position that Jack seemed to wear quite well. And why not? Not only had Jack worked hard, he had also throughout all of his life treated people extremely well. He deserved everything he had and probably more. In the eyes of all that knew him Jack was still a hero. He was respected and admired. A textbook model of success.

Driving past the Genuine Deli I turned into the parking lot of the run-down industrial complex located on its south side and in doing so caught sight of my cousin sitting at our usual table. Upon seeing him I immediately looked away and slumped down in my seat, ludicrously hoping this would prevent him from seeing me. Like my slumping down was in some way going to inhibit his ability to recognize my car - how's that for solid thinking?

Still, I did hope he hadn't noticed my choice of parking lots. For I knew, looking at Jack as he comfortably chatted away with Barb, our regular server, that his Mercedes would not be more than twenty yards from his present location. It didn't matter if it was double-parked, parked in a fire route, or merely blocking in some other car, it would not be more than twenty yards from his chosen point of entrance. I also knew that, no matter what parking infraction Jack might have committed in following this lifelong strategy, his car would neither be ticketed nor damaged during his stay at the Deli.

I, on the other hand, would endure the long walk back to the patio, and Jack's sarcastic cracks about our respective parking acumen, secure in the knowledge that the Lexus would attract every seagull, pigeon and crow within a half-mile radius. Such has been the status of my life in 1993.

After bringing the Lexus to a halt, and seeing just how far I had parked from my final destination, the uneasiness I'd been feeling all day began to grow. I hadn't realized when I chose this lot (a choice I felt compelled to make because the previous week some idiot had parked his car within ten feet of the Lexus) that it angled away from the restaurant the way it did. The result being, I was now positioned about three hundred yards away from where Jack was sitting.

Stepping out of the car and looking across the two parking lots I would now have to negotiate in order to reach the Deli, I couldn't believe what I had just done. I mean, not wanting someone to hit the car was one thing, but parking it in a different postal code to prevent this, sort of bordered on the insane.

What in the hell was I going to do now?

Looking away from the restaurant while I tried to formulate a plan that would allow me to get there without looking like a complete ass, I pushed away from the Lexus and began walking towards the dilapidated structures that were at least in the vicinity of my mis-parked car. It was a short walk, though given the circumstances not a very pleasant one. And after arriving at a spot from which I could easily survey the entire area, I wrapped my arm around a headless lamppost that stood at the side of a badly littered loading dock and latched on to it for support.

The buildings that comprised this once busy industrial mall were about twenty-five years old. They were an unimaginative combination of brick, mortar and concrete, that had been quickly slapped together in order to facilitate some function of the city's once bustling economy.

However, as evidenced by their crumbling outer faces, the purpose of these ghostly shells at this point in time, much like my reasons for staring at them, were virtually non-existent. Most of them had been vacant for a couple of years now, and were likely to remain unoccupied for several more. They were old, outdated relics which in less than three decades had outlived their usefulness. Nothing could save them now. They were too far gone, and it was only the expense of knocking them down that had saved them from the wrecking ball.

Growing weary under the heat of the afternoon sun, I closed my eyes before awkwardly leaning my head against the lamppost's grimy concrete surface. And it was while I was standing there that I started to get a sense of what had been bothering me all day.

The whole time I had been pondering this question I had assumed that the cause of my consternation was tied to the terrible financial whipping I had taken over the past three years, as well as the toll of having to deal each day with the many legal entanglements my downfall had caused. But as I stood there - tethered to a post in the middle of a vacant parking lot I had no business being in, I suddenly began to suspect that maybe this was not the case.

And I began to see that what was bothering me was not so much any regrets I might have about my recent past, but rather the fact that I was dealing with all of this at a time when I couldn't seem to do anything right. And I do mean anything. Hell, two weeks shy of my thirty-sixth birthday I couldn't even successfully park an automobile in the right goddamn lot.

Chapter Three

CHAPTER THREE

AFTER FINALLY UNLATCHING myself from the lamp-post I did eventually make my way to the patio of the Genuine Deli, but not before attempting to give purpose to my prolonged stay in the vacant lot by pacing off the width of one of its loading docks. I knew I shouldn't have done it, but this knowledge alone didn't seem to be enough to stop me. And before you could say "who's the biggest fucking nut in the world" there I was, arms stretched out beside me, tiptoeing through enough garbage to start a landfill, in order to ascertain that the dock was approximately ten feet wide. Or, about the same width as every other loading dock in the city.

Of course this pathetic ruse only made the long walk to the restaurant seem even longer, so long in fact that I wound up sprinting the last fifty yards. Dashing across the black asphalt, I didn't know if I was running towards the Deli, or away from my own stupidity, I only knew that I had to run. And it wasn't until I arrived at the restaurant steps that I felt even a slight sense of relief from myself.

Stepping up to the patio, I began to feel as though I had finally reached a safe harbour, taking a small measure of comfort in the knowledge that very soon now, the afternoon's intake of alcohol, and a long conversation with my oldest confidant, would gradually rescue me from my own feelings of inadequacy.

It was in the safety of this thought that I moved forward to join Jack, my spirits brightening further still as I noticed a large orange beverage (a double Screwdriver to be sure) sitting in front of my unoccupied chair. *Whoaaa baby, come to Papa.*

Crossing the patio under the day's brilliant sunlight, I returned the restaurant manager's friendly wave before shifting my attention to my cousin, and greeting him with all the enthusiasm I could summon.

"Hey, Jack, how's it going?" I called out while still several feet away from our table. "Hell of a day, huh?"

Having reached the safety of the patio I was feeling a bit better, but just to keep things moving in that direction I figured I'd try to control the conversation in order to keep it away from my activities of the past few minutes. At least until I had a drink or two.

"Ahh, things are pretty good, I can't complain," Jack answered, before looking towards the parking lot and adding, "What were you doing...?"

Sensing danger, I cut in right away, "So, is Thatch coming by?" I asked while sliding my chair out from the table.

"Yeah, but not till later on. He said he'd..."

Slipping into my chair as Jack filled me in on Bruce Thatcher's plans for the evening, I removed a crumpled pack of Players Light from my jacket and tossed them out onto the middle of the table.

"Anyway, he figured he'd be here sometime after seven," Jack finished up clumsily, as the cigarettes slid to a halt in front of him.

Listening to Jack speak, I noticed a slight thickness to his words which caused me to suspect that his current drink was not his first of the day. And when he picked up the package of cigarettes and quickly popped one in his mouth I became certain that it wasn't. Jack and I had both smoked, on and off, since we were teenagers. But Jack was strictly a social smoker, that is to say he smoked when he drank. I'd never seen him light up unless he had at least three or four drinks in him. But what the hell, he was of legal age, so, after handing him a lighter, I took a small sip from my drink and went on with the conversation.

"So, what's up, anything new to report?"

"No, everything's quiet," Jack responded, as he puffed away on his cigarette. "How 'bout yourself, your battles with the *pezzono-vante* go okay this week?"

"Yeah, they went just fine, thank you, and spare me the Don Corleone horseshit please," I answered passively as I took a larger swallow from my drink.

The *pezzonovante* he had referred to was the demeaning term for the bureaucrats and establishment types who periodically intruded on the lives of the characters in *The Godfather*. The same people my cousin knew were circling around me.

Looking up from my drink I could see Jack resting his head against his thumb and forefinger in the same manner as Mario Puzo's famous Mafioso Don, and before I could protest further, he carried on in his best Marlon Brando.

"I'm sorry for your troublez. I know how you feel, and I think maybe itz time we made dese foolz an offer dey can't refuze."

My cousin is a very talented fellow, and his ability to mimic other people is remarkable. He could do anybody - teachers, relatives, athletes, movie stars - you name it. He'd been doing it ever since we were kids (Brando was his favourite), yet as amusing as this was to see, on this occasion I could tell he was doing it not to amuse me, but because something was bothering him.

It was at this point that Barb arrived at the table and present-ed us with another round of drinks. Having not yet finished my first, it seemed her arrival was a little premature. But since Jack was already in need of another and because I didn't want any future service slowed on my account, I tipped my head back and downed the remainder of my drink.

Barb was probably about twenty-three or twenty-four and was truly stunning to look at. She stood about five foot five, had long blond hair, haunting green eyes, and a smile that could light up a city. On top of her gorgeous good looks, she had also been blessed with the kind of figure that most pin-up girls could only dream about.

"Hey guys, here we go… one Bloody Mary, one Screwdriver - both Deli Size," she greeted us before glancing at Jack and adding, "So, he finally decided to show up, eh?"

Offering her my empty glass, I accepted the one she handed me not understanding what she meant by this, and it wasn't until

31

she turned to Jack and resumed what seemed like an ongoing conversation that I realized my cousin had probably been there for quite some time.

Barb was dressed in a teal-coloured Genuine Deli golf shirt and long off-white shorts. The shorts were fastened around her waist by a thick black belt, and hung baggily down around the top of her knees. Her ensemble was completed by a new pair of low-cut Nikes, and white ankle socks that clung tightly to her well-tanned legs.

"So, are you guys here for the night, or are you going to break my heart and leave early like you did last week?" she inquired as she scooped up the ashtray from the far side of the table.

"Depends if the service is any better than it was last week," Jack answered with a smile.

"Then I shall respond obediently to your every request," Barb replied.

"Well, I must say I like the sound of that."

Listening in as Jack and Barb began to tease and taunt one other in their usual manner I stayed out of the conversation and took the opportunity to put a significant dent in my second drink. There are just some days when they sure go down easy.

However there did come a point when I noticed Barb playfully tap Jack on the head with her serving tray after he offered to "pinch hit" for some guy, if she agreed to buy him dinner at a nice restaurant first. And after watching her react in such a light hearted way to his little joke, I (now starting to feel the early manifestations of a nice little buzz) decided to join in on the fun by declaring that I too was available for pinch hitting duties. How's that for a razor sharp wit?

Of course at the time I said it I assumed my wedding band made it clear that I was only kidding, but the nervous smile Barb flashed after hearing the comment suddenly made me feel like maybe I'd struck a nerve or something. And when she picked up her tray and danced off to her next table without so much as another word I felt pretty certain that my comment had indeed offended her.

Waiting until she was out of range, I looked to Jack to see if he had some sort of an explanation for what had just happened.

"What?... What, did I say?" I protested as if Jack was some sort of bar room judge.

It was a little distressing to find that I was now offending people without really understanding how - especially Barb. She was as friendly a person as you'd ever want to meet and extremely fast on her feet when it came to deflecting the flirtatious banter she encountered each day. So how could I have offended her so easily?

Ignoring the urgency of my request for his insights, Jack simply rolled his eyes and shrugged. "I don't think it's anything to worry about Hannibal old buddy. Just enjoy your drink and relax."

"What do you mean, just enjoy my drink and relax? What just happened there? I didn't say anything," I continued on until I realized Jack wasn't really listening.

"Hannibal," Jack started before reaching for another cigarette, "How is it that someone as smart as you is always the last person in the world to figure out what the fuck is going on?"

"I'm the what?" I asked nervously, like I was about to become the butt of some practical joke.

"You heard me, ever since we were kids... Oh, never mind. But it's so obvious. Haven't you noticed that our little pal Barb has a crush on you?" Jack explained, as if telling me something that was common knowledge. "Who do you think I was offering to pinch hit for?"

"She what... Barb? You were gonna pinch hit for...? - Get the fuck out of here," I bumbled while reaching for a cigarette myself.

"No, I'm not kidding, I kind of thought so last week, but I got here early today and she starting asking about you the moment I arrived. And believe me, if you gave the word, well, she'd be into it," Jack stated matter-of-factly, before waving his drink at the parking lot behind me and adding with a laugh, "And for chrissakes, looking at where you parked your car, I'm sure nobody would notice if you just strolled her over there."

Listening to Jack, I blanched a bit at his reference to my mis-parked car, before considering the news he was relaying to me. Barbara Sutherland, - lovely, beautiful Barb had a crush on me? Why?

It wasn't that something like this had never happened before. In fact there was a time in my life, about a decade ago, when this kind of thing happened fairly often. But it had certainly been a long time since anyone other than my wife had declared affection

33

for me and as I sat there thinking about it I realized that the only other time it had happened in recent memory, the declarer… had been a guy.

"Whistle her over to my car? You're a sick man, Jack," I protested mildly, feeling flattered but trying to appear unconvinced and unconcerned by this surprising bit of news.

"Well, I can only tell you what she told me. Anyway, as nice as Barb is, if I was married to your wife, I suppose I wouldn't be tempted either," Jack concluded, as if he shared my nonchalant view of Barb's possible interest.

Then, while still fixing his gaze on the vacant lot behind me, Jack suddenly switched gears and inquired curiously, "By the way, what were you doing over there earlier, have you got something goin'?"

Listening to the question, a question I suppose I knew was going to come up sometime, I fired up the cigarette I had been holding, while I tried to figure out an answer.

Beyond the curiosity in Jack's words was a discernible measure of hopefulness as well. He knew the last couple of years hadn't been my best and looking at him as he waited for my reply I could tell he was hoping that maybe I had pulled a rabbit out of my hat. That maybe, just maybe, I had put together some deal that would require me to resurrect one of my former companies and reclaim some of the ground I had lost in recent times.

It was this element of hope that was the troubling part of my cousin's question. How was I supposed to explain to a concerned party such as Jack the reasons behind my measuring a loading dock I never had any intention of using and not expect him to become even more worried about me? How could I explain to him in thirty words or less something that might take a competent doctor several years to explain to me?

Drawing weakly on the cigarette, I inhaled slowly as I pondered the question, until this prolonged drag trailed off into an interminable silence. What to say? What to say? What to say? I couldn't seem to find any kind of answer, and it wasn't until Jack reposed his question that one finally poured out of me.

"Have I got something going?… No, no, just losing my mind," I replied obliquely, as I turned to watch Barb drop off a couple of drinks at the table beside us.

Chapter Four

CHAPTER FOUR

BY THE TIME SIX O'CLOCK rolled by the patio at the Genuine Deli was standing room only. Over the previous ninety minutes the place had swelled to capacity and beyond, to the point where there was now a small line-up amassing at the short stairway behind me. And all around us tables full of consuming patrons escaped to the weekend with an audible passion.

Sitting amid the clatter I tried to feign interest through the moderate haze of my fourth double vodka as Jack restated his view on whatever it was we were talking about. But inside my head I was a thousand miles away, privately pondering the significance of a couple of unrelated matters.

The first was Jack himself - something was definitely up with him. As the afternoon had worn on the conversation between us had become more strained than I could ever remember it being. Even when we switched to topics we had been discussing all our lives - like the Toronto Maple Leafs, or the Blue Jays, or politics, or women, or music or anything else we tried - all of it led from one dead-end to another. And I could tell that he was growing more and more uncomfortable with the silence that accompanied each conversational impasse.

The other was Barb, and why I kept watching her from

beneath the safety of my dark glasses. She had dropped by a number of times throughout the course of the afternoon, sometimes to deliver drinks, sometimes just to see what we were up to, and each time she did I found myself becoming more and more distracted by her.

It was a distraction that was tough to define. It wasn't that I wanted anything to happen between us. I really didn't. My wife had been the only woman in my life for almost eight years, and regardless of whether what Jack told me about Barb was true or not, I didn't really care. I loved my wife, and couldn't see myself betraying her with another woman.

But there was something about our young waitress that had me monitoring her every move, and while I couldn't quite figure out what it was, I knew I wasn't imagining it either. It was like her possibly having feelings for me had suddenly given her some kind of a hold over me, and I couldn't understand why.

"So, did Caroline and the kids get off to the cottage okay?"

"Hmm?"

"Caroline and the kids, did they get away okay?"

Looking over at Jack and hearing that we were once again moving on to new territory, I took a second to refocus my thoughts before considering his question.

"Yeah, at about noon," I answered, as I began fidgeting with my tie.

"How long are they gonna be up there?"

"About three weeks, I'm heading up on Tuesday," I replied with forced casualness, unable or unwilling to mention that I had sold the cottage over a month ago and that my family's current visit would end when I handed over the keys to the new owner.

"Good, that should be a great trip for you guys," Jack responded optimistically before I cut him off.

"Yeah, it should really be one to remember," I answered quietly, the day's liquor trivializing the deep regret I felt about having to sell my family's summer home.

Accepting my answer with a pleasant tip of his glass, my cousin then slipped back into his chair and hopefully suggested, "Well then, let's make a night of it. Thatch should be here in about an hour, so what the hell, huh?"

Reaching for the package of cigarettes we had ordered with

our previous round of drinks, I let Jack's words bounce around a bit before responding. "Let's make a night of it."… "So what the hell, huh?" The implication couldn't have been more clear. *We've got nothing better to do in this whole wide world, so let's just sit back and get pissed.*

But even after considering the implications of Jack's suggestion I still couldn't come up with a reason to resist the invitation. So, after unwrapping the cellophane from the small blue and white cigarette package I offered three simple words of consent, "What the hell."

It wasn't a great reason for staying, but it was the one that fit.

Having agreed on a course of action (or inaction) for the night, the commitment to remain together at the Deli seemed to soothe much of the edginess that had prevailed earlier in the afternoon. Now that each of us was assured that our time together was not going to end abruptly, Jack and I were able to unburden ourselves from the trappings of forced conversation, which allowed a more comfortable pace and rhythm to set in at the table. There were still periods of silence between us, but as they occurred each of us was able to lean back and more comfortably ride them out under the early evening's tranquil sky.

We retraced a couple of the inconsequential topics we had fumbled through earlier and while we both seemed to be avoiding any kind of serious dialogue, as the time passed, other than the fact that I occasionally caught myself studying Barb like the answer to some great mystery was written across the back of her ass, a discernible feeling of normalcy did set in at our table.

"So I guess you've got a birthday coming up, what's that make you thirty-seven?… Thirty-eight?" Jack asked, perfectly aware that I would be thirty-six on the fourteenth of July.

"You better hope not, that'd make you forty-one."

"Ouch, I guess it would, wouldn't it? Well let's just say you're twenty-nine then, no point in rushing these things."

"That's okay by me, but I gotta tell ya, just the other day I caught myself admiring a minivan, so I've got a feeling that my twenties are long gone."

"Well, you do have three kids Hannibal, so you had to know that a minivan was comin'."

"Never!" I declared earnestly, as if taking an oath.

I don't know why I had always been so intent on avoiding the world of minivan drivers. Not only was I a primary candidate for one, but half the people I knew had 'em, and loved 'em. Yet I held them in about the same regard as a bad case of the pox - though I had never driven one.

"Thirty-six. You know it doesn't really bother me," I started out, before stopping to confess. "We'll maybe it bothers me a little… but I guess there's not much point in complaining to you about it."

Jack would be thirty-nine on Christmas Day, and if I were to be objective about it I'd have to say he looked his age.

"I remember turning thirty really bothered me. No reason for it, it just did. So I wouldn't worry about it too much, everyone has a year or two that gets to them a little bit."

Jack paused for a second and before I could jump in, he added, "Even Nana, remember a couple of months ago at Nana's birthday party? Well I walk up to her and I ask how it feels to be ninety-two. And she looks at me and says she doesn't know. She never knew any one that old to compare it with, but she certainly thought it sounded old. And I'm thinking to myself, Christ Nana, you've always been old, haven't you? Turning ninety-two can't be that big a shock, I mean, you just spent a whole year being ninety-one. But then it dawns on me, in her head she's still a young girl. Just like you and I still feel like we're in our twenties, so does Nana. So does everyone I guess. Nobody actually believes they're as old as the calendar says they are. But the calendar doesn't lie. Look at me, I look thirty nine, don't I?"

When he was thinking straight, and he usually was, Jack had this way of framing everything he addressed and making it universal. In his mind few things were unique, everyone more or less thought and felt the same about most things - even age.

"I suppose that's true."

"It is. So if having a birthday is bugging ya, you should just throw yourself a big bash."

"I don't think so."

"You should? Have a big one. Christ, everyone we know could use one right about now. So let's have a party – we'll even invite Oprah," Jack added with a grin, his reference to Oprah inspired by a recurring dream he knew I'd been having.

"Yeah, well I'm not up for a party this year… and even if I were I sure as hell wouldn't be inviting Oprah. Besides, I'm not really sure I deserve one… I've just been doing the weirdest things lately."

"Oh yeah, like what?" my cousin asked as he waved at Barb to bring us another round.

"I dunno, like last Tuesday, I was just sitting around, typical day, nothing to do, so I decided to go out on the front step and have a smoke. And while I'm sitting out there, the three boys from next door come running out of their garage, hop on their bikes, and go peeling off up the street. But the youngest kid, I don't know what his name is, only gets to the front of the house, before he jumps off his bike and starts calling out to his brothers for help."

"Right."

"Well, of course they don't even turn around. They just keep racing up the street and around the corner. So after his brothers are out of sight this kid starts pushing his bike back up the driveway, and just around the time he starts crying I notice that the little fella has a flat tire."

"Okay."

"Now, the boy is probably only about eight or nine, and as he disappears into his garage I figure he's crying because he doesn't know how to change his tire. So I start thinking to myself, come on now, get up and help the kid out. I mean, he's my neighbour, and I certainly have the time, right? So I get out of my chair and start heading over, but before I get there, I stop just to do a quick mental review on tire changing. You remember those old red CCM's that we used to ride? We must have changed the tires on them a hundred different times, right?"

"Sure, at least."

"So now I'm standing on my neighbour's lawn trying to remember… loosen the back wheel, remove the chain, take off the tire, grab a dull knife and work out the inner tube, submerge the inner tube in a bucket of water and infl…" I rambled on until Jack mercifully stopped me.

"Hannibal, I know the drill. I'm the one that taught you how to change a tire, remember?"

"Yeah right, that's true, okay, so anyway, now that I've got it clear in my head how to change a tire, I start looking at the kid's bike and it didn't take long to realize that this thing didn't look anything like my old bike. First of all it was orange, which I didn't really like, but I figure, okay, so it's orange, I can get by that. The next thing I notice is that even though it was this really sleek little number, it had tires on it that had to be the width of my hand... almost like mags, you know... but I'm still thinking I can handle this. I mean I'm a grown man, right? Until I look really closely and I see that this bike must have four or five hundred gears on it."

"The bike had four or five hundred gears, Hannibal?" Jack inquired dubiously.

"Okay, let's say twenty-five. Either way, the point is, in as short a time as it has taken me to cross my front lawn I've managed to convince myself that this kid's bicycle could... I dunno... fly or something. And I start thinking, hey, what if I can't do this? I mean I haven't changed a tire since the late sixties, maybe things are different now. What do I know? Maybe this kid was in his garage looking for some 'Inflato Tire In A Can' shit or something like that. You know, some new product he'd simply attach to the tire, press a button – and presto... he'd have an instantly repaired tire.

"And then all of a sudden I picture myself standing in front of this kid with a rusty old bucket in one hand, and an air pump in the other, explaining to him how when I was a boy I got a quarter a week for allowance, and that chocolate bars were a nickel back then. And the kid would just be looking at me like I was some thousand-year-old dinosaur with bad breath and spit coming out of my mouth. You know, the way we used to think of old man Watson. So I thought, hey, I don't think I can handle this. So ya know what I did?"

"No, what?"

"I went inside and had a nap. Can you believe that? After losing an uncontested battle of wits with a child's bicycle tire I needed a nap." I concluded with a defensive laugh.

"Hey come on, that's no big deal. So you didn't change the tire, who cares?" Jack answered kindly, before breaking off as Barb suddenly appeared beside him.

"Yeah, I know but..."

"Sorry about the delay, but the bar is just swamped. One Caesar, one Blue Light. You guys having a good time?"

Barb, I'd forgotten all about her. She looked quite different than the last time she'd dropped by. Her long hair was now tied back, and a drop in the early evening temperature had caused her to put on a company sweatshirt. Though neither this change in appearance, nor my bewilderment over why I refused to confront the bicycle tire, did anything to shift even a small portion of my attention away from her.

Over the course of the afternoon, I had continued to monitor her surreptitiously as she tended to her duties around the patio. Which was probably ill advised enough on its own, especially since more often than not Barb had caught me watching her. However the impropriety of these furtive glances paled in comparison to the increasing level of obnoxiousness I had displayed each time she stopped at our table... including twice when I actually referred to her as "Babe" and the last time when I told her, and I said it while trying to impersonate the man, that I had better switch from Screwdrivers to beer because "if I have any more orange juice I'm gonna start talking like Bing Crosby." To which Barb merely smiled politely before asking, "Bing Who?"

It was after the crack about Bing I began to realize that the reason I was acting like such an ass around Barb was because after hearing that she might possibly like me, I felt a certain obligation to act in a way that would justify her feelings. Otherwise she might stop liking me... which I didn't want to happen. It didn't make a whole lot of sense, but just because I didn't want her liking me in the first place, didn't mean it wouldn't bother me if she were to suddenly stop.

Having finally figured this out, I had been looking forward to her return so that I might do a little damage control. Now that I understood why I had been acting like such a fool I had decided that the easiest way to stop this sophomoric behaviour would be to simply keep my mouth shut each time Barb stopped by. What could be easier than that? So, after graciously accepting the beer she had brought me, I sat back and privately committed myself to remaining perfectly silent during her stay at the table.

"We're having a great time, how 'bout you?" Jack replied in a slightly slurred though friendly manner.

"Not too bad, except, honestly, nobody tips anymore. Ten percent is the most you ever get, 'cept for you guys, of course."

As Barb and Jack began to chat, I was at ease within my self-imposed silence and felt no compulsion at all to join in on their conversation.

"Oh well, sign of the times I guess," Jack replied before looking over at me and adding, "Listen Barb, maybe you could help us out here."

"I'll do my best."

Jack leaned back in his chair to create a comfortable conversational distance between himself and our attentive young waitress.

"My ugly friend here has a birthday coming up and he's a little uptight about it, so I thought you might have some words of wisdom that could help him out."

While listening to Jack, Barb fixed her enchanting green eyes on me before responding with a smile, "I thought he was a little off today. Well, let's see now, just how old is he going to be?" she replied as she casually placed her hand on my shoulder to help support herself.

"Twenty-nine!" Jack declared, his eyes moving directly to mine to see if I would contradict him.

"Twenty-nine, eh, well I figured he was about twenty-seven, so obviously he's looking just fine," Barb playfully squeezed my shoulder, adding, "Feels fine too."

Looking up at Barb, I thought I should chime in and tell her that Jack was just bullshitting, not only about my age, but also about my giving a damn about it. But before I could she just continued on.

"So what's the problem then?"

"Nothing, he just feels like he's getting old that's all."

"Oh, that's crazy."

Having been silenced, and perhaps for the better, for it certainly erased the possibility of my calling Barb "Babe" again, I decided to continue on with my plan, and let Barb and Jack sort this one out on their own. I didn't really care what they talked about. So long as I was no longer trying to act like the captain of the high school football team in front of Barb, none of what she and Jack talked about mattered to me. I was back in control.

However, as Barb finished expressing her view on my "twenty-ninth" birthday by suggesting, "So don't worry about turning twenty-nine Hannibal, I'm going to be twenty in August and it isn't bothering me," she punctuated her message by sliding her hand off my shoulder and running it down the length of my upper arm. And as it came to rest on my bicep I found myself flexing the muscle so fucking hard it's amazing the neck of the beer bottle I was holding didn't snap off in my hand. So much for being back in control.

After delivering these words of advice, Barb then dutifully shuffled off to the bar, leaving me and my flexed bicep to work out my psychological shortcomings on our own.

Watching her leave I slowly began to relax my arm, while deliberately avoiding Jack's heavy stare. I wasn't sure if Barb had noticed how purposefully I had hardened my arm for her, but I felt pretty damn certain that Jack had seen what I had done.

Reaching for the cigarettes, I continued to evade his eye, and it wasn't until I stood up to make my first embarrassed step towards the restrooms that I finally looked at my cousin and made the following request.

"Don't say a word, not one word. Not now… and not when I get back."

Chapter Five

CHAPTER FIVE

Upon RETURNING TO THE PATIO I could see two menus sitting side by side on our table, however Jack had vacated the area. He was standing in the back corner talking to three guys who looked like they'd just stepped off a golf course.

Walking clumsily across the patio I noticed that their conversation more resembled a sermon, with my cousin at the pulpit, than a four-way dialogue. But it wasn't until I sat down, and saw the level of animation in Jack's face, that I realized what was going on. I had seen that look a million times before. Jack was telling these guys a joke.

Sitting down, I focused in on my performing cousin and began trying to sort out which of his many jokes and stories he had selected for his captivated trio. But before I got too far into my observations Jack turned his head to one side, as if addressing an invisible person standing beside him, and delivered the punch line.

"See, I told ya, ya fucked a penguin."

As soon as he said it, the three men burst into laughter, and taking this as his cue to return to our table, my cousin bid them adieu with a patented half grin and a casual wave.

Watching him as he neared our table, I had to smile a little myself. I'd never heard the penguin joke before, but I knew that few people could tell a story like Jack. And it was always fun to watch him work a crowd.

Slipping into the chair beside me, Jack's return was very low-key. Which left it up to me to find out why he'd stepped across the bar.

"Who were those guys?" I asked after allowing Jack a moment to peruse the menu.

"I don't really know. The heavy guy remembered me from some mutual fund seminar I gave a few years ago at Flynn & Gunn. He called me over. They're all doctors, believe it or not, and as you know, in my business, there's gold in those medical types."

Listening to Jack's words, they simply didn't ring true.

"Jack you're a publishing mogul now, how are a couple of fat doctors gonna help you?"

"Oh yeah, well you know the old saying cousin, old habits die hard. Cheers," he said, not really looking at me.

"Cheers."

The culinary offerings of the Deli were a mix of old restaurant standards combined with several trendier items. There were of course soups, sandwiches, burgers, and chicken wings for your basic meat and potato types. There were also fajitas, nachos, noodle salads, and a vast array of seafood pasta dishes for your more adventurous types. Such attempts at creative cuisine were wasted on Jack and myself. Then again, menus were wasted on Jack and myself. We both ordered burger platters and another drink.

Not long after placing our food order, I glanced down at my watch and took note of the time. It was 8:30 p.m.

"What time did you say Bruce would be coming by?"

"He said anytime after seven," Jack responded as he checked the time himself. "Huh, he must have got tied up somewhere."

"Ahhh, no big deal, he'll get here when he gets here. You can never tell with Thatch, he may not be able to find the right socks, or something like that," I answered in reference to Bruce's annoyingly fastidious dressing habits.

"Yeah really, or maybe he just decided to re-floss a few times before leaving the house," Jack stated with a laugh, before catching himself and quietly adding, "Ahh, poor Bruce."

"Poor Bruce, what do you mean poor Bruce?" I started to ask as I caught sight of Barb coming towards us.

Jack ignored my question, opting instead to greet Barb as she pulled up beside him. "Whoa, slow down Barb. What's the rush?"

"Oh, I'm just in a hurry to see you two," she beamed as she placed three thin shooter glasses on the table. "And these are for us, courtesy of those three guys over there," she added, pointing at Jack's doctor friends.

"B-52's! Who in the hell still drinks these things," I protested in what I assume was another adolescent attempt to somehow impress Barb.

"Sorry, but they were very specific about what to bring you."

"Easy Hannibal," Jack instructed. "Those guys don't know it yet, but they'll soon be my three newest clients."

Then, peering over my shoulder he lifted his glass to toast the doctors, before downing their syrupy gift.

With Barb and I watching, Jack then let out a satisfied gasp while nodding approvingly. It was as if he were saying, "Thanks guys, that really hit the spot", which was surprising.

I knew Jack didn't like B-52's, so I couldn't figure out why he was being so gracious. His actions went beyond politeness. Jack was selling these guys. But what was he selling them? What would three doctors need with a bunch of religious literature? Judging by the joke he had told them, these guys were not holy rollers. What did he mean by his three newest clients?

Turning my attention to Barb I could that see she was waiting for me to join her in the downing of the remaining shooters. So, after casually clinking my glass with hers, I quickly drained it, before looking at Barb and watching as she tipped back the creamy contents of her glass.

Though having reverted to my no-talking strategy after my stupid comment about the B-52's, I was definitely staring at Barb again. And this time my gentlemanly silence did not seem to grant me the manners to stop focusing on the thick nipple imprint that pressed out through the heavy material of her sweatshirt.

Having drained her glass, Barb then contentedly ran her tongue along her upper lip to wipe the drink's residue, before flashing her trademark smile and declaring, "Hmmmm, those have got to be my favourite drink of all time, I could drink them all night."

After hearing the comment, it was only because she was looking straight at me that I felt any inclination to offer a response. But because I wasn't sure I might not answer her by saying something asinine, like, "I think I might enjoy just watching you drink them all night - Babe", I decided that remaining resolutely silent was still my wisest course of action.

"Barb," Jack started up, "next chance you get, send them a round of whatever it is they're having. And if they should send us a second round, no matter what they say make mine a Chivas."

"Right, that's two spritzers and a Tom Collins for them, and a Chivas for you if they respond - got it. B-52 okay for you Hannibal,… if they send one over?"

Of all the things I wasn't sure of at this point in the day, the one thing I did know was that I didn't want another B-52. However, I could also tell by the look on Barb's face that she was anxious to recruit me as a new supporter of her favourite drink, and would feel quite validated if I were to accept this offer of confederacy. Still, I didn't really think I could stomach another, and it definitely was time to start squashing any nuances of courtship I may have perpetuated throughout the day, so, the answer was an obvious one.

But just as I was about to tell her to make mine a Chivas as well, the words, "A B-52 would be just great, Babe," suddenly popped out of my mouth. (Aren't there just days when you could just shoot yourself ?)

"Spritzers and a Collins," Jack snorted derisively, "perfect."

"Who are those guys Jack?" Barb asked as she finished writing something on her order pad. "The one in the glasses seems really creepy. And I can't go near their table without each of them calling the other doctor at least twice - like I'm suppose to care."

"Don't sweat it my dear, they're harmless, and don't worry about all their 'doctor talk'- just means they're probably dentists."

"Yeah, okay, but who are they?" she persisted.

"Them? They're, now if I tell you, you have to promise to keep it to yourself, okay?"

"Okay."

"Promise?"

"I promise." She leaned in very close to him.

"They're money in the bank, gorgeous," Jack proudly announced, his face a mask of uncontested happiness.

After hearing the answer Barb just shook her head before leaving to continue on with her evening's duties.

Watching her depart it was obvious that our young waitress didn't understand that, to his way of thinking, Jack had told her the God's truth. He had told her everything he knew and everything he needed to know about the gentlemen she had asked about.

However just because Barb didn't understand Jack's answer didn't mean that any of its meaning was lost on me. After watching her shapely backside disappear into the restaurant, I quickly turned my attention to Jack.

"What the hell are you talking about, money in the bank? What's going on with you?"

Jack, obviously caught off guard by my sudden inquiry, slowly slid back into his oversized lounger and I watched as a deeply reflective look came over him.

"Hannibal…" He paused. His body was now pressed squarely against the back of his chair and drawing in a deep breath he turned his face directly up to the sky, before slowly exhaling into the night air. Lowering his head to face me, he continued. "When I called you here a few weeks ago, I wanted to talk to you about a couple of things…" Weakly his words trailed off into silence. Again looking up and pausing, Jack struggled once more to take in some air, and this time when he did, I noticed his lower lip was starting to quiver. Watching him carefully I felt a horrible queasiness in my stomach as a look of utter sadness and torment continued to spread across my cousin's face. *Oh God, what's going on here?*

"Jack, Jack… what is it?"

I asked the question as calmly as possible, trying to help Jack snap out of the morose mood he was sliding into.

Come on Jack, please snap out of it.

I was still waiting for him to respond when the tension of the moment was defused as a young Oriental kid arrived with our food.

"Okay, two burger platters and your drinks are on the way.

Can I get you anything else? Mustard, ketchup, anything?

"No that's fine, thanks," I answered, looking directly at Jack.

"Enjoy."

The change of conversational pace brought on by the timely delivery of our dinner order was just the reprieve Jack needed to collect himself and begin again.

"Ah, I don't know what to say Hannibal, everything is just… I've made a mess out of everything and I just don't know what to do."

"What do you mean, you've made a mess out of everything? What are you talking about? Is it the company? Is your company in trouble?"

I don't know what it was that made me immediately suspect Jack's problems were business related. It must have been the expression on his face when he said, "I've made a mess out of everything." It was a look somewhere between panic and confusion - like he was caught in somebody's gun sight and had no idea why. It was a look that had started spreading through the city like a plague almost three years ago as layoffs, foreclosures and bankruptcies began to confirm that the long predicted economic recession had arrived. It was also the same look I woke up with every morning.

"The company… that's funny, yeah you might say it's in trouble. The bailiff read its last rites a couple of weeks ago. It's as dead as Abe Lincoln's nuts… along with me, my home, my car, my credibility, everything… Uhhhhh, I don't know how I could have been so stupid?"

Jack was shaking his head as he spelled out the details of his situation, but as he spoke, he seemed to be regaining his composure. I listened to him as dispassionately as possible, so as not to upset the flow of this shocking news but for all my outer serenity, my insides were churning into knots. Jack was in a substantial amount of trouble.

"Look, Hannibal, when I asked you here a couple of weeks ago, I was hoping that you could help buy me some time or something. But I want you to know up front that I don't want anything from you. I know you're fighting your own battles, I just need… I dunno, to talk to someone, I guess.

"Like I said the company is gone. It ceased operations on the tenth. I don't know what the full balance is of the outstanding executions, but I figure when all is said and done, it'll be over four hundred thousand."

Hearing the figure, I asked as unobtrusively as possible, "Are those all corporate judgements, or are any against you personally?"

"I don't think so, but frankly I didn't defend any of the actions, so I'm not sure. Why?"

"Well that should be easy to find out. How about corporate assets, anything left?"

"The last one was my car. I flipped it into my name in April, so I don't know if they can grab it or not," my cousin replied with a shrug.

"They probably can. Are there any liens against the car itself?"

"Yeah, I refinanced it through a leasing company last year for $25,000. They're definitely looking for it. It's about four payments behind. I park it at a friend's."

"What's it worth? I mean, is it even worth twenty five?" I inquired, noticing that I was once again fidgeting with my tie.

"Tops."

"So if they grab it there's no real loss there... I mean it's the leasing company's car anyway."

"No loss, except for the fact that I need a car," Jack responded somewhat indignantly.

"Sorry man, I just meant that strictly speaking..."

"I know what you meant, don't worry about it."

As Jack and I continued along surgically analyzing the material sum of his life's work, the early dramatics of the conversation were quickly forgotten. This was now strictly business, and there were serious questions to address. What to save? What to cut loose? Who to screw? Who to make a deal with? It wasn't pleasant stuff, but once immersed in it, it became no different than any other conversation. Barb dropped us off a couple of drinks (and for the first time all day I managed to accept mine without doing anything stupid). We did a little work on the burger platters, and in a short time a relative calm returned to the table.

"So what's the story on the condo, how does it tie in with the demise of Good Word Printing?"

"I remortgaged the place in 1990. It had appraised for $300,000, so I took the first mortgage from $100,000 to

$200,000 and used the cash for operating capital. I did this all privately through Michael Kilroy. The problem is that the place is now only worth $215,000, so I can't use it to re-capitalize. And I'm three payments behind. The monthlies on the place are about $1,960, and I'll be four payments behind next week. So Kilroy has started foreclosure proceedings. And it gets worse. I'm two and a half years behind on the property taxes to the tune of about $8,600. I'm about nine months behind on the building's mainte-nance fees, for say about $3,200. I gotta owe over $220,000 on the place in total and I'm not making squat."

Joining in, I decided to tell Jack what I'm sure he knew was obvious.

"Well there's the first step right there. What can you do about generating income? Any options?"

"Yeah, sure, about six weeks ago I went down to Flynn & Gunn. I've always kept in touch with Jim Nasso. You remember him?"

"Sure," I responded, not recalling whether I remembered him or not.

"Anyway, I tell him I miss the business and might wanna come back. You know, just feeling him out."

"Was he interested?"

"It's not really a matter of being interested. They'll hire just about anyone in that business. In the end it's all commission work, right? So they'd hire a fucking monkey if they thought they could make some money off him. The problem is, I'm so goddam broke I've got to get him to agree to some kind of a draw, but if I look too desperate I don't know what he'll say."

"So, what happened?"

"Jim's a pretty decent guy, and he must have sensed that something was up because before I even bring up the draw he offers me the top salary allowed - a G-note a week."

"A thousand dollars a week is the top salary down there?" I stammered in surprise. As soon as I said it, I started to worry that Jack might interpret my quick remark as condescending, but it just rolled right off him.

"Yeah, I know it sounds like shit, but remember it's really all commission. That salary, or draw if you prefer, is only good for three months. After that your billings should be earning you at least twice that much or they really don't want you around."

"I see."

"Anyway, I get the job lined up, but I've been out of the business so long I've got to retake the licensing test. It's no sweat, but they only offer the test every two weeks. So I don't get a chance to write it until early June. Then you have to wait for the results, and send off a bunch of other information to the securities board. Then you have to wait again until they mail you your license, and I can't write up dime one without that license."

"So how did you do?"

"Fine, like I said, the test is no sweat. But… the license still hasn't arrived. They figure it'll be in next week. So I can start sometime after that."

"That's great," I answered, relieved that at least Jack had options.

"Yeah great, if I start in the next week or so, that means by the middle of the month I'll have a thousand dollars. In the meantime, beyond what I've already told you Revenue Canada says I'm into them for $22,000. I've cashed out every stock, bond and RSP I've ever owned, and several of the city's finest collection agencies along with two credit card companies are trying to crawl up my ass to see what organs they can remove. But hey, in just three weeks I'm gonna have a thousand dollars! Fucking great."

I could see the frustration once again growing in Jack as he replayed the details of his financial situation. It was a frustration that ran so deep, his gestures and body language suggested that a violent outburst was lurking just beneath the surface. It was like he wanted to strike out at something, and it was only the lack of a clear target that controlled his simmering rage.

"Oh, and here's the funny part, you can laugh at this if you want to. You remember when we were picking up Uncle Talbot's belongings… remember sorting through all his possessions the day after we buried the miserable prick? Everything the man owned was given to him by the Good Shepherd, right, and every cent he had was a government hand out, right?"

"Right."

"Well old buddy, you would have to triple my current bank balance to match the lofty sum left by our dear departed Uncle. Can you believe that? And it's not like I have to tell you how old he was when he died."

Talbot MacEachern was our uncle. He was our mothers' youngest sibling, and only brother. We never really knew him that well. He was kind of a thug, and even his sisters didn't want him around because he was also a world-class booze hound. So complete was his loyalty to the bottle that he managed to blow out his liver and both kidneys before his fortieth birthday.

He died in 1979 at the age of thirty-nine, or about the same age Jack is now. At the time of his death his body was so eroded by the relentless assault of alcohol that there was almost nothing left of him. He weighed less than one hundred and ten pounds and the only suit we could find to fit him for burial was my first St Ignatius uniform. (I remember how Jack's mother had insisted that we remove the school crest from the blazer so as not to disgrace it by laying it to rest with Talbot.)

The day after the funeral, Jack and I were dispatched to the rooming house Talbot called home in order to clean out his limited belongings. Home in this case was a filthy one-room hellhole on the first floor of an old four-storey building in Parkdale, which was distinguishable from a public outhouse only because it smelled worse.

After finding his apartment, Jack and I were both disgusted that Talbot could have lived in such squalor. The apartment was a small twelve by twelve-foot square, and even given its limited size seemed sparsely furnished. One unmade bed, a chair, an old television, and a coffee table constituted the full range of appointments.

The man owned next to nothing. Even the dingy furniture belonged to the building's management, and a scraggly superintendent stood guard as we carried out our business. It was a terribly depressing setting, and I have never forgotten the smell of the place. It was the unmistakable stench of failure.

It was while I was hurriedly stuffing some dirty laundry into an old duffel bag that a bankbook fell out of a shirt pocket. At first it was surprising to see that my uncle even owned a bankbook. But not only did he have one, it was recently updated. The previous week he had made a $3 deposit. Looking at the figure I couldn't fathom why anybody would walk to a bank to make a $3 deposit? But as the book's pages revealed a pattern of corresponding deposits and withdrawals, all between two and five dollars, it occurred to me that the kind of person who would make a $3 dollar deposit was the kind of person who only had $3 to deposit. It was so sad. All of a sudden my dead uncle had become a real person. The balance of the account was forty-one dollars and twenty-three cents.

After gathering up Talbot's clothes, the only other item we took was a framed picture standing on the apartment's grimy window ledge. Jack had spotted it and tapped me on the shoulder to point it out. When I first saw the damn thing I honestly couldn't believe it. Neither could Jack. And as we started towards the window, my cousin and I approached that picture as one would approach a ticking bomb.

Though I had never seen the picture before I remembered the day it was taken very well. It was Christmas Day 1963, Jack's ninth birthday as a matter of fact. And as strange as it was to see, there it was, staring back at us from beneath the aged frame's broken glass, the unabashedly happy faces of Jack and myself, clinging proudly to Uncle Talbot.

I knew that it was '63 because the picture was taken at Jack's house and our Christmas dinner was held there only once. I recall the year because of an argument that broke out prior to dinner over the recently assassinated John F Kennedy. As we sat down to eat, my grandmother, who probably loved Kennedy for no other reason than he was Catholic, made the mistake of suggesting that we observe a moment of silence in his memory.

All present that day were great admirers of the President with the exception of Jack's father, who decided to observe the moment by mumbling into his glass of unmixed scotch, "Moment of silence, it's too bad they didn't get the son of a bitch three years earlier."

And the brawl was on.

Staring at the photograph I couldn't believe how young Talbot looked. He was only twenty-three at the time but in that picture he could have passed for seventeen or eighteen. His long hair was slicked straight back and stood out in sharp contrast to the merciless brush cuts sported by his two adoring nephews. His perfect smile, the kindly result of a full set of dentures, offered no hint of the hell his life was to become. He looked young and happy, a far cry from the ghoulish eyesore we had just buried.

I remembered that while he hadn't brought either of us a gift that day, when Jack and I went outside to set up his new hockey net it was only Uncle Tab who ventured out to join us. Jack and I, both having donned our prized Maple Leaf jerseys (with matching toques of course), had barely assumed our respective roles of Mahovlich and Bower when, sliding onto the road, his pointed black shoes desperately searching for traction in the snow covered asphalt, came Uncle Talbot.

In retrospect I'm sure he was half in the bag. But that didn't matter. What mattered is that he had shown up to play. And play we did.

For hours Tab and I peppered Jack with uncountable slap shots, before Tab assumed the goal stick and proceeded to put on a goaltending performance that would have been worthy of the great Bower himself. Time after time and from every conceivable angle Tab made one spectacular save after another on his two determined nephews.

It was only after darkness had covered the street that we reluctantly packed up the net and headed indoors. But not before Mahovlich (me) put one last shot past Plante (Tab), the dreaded netminder of the hated Montreal Canadians. It was of course an overtime goal, and clinched the Stanley Cup for the Maple Leafs. It was the sixth time that day in which the city's storied hockey franchise had prevailed over the Habs, and the fifth time that the Big M had scored the winner. And I've never forgotten the way Tab parted his legs ever so slightly to allow the winning goal in, as Jack's screams of "He shoots! He scores!" echoed throughout the neighbourhood.

Christmas Day, no school, scoring the winning goal, and an adult to play with. It was the greatest day a six-year-old could have.

Looking down into that old picture I felt ashamed that I hadn't thought of that Christmas during my family's period of half-hearted mourning over Talbot's passing. I should have mentioned it. Somebody should have said something nice about him. Jack must have been thinking the same thing, because when the old superintendent told us, "Hurry up, I don't have all day," Jack shot him a look that would have stopped a freight train.

God it was sad. A small duffel bag of clothes, $41.23, and a picture (which Jack kept) of two nephews he hadn't seen in more than a decade was all that thirty-nine years of life had amounted to.

"That's right… thirty-nine. Thirty-nine years old and save some nicer clothes and some furniture, if I died tomorrow my life would have amounted to about the same as his."

Jack's words were once again becoming more reflective than angry. The rage in him seemed to be receding, so I took the opportunity to jump into the conversation.

"Well not quite the same as his. Tab had more cash," I answered, cautiously smiling.

"What?" Jack looked perplexed then, smiling back, he added, "You son of a bitch. Well, I guess I did say you could laugh."

"What am I going to laugh at? I just realized I'll be picking up the bill here today."

"You're a riot, Alice," Jack said. His mood was lightening, but for understandable reasons he was still far from happy.

"Seriously man, it's just all so humiliating. Honestly, from the moment I wake up I feel like I'm suffocating and when I go outside for air it feels like someone is trying to slip a rope around my neck. I just can't stand it. I feel so stupid. I should have gone back to F & G a year ago. No, I never should have left in the first place. I'm a dead man, a grand a week ain't gonna solve nothing."

The words weren't out of his mouth when Barb arrived. She was looking mighty pleased with herself as she pulled up to the table and set three small glasses down in front of us.

"Here we go, two B-52s and a Chivas." Then without hesitating she picked up her glass and asked,

"So, what shall we celebrate?"

You had to admire the ease of being twenty.

Chapter Six

CHAPTER SIX

I'M SITTING IN THIS VERY FOGGY ROOM, and some guy is talking to me. Although I can't really see who it is, I feel quite certain that I know the voice from somewhere. Then, as the fog begins to lift, I realize it's not a guy talking to me at all. It's Oprah.

There I am, sitting on *The Oprah Winfrey Show*, - the only guest in sight. I haven't got a clue what I am doing there and at this point Oprah and the entire audience are just staring at me. They seem to be waiting for me to say something.

Being completely lost, I look towards Oprah and ask, "I'm sorry, but can you repeat the question?"

Oprah tucks her head down a bit, almost like a turtle pulling its head into its shell, or in this case into the black judge's robe she is wearing for today's show. Along with the robe, Ms Winfrey is also wearing my wife's engagement ring and what appear to be Dorothy's ruby slippers from *The Wizard of Oz*.

Oprah seems a little perturbed by what she believes to be my lack of attentiveness and while giving me that authoritative but sensitive look of hers she pulls the mike up to her lips to repeat her question.

At this point I am desperately searching the audience for

Caroline, or Jack, or even Bruce Thatcher, somebody who might be able to tip me off as to what I am doing there. But alas, there is nobody in sight that I can even remotely recognize. Then again, why would there be? I must be in Chicago.

With the exception of two black men in the front row, everyone in the audience has this fiercely compassionate look on their face. They seem quite interested in me and in my story. Whatever that might be? However, the two black guys are looking at me like I'm pitiful.

Suddenly, blasting out of the studio speakers comes the sound of Oprah's hurried voice.

"So, Hannibal... you feel that you have honestly come to terms with the fact that your wife has been unfaithful to you. How were you able to do this?"

Hearing the question for the first time, I turn to Oprah as quickly as I can. She has the mike in her right hand, while her left arm is extended directly out beside her. The palm of her left hand is completely opened, as if trying to assist me in formulating an answer. Still nothing will come out.

Through the silence that follows, Oprah and the audience continue to stare at me, and when it becomes clear that no response will be forthcoming, a deeply confused look crosses Ms Winfrey's face.

It was plain to see that my performance was starting to piss Oprah off. She has become extremely agitated, and is looking at me like I'm some sort of simpleton. But what was I supposed to do? It's not that I don't understand the question, it's just that I'm so dumbfounded by the whole situation that I don't know what to say. What am I doing on *The Oprah Winfrey Show*?... And how does she know my name?

In complete panic I start to *ad lib* an answer, hoping that it might jog my memory.

"My wife had an affair... and at first, well of course, you know... I mean..."

I'm sort of shuffling around in my chair, looking down at the floor and mumbling like an idiot, when somebody suddenly takes my hand and gently squeezes it.

Startled, I look across to my right and from out of nowhere a stunning blonde has appeared on stage. She's caressing my hand,

and looking at me in such a reassuring way that I begin to think that maybe she's here to help me? Then I realize that this is my wife. I mean, not my real wife, but my wife in the dream.

Now at this point, I see an easy out for myself and I start thinking that I should tell Oprah that there's been some sort of mistake. They've got the wrong guy. This beautiful woman on my right is not my wife and I don't know what I am doing here. So, if you'll just lend me your ruby slippers, I'll be out of here in three clicks. But the words just won't come out. I just sit there staring at my 'wife', wondering who in the hell is she?

Suddenly Oprah's voice comes blasting through the speakers once again.

"We'll be right back - to see what happens when Hannibal meets Bob, Amanda's former lover, for the first time."

What? I'm going to meet Bob? Now I'm supposed to sit here and meet the guy who's been banging my wife? I don't think so. Where's Oprah?

Amid the buzz of the audience and the motion of various stage and technical people, Oprah ambles down to the stage, and puts her hand on my shoulder.

"Come on now Hannibal, we covered all this during rehearsals. I know this is not easy for you, but try to pay attention."

Ms Winfrey has become quite frazzled by my poor performance. The show was bombing and she was trying to find a way to pull it back together. So, when I started to tell her that there'd been some sort of mistake, she immediately cut me off.

"Relax Hannibal, we'll come back to Amanda... then introduce Bob... and you just jump in whenever you want. Okay?"

She seems like a genuinely nice person, but the thought of one of her shows bombing has her in a state of panic even greater than my own. So I figure, what the hell, I'll help her out and play along with the storyline. After all it's not my wife old Bob-O's been shagging, so what do I care? I even start to figure that maybe I can have a little fun with the whole situation.

Amanda squeezes my hand and smiles. "You're doing just fine honey," she announces like she couldn't be prouder of me.

Amanda was simply drop-dead gorgeous. She had a model's smile, full, pouty lips, and deep blue eyes that seemed like they could look right through me. She was very tall, and was wearing an extremely short black mini-dress, which only marginally covered the upper regions of her shapely legs. Her legs were quite a distraction, and the fact the exotic silk that covered them was monogrammed with my initials made it even more difficult to stop staring at them.

Looking at her, it sort of broke my heart to think that she had cheated on me, and I started thinking that maybe I knew her from somewhere.

When the red lights come flashing on, Oprah is perched on a step, way up in the audience. Turning her attention to Amanda, Ms Winfrey wonders aloud, "So Amanda, do you feel that your initial attraction to Bob was to fill a certain emotional void in your life, or to fulfil a wanting physical need?"

Pulling my eyes away from Amanda's legs, I look up in amazement at Oprah. Geez, what a loaded question? Oprah Winfrey had just asked my wife in front of a national television audience if she enjoyed doing the wild thing with another man because I was a cold, humourless and intellectually barren android... or if she did it because I was, shall we say, less than inspiring in the sack?

If this wasn't a dream, a guy could really take offence at such a question. But for some reason I just smile politely.

As Amanda begins to rhyme off Bob's many ingratiating qualities - his kind heart - his ability to listen - his coming around at a time when she really needed a friend - his special sense of humour (he was the funniest man she'd ever met) she ended her answer by adding with the slyest of giggles, "As for the physical side of my time with Bob, let's just say it was WONDERFUL."

Let's just say it was WONDERFUL. The word hung in the air like a misdirected curve ball. And looking towards Oprah it was clear that she was going to tee off on it.

Seeing the opening she had been waiting for, Oprah had a smile on her face that went from ear to ear.

"Ooooooh girl, it sounds like you sure had yourself some fun with old Bob."

As Oprah begins leading the crowd into a series of lascivious "Ooooohs" and "Aaaaahs" I suddenly realize that with the exception of the two black guys up front, the studio audience is made up entirely of women. They are all facing each other going... "Ooooooh, it was WONDERFUL... Aaaaaah." The two gentlemen up front continue to look at me with obvious scorn.

The sexual energy brought on by Oprah's question causes Amanda to press her knees together, and she starts kicking her high-heeled shoes up and down on the stage floor. Tossing her head back, she closes her eyes, and through clenched teeth, my "wife" begins to shudder uncontrollably. You didn't have to be Einstein to realize that Amanda was reliving one of the many sexually explosive moments she had shared with Bob.

All of a sudden I couldn't see the potential for fun in my miscast role on today's show. And as Amanda struggled to regain her composure, Oprah kept egging her on.

"Whew,... A-MAN-DA, oooooh girl... I see we really are talking WON-DER-FUL. Are we talking... intense, like the earth moved WON-DER-FUL?... Are we talking multiple WON-DER-FUL?"

All Amanda could do was kick her heels harder into the floor and nod in acknowledgement of Oprah's leering queries.

The women in the audience had positively gasped as the word left Oprah's mouth... WON-DER-FUL. They had all dreamed about WON-DER-FUL. They had all dreamed of intense and multiple visits to the very core of their sexuality. Yet their girlish reaction to Amanda's trips to WON-DER-FUL suggested that most of them had never reached this point of ecstasy... for, no doubt, they were generally married to slunks, like me, I suppose.

It took several moments for Oprah to bring the crowd back under control, but not before sarcastically chastising them, "Whoa ladies... you're bad, you're all being bad. I think some husbands are in for a real treat when you all get home tonight."

The audience squealed in delight. Oprah had really played it to the hilt. The show was back on track, and flying, and Ms Winfrey couldn't have been happier.

And Amanda,... Christ, Amanda looked like she was ready for a cigarette.

Sitting quietly, I couldn't figure out why Oprah had whipped the crowd into such a frenzy at my expense. *I* was the one playing out this little charade so as not to ruin *her* show. *I* was the one doing *her* a favour. Who was she, to serve up my balls to a national television audience? The two guys up front continue shaking their heads in disgust.

Well, now I'm not just going to sit there and be Oprah's whipping boy. Two can play it this way. So I decide that when it's my turn to speak, I will call Ms Winfrey a fat bitch, who can only get any action at all because she's worth a couple of hundred million bucks. Yeah, we'll see how she likes a taste of her own medicine.

So when Oprah asks me if I have any comments on Amanda's summary of Bob, I smile ever so smugly into the camera, and prepare to broadside my unsuspecting host. But at the last second I just look straight at my shoes and say, "No, I'm just looking forward to meeting him."

Damn, what an asshole, I can't believe I said that.

The guy that's been defiling my wife sounds like such a good guy that I just want to meet him.

Hannibal, what in the hell are you doing?

Then before I know it, from my left side, Bob comes prancing out onto the stage. He's this tall gangly guy with dark hair, and a nose that looks like a Buick. He's wearing a green leisure suit and he's got something in his hand. It's a video camera. Holy shit, does he have movies of him and my wife together? Are they gonna show them?

That's it. I better do something. I'm already sitting there like the single biggest stooge in the history of American television, and now this guy thinks he's going to show porn movies of him and my wife together. I don't think so.

So I figure I'll just punch the guy. Who could blame me? As soon as he's within range, I'll let him have it. I mean what are they going to do, arrest me? It's a dream for crying out loud.

As Bob approaches, unaware of the danger he is in, I rise to make my stand. But when he does pull into range all I do is offer him a hand to shake. I try to shake the guy's hand. Can you believe that? And he doesn't even shake it. He ignores my friendly gesture and brushes by me like I'm not even there. Then he and Amanda lock in this long, loving embrace and begin twirling around the stage to the frantic applause of the audience. All the while I'm still trying to get his attention so that I can shake his hand.

Oh God, Hannibal, what are you doing? Hit the bastard!

When Bob sits down, things get even worse. Upon getting a closer look at him, I realize that he doesn't have the video camera because he intends to show movies of him and my wife together. He's got the video camera because he's Bob Saget, host of *America's Funniest Home Videos*. Bob Saget, the most irritating man on the planet, was my wife's lover. She preferred him - to me. This was really humiliating. I think I felt better when he was just a guy named Bob, who was here to show some dirty movies of my wife.

And when old Bob immediately goes into his routine, that goofy shtick he does on his show, guess who laughs the hardest? Laughs the hardest, hell I was the only one laughing at all. While Oprah, her audience, and even Amanda were appalled by his cornball delivery of several ancient jokes, I laughed like the man was Jackie Gleason.

I laugh at everything the idiot says. And no matter how hard I try to stop, I just can't. I know he's about as funny as getting hit by a car, but I just laugh and laugh anyway. It was so frustrating, and so humiliating. *Why doesn't somebody just step forward and shoot me?*

By this time, the two black guys have become so embarrassed for me that they get up to leave. And even though I just want to crawl out of the studio with them, I can't seem to move. It's like I'm chained to my chair.

I have to sit there and listen as Bob tells me in a most patronizing way that I shouldn't feel threatened by him. He confesses that he was only using Amanda for sex, and that since he was now probably finished with her... I could have her back. He also hoped that he hadn't caused me any problems, but if he had ..."*c'est la vie.*"

C'est la vie - c'est la fucking *vie.*

Now at this point I see that my only hope of reclaiming any self-respect or dignity from this whole exercise would be to strangle Bob with his leisure suit before killing myself.

But instead, I assure him that there are no hard feelings and in fact... maybe I should thank him, as he has helped me learn a lot about myself. I thanked him. Can you believe that?

God, Hannibal, get up and say something. Stand up for yourself. Come on, you idiot, take charge. If nothing else, at least belt Oprah.

The frustration was killing me. Why couldn't I do anything?

Finally, after forcing myself out of my chair, I tear the microphone off Bob's six-inch lapel and begin to address the stage's main camera. Speaking clearly and deliberately I announce,

"Oprah, there's a couple of things I have to say here and I don't want anyone to move until I have set the record straight. I'm not sure how I got here, but I want you all to know there's been a terrible mistake..."

It really felt great to finally have the words I was trying to say, actually be the ones coming out of my mouth. What a relief, but just as quickly as I got started Oprah cuts me off.

"You'll have to save it for tomorrow Hannibal."

Then, turning to a side camera, she continues, "Please tune in tomorrow when Hannibal will be joined by Doctor Joyce Brothers, to discuss his obsession with wearing women's clothes."

Then, as security guards are wrestling me off the stage, Oprah breaks into song. As fog begins to fill the room she performs this really dramatic rendition of 'Somewhere Over the Rainbow'.

Then I wake up.

Chapter Seven

CHAPTER SEVEN

As I OPENED ONE EYE, the faintest beginnings of morning light allowed me to recognize one of the wooden beams that decorate the ceiling of my home's main floor den. Happily reassured by this information, I immediately closed the eye. I was home. Thank God, I was home.

I could tell by the room's almost total blackness that it was approximately five a.m. – which was not surprising. For the past few weeks, regardless of what time I went to bed, I hadn't been able to sleep in any later than five. And, as I lay there on the couch, unable to block out the random chirping filtering into the house from the backyard, it became clear that even sleeping in a drunken stupor had done nothing to fool my misguided body clock.

It was five and once again I was up - sort of.

With my eyes still tightly closed, I tried to ascertain what other clues to my existence my remaining senses might provide. I was definitely lying flat on my back on the room's only couch. A restricted feeling around my shoulders told me that I still had my shirt on. Which meant I was probably still fully dressed. Which seemed about right - given the amount of alcohol I had consumed the previous night.

In order to confirm this suspicion, I reached one hand down to my hip, and briefly ran it across the front of my pants, before moving on, and concluding my inventory check by rubbing my feet together and determining that I was still wearing both socks, and one shoe.

My sleeping attire confirmed, I turned my muddled thoughts to my physical condition. I felt certain that my eyes and hair would have that really hung-over look, but my head, while pulsing slightly and extremely fogged, had not even a trace of an ache to it, the fact that I was still drunk preventing any pain from setting in. On the other hand, my mouth was definitely experiencing that dry woolly feeling that follows a night of heavy drinking.

Taking my left arm, which was dangling freely off the side of the couch, I brought it up to my head and gently rested it across my eyes. The weight of the arm contained the head's pulsations as I made my first attempt to rise to a sitting position.

Grabbing the back of the couch with my right hand, I started to pull myself up but as my upper body rose I could feel my tie tightening around my neck. It had somehow gotten wrapped around me in such a way that when I pulled up it pulled down.

Rather than taking any immediate action against the trapped garment, I simply slid back down the couch and with my left arm still resting comfortably across my face I just lay there, wistfully dreaming of orange juice and coffee.

A minute or so later, after blindly fumbling around with my tie, I decided on a different course of action and simply rolled off the couch onto the floor beside me. Landing on my hands and knees on the room's Persian rug, I purposefully steadied myself and groggily prepared to rise to my feet. However, my body still wasn't quite ready to meet this rather meagre challenge.

Resting in a standard four-point position I waited for some evidence of motor-skills to return. But they were slow-a-coming. I felt like a pummelled boxer must feel after being knocked down. And seeing myself this way I used an imagined ten count as motivation to quickly rise to my feet.

I was up, and though no visible opponent was in sight, the fight could continue. What to do first?

Resisting an impulse to sit back down on the couch, I instead staggered towards the kitchen, and the relief of a cold drink.

Reaching into the fridge I squinted slightly to protect my eyes from its interior light and through my fractured gaze quickly spotted a juice container. Removing it, I clumsily cracked it open and, without even considering the use of a glass, promptly downed at least half a litre or so. Whew, I felt like shit.

Heading back towards the den, juice box firmly in hand, I paused to take a quick trip out to the driveway. I was pretty sure I wouldn't have driven myself home the previous night, but I wanted to check to be sure.

Arriving at the front of the house I discovered, as I had hoped, that there was no car in the driveway. However, I did find one of my shoes sitting peacefully in the space normally occupied by the Lexus. And while I felt relatively confident that I hadn't driven the shoe home from the Deli, given my lack of recollection into the night's latter events I couldn't definitively rule it out as a possibility.

Picking up the shoe I felt more than slightly troubled as I removed it from the driveway and returned to the house.

The recent upturn in my consumption of alcohol had given me many reasons to feel embarrassed about my actions lately. But the blank spaces in my memory of last night left me feeling particularly uneasy.

I could remember Jack telling me that he was in big trouble. I think that we agreed that he needed to come up with $8,500 by some given day, or something bad was gonna happen. Oh yeah, his apartment, he'd lose it to - Michael Kilroy? That can't be right.

What else had happened? Did Bruce Thatcher ever show up? I could remember we were waiting around for him, but I couldn't recall actually seeing him. Did he show up? He must have. Maybe he drove me home?

And Barb, what was I doing with Barb? She was sitting down with those B-52s sometime after last call. What were we talking about? She needed some help with something. What was it? And was I talking to her down by my car?

I figured I'd have to talk to Jack about filling in a couple of blanks from the night before. Jack,... holy shit. What was I going to do about him? Was Michael Kilroy really putting the screws to him?

It was close to six before the first real traces of sunlight were visible on the horizon. Having made coffee, I filled a large mug to capacity and carefully eased my way through the den's sliding glass door.

Out on the backyard's multi-tiered cedar deck, I momentarily considered stepping into the jacuzzi but, lacking the energy to take off my clothes, I opted instead for a semi-reclined lounge chair on the deck's top level.

Gingerly lowering myself into the chair's elasticized fabric, I sipped heavily on my coffee. The dark brew tasted nothing like coffee was meant to taste. Though I had made it much stronger than usual, its deep flavour was no match for the grungy after-taste of the liquor I had consumed the previous night. Though, as bad as it was, I was determined to finish the beverage for its per-ceived sobering qualities.

The taste of the coffee aside, there was a nice breeze blowing across the yard and having found a comfortable position in the lounger's lazy folds, I crossed my arms over my midsection, and enjoyed the wind's invigorating movements. Closing my eyes, as the wind danced pleasantly across my face, I began to sort out the most pressing matter that had come up last night. Jack, where was I going to come up with some money for Jack?

Far more painful than the shock of hearing how badly Jack had fallen was the realization that I was in no position to help him. Though I had been able to hold on to some of the assets I had acquired in the eighties, I had almost no cash left. My success in holding on to anything these past few years had been based strictly on negotiated deferment of debt, various legal manoeu-vres, and the strategic placement of several assets in my wife's name. Nothing had been rescued as a result of sustaining a serious cash flow. It had all been done with smoke and mirrors.

The deep well of cash that once protected me from so many of life's problems had run dry. Bone dry.

While my asset base was still significant, my equity position in what remained was already way below the comfort level of my many creditors. I was simply too deeply mortgaged to wring any cash out of my remaining holdings.

Cash, the undisputed king of all assets, how could I lay my hands on $8500 for Jack – quickly?

Damn, it was frustrating. Where had all the money gone? Mine, Jack's, everybody's? There was a time in the not so distant past when the money Jack needed would be about the equivalent of a week's pay. But in 1993 the cold, hard truth of my life was that $8500 was more money than I'd earned since the beginning of the year.

Trying to escape this thought, I slumped deeper into the recliner and tried to go back to sleep. But it just wasn't going to happen. The first evidence of what *was* going to happen was only just beginning to pound away from beneath my left temple.

Chapter Eight
CHAPTER EIGHT

AFTER GRADUATING FROM UNIVERSITY in 1981 the job market offered few opportunities for young business students from the University of Western Ontario. The economy was hopelessly stalled in recession, still unaffected by the forthcoming miracle of Reaganomics. And the only opportunity I could find that even faintly resembled a white-collar job was selling life insurance door to door.

Uninspired by this bleak prospect, I decided to put my business career on hold for a while and opted instead for a job as a courier at a downtown delivery firm. It wasn't the glamorous start to a career I had envisioned while still in school, but it wasn't a bad job.

My duties at AMB Courier were simple. Pick up a package at Building A and move it in the most expeditious manner possible to Building B.

The assignments couldn't have been more clear. And the pay was excellent. Most weeks, a good hustler could clear a solid $600 to $700. Combine all of this with flexible hours, and an extraordinary perk that was built right into the job, and it didn't take long to figure out that there were a lot worse ways to earn a living than being a courier.

I hadn't realized it at the time I signed on with AMB, but couriers basically have unlimited access to women. And I was no exception. All I did all day long was pick up and drop off packages to receptionists and secretaries right across the city. So I quite literally had to meet women in order to do my job. And while between the hours of nine to five my relationship with all of these new acquaintances may have been strictly business, after hours that wasn't always the case.

Within three months of becoming a courier I had a more extensive network of friends than I had developed all through high school and university. And most of them were women. It was amazing how often a two-minute chat while filling out a delivery form would lead to getting together for a drink after work.

It happened at least three times a week. And while at the time I was setting up these post-working-day rendezvouz I kept hoping that, in spite of my general ineptness, inexperience, and lack of confidence in such matters, one of these get-togethers might somehow lead to sex, in the end something even more remarkable than sex kept happening.

These girls started to become my friends.

Girls as friends, talk about a brave new world! For me it was anyway. I don't know if it was my parochial background (how many girls can one really meet while attending an all boys high school), or if it was the fact that generally speaking I had always been something of an introvert, but up until the summer of '81 I had really never had any female friends.

Yet that first summer at AMB I had a core of five or six girl "friends" whom I hung out with all the time. And what a great summer it was.

Most weeks it was all I could do just to keep up with the social opportunities my new friends arranged for me (or at least brought me along to). Parties, dinners, movies, restaurants, bars, malls, cottages, camping, beaches, picnics - it never stopped. Everything was just go – go – go.

It was great. Not only did I always have something to do, I always had someone to do it with. Even on slow nights some pretty nice things were liable to happen.

I recall one particular evening when a sprained ankle left me unable to attend a big party that was going on down at Centre

Island. Well, I had barely started sorting through the various fast-food coupons that were scattered around my apartment when Julie Newton, the undisputed ringleader of most of my activities that summer, arrived, unannounced, at my apartment, with dinner, magazines, cigarettes, chianti, vodka, and an armful of Rolling Stones tapes.

And by the time Mick and the boys had broken into the second verse of 'Tumbling Dice', I was sitting comfortably on the couch with a plateful of chicken wings in one hand, and a rather large Screwdriver in the other. Apparently the night wasn't going to be a total write-off after all.

Even before dinner was over, two other girl friends had called (Lisa Ramsey and Kathy Hill) just to see how I was feeling and to say that they would drop by the next day.

By comparison, the only male friend I had that called was Rick Connelly, my best friend at AMB. And he just called to see if – since I was laid up anyway - he could borrow my van.

I couldn't really hold it against Rick – his asking for my van while I was out of commission. After all, I probably would have made the same request of him had our situations been reversed. Still, his request did underscore the difference in expectations between friends like him, and friends like Julie Newton.

I think Julie and I became pals for life that night. We drank Screwdrivers (her drink of choice) and smoked cigarettes non-stop till four in the morning, and solved just about every world problem we could think of along the way. No topic was off limits – men, women, sex, likes, dislikes, hopes, fears, dreams, and we spent about seven or eight hours covering all of it before Julie fell asleep on the couch.

At the time Julie dropped off we were right in the middle of one of her favourite topics of conversation.

Why I didn't have a girlfriend?

She wasn't lobbying for the job or anything like that. Julie was a babe, and popular too. I'm not sure I ever met a woman who attracted guys the way she did. But she had been attached – on and off – to her high school sweetheart, Mike Bell, since early in the tenth grade. And though the couple had broken up on at least a dozen occasions, the fact that they always wound up back together had caused Judy to accept the fact that, sooner or later, she was going to marry "the big, dumb asshole".

However attached or not, Julie still enjoyed talking about how other boys and girls played the game – especially about men, and why some guys had a way with women, while others couldn't get laid if they were standing on a corner handing out thousand dollar bills. To Julie, it was all so simple and it all came down to this. If a man was A - "normal" (no major hang-ups or insecurities) and B - "easy to talk to", he could be "ugly as hell" and nine women out of ten would love him until the day he died.

It was a theory of hers I had heard many times before, though never how it applied directly to me. But on this particular night Julie Newton decided to apply it. And since she felt I was both "extremely normal" and "super easy to talk to", it confounded her why I didn't have a girlfriend? Especially since, as her final words of the evening (before succumbing to the vodka as well as the late hour) put it – "and you're sure not ugly as hell."

Normal, easy to talk to, and not ugly as hell – how could any woman resist a man with such credentials?

Julie Newton fell asleep before I had a chance to ask her why she thought I didn't have any major hang-ups (I thought I was full of them). So we didn't quite reach any conclusions as to why I didn't have a girlfriend. But I do remember that as I removed her shoes, and draped a blanket across her shoulders, I did so feeling extremely fortunate to have a friend like her.

I really thought she was great, and it wasn't just her general assessment of me that made me feel that way. Words such as "extremely normal", "super easy to talk to", and "not ugly as hell", are not really what you would call breathtaking words of praise. However, even at the time I realized they were the most affectionate ones she could use, given the bounds of our platonic relationship. And they did serve their purpose. They made me feel pretty good about myself.

Julie had a gift. She had a way of making people feel a little bit better about themselves. And it was one that she shared with me almost every time we got together.

Julie Newton and I might have become life-long friends had this particular night never happened, but I always felt pretty certain this was the night that clinched it. We hung-out together constantly after that - mostly in a group. But no matter how large a group we gathered in, I always understood who my best friend in the crowd was. It was Julie – hands down, going away.

Years later not only did Julie Newton-Bell set me up with the woman I was to marry, she also donned a tuxedo and stood as an usher for me at our wedding. Now how are you going to beat a friend like that?

Around the same time as I was developing such relationships as the one I enjoyed with Julie Newton, my position as a courier was also the catalyst that led me down another unfamiliar path.

It wasn't something that had started happening immediately, but toward the end of my first year at AMB, I was also beginning to meet, with surprising regularity, a number of girls who – there's really no other way to put it – fucked my brains out. It must have been them fucking my brains out because I really wouldn't have known how to fuck theirs out.

At the time I joined AMB, while not being a virgin, I wasn't exactly a man about town either. And any knowledge or insight I may have gained into human sexuality during any of my previous experiences was not only extremely limited, I was also haunted by a deep suspicion that most of it was just plain wrong.

Prior to becoming a courier there had been five girls (six, if no rules in regards to minimum duration are applied as a qualifier) in university and two in high school with whom I had "done it". And it was all "done" the only way I ever understood it could be done.

First you'd have to meet the girl, then you could ask her to a movie or something, after which the success or failure of the date could be easily assessed based on the amount of necking you did on the way home.

This first date then would be followed by a number of follow-up dates, each one featuring a more risky groping session, as you inched your way towards a committed relationship garment by garment. Until finally, as a couple, assuming you had been able to stand the sight of each other long enough, you were finally able to set aside your guilt and your preconceptions and, almost in an apologetic way, actually get around to "doing it". (The final act being carried out with only a minimal amount of enjoyment, and even less imagination – you know – faces together at all times, and no loud-breathing, come on now, everybody be a good Catholic.)

However, shortly after entering the world of AMB, I found that much of the ritualistic behaviour of my university years was extremely out of fashion. In the pre-Aids era of the earlier 80's commitment, morality and conscience were not exactly the major buzzwords of the time. These were the *Dallas* and *Dynasty* years, and not only was everybody screwing around, they were doing it at the drop of a hat.

Shortly after settling into my new circle of friends, I began to observe first hand that in most work places the office stories were about the same. Affairs, trysts, and nooners were damn near as routine as the morning mail. The only difference being that not everyone got mail.

Even while being a relative novice to this whole experience, it would have been impossible not to notice what was going on around me. And bolstered by the recalcitrant attitude of the times, (as well as the security of having my girl "friends" to fall back on), I too started to spread my wings a bit and began breaking a little new ground myself.

And why not, not only had the damning rules and expectations of my past been washed over by the "me first" attitude of the eighties, I also had it on good authority that I was "extremely normal", "super easy to talk to", and "not ugly as hell". A man made for the times – right?

The first girl I slept with while working at AMB was a legal secretary named Stephanie Trimble. She was the friend, of a friend, of a friend, of somebody or other who had ventured into a mid-town bar called Hector's, where a bunch of us used to congregate most Friday evenings.

And while I remember her as the first women who ever "fucked my brains out", there was something else about her that I recall even more clearly than the sex. (While I may have been a mere freshman, by comparison Stephanie Trimble had her Ph.D. in sex. She assumed positions, used techniques, and performed acts, in ways that I would never have dreamed of initiating. And she did it all with a casualness that was almost shocking to me at first - not that I wasn't shocked enough to find myself having sex with someone I'd just met three hours earlier.)

The sex aside, the thing I remember most clearly about

Stephanie was a story she told me that night which seemed to make all of what we had just done - seem normal.

Deep into the middle of the night, Stephanie informed me that the previous year she had spent at least three afternoons a week in her boss's office, propped up on his desk, resting on all fours. And that it was from this position, which was her favourite, that she and her boss would spend large parts of the day fucking like a couple of old hound dogs.

She swore that her boss, a senior partner in the firm, had chosen his particular office for no other reason than the privacy of its outer view. And that even when taking simple dictation he would often request that she slip out of her dress and complete her assignment clad only in her bra and panties.

As she was telling the story, I mistook the look on her face for one of anger and so, ever the hayseed, I interrupted to ask why she put up with that sort of treatment.

After processing my question, Stephanie sighed impatiently, before explaining that the reason she put up with it was because she thought she loved the guy. Then looking slightly reflective, she added, "Until, the old shit told me he was going back to his wife."

After Stephanie told me the guy had dumped her I started to feel a little bad for her situation. And for a brief moment I almost felt like I wanted to come to her aid, and defend her lost honour. (Although my Catholic value system was very unclear as to how I should do this – I mean, after all, hadn't I just spent the previous two hours dishonouring her myself?)

But as she finished her answer by informing me, and she informed me with a giggle, that after the "old shit" told her he was going back to his wife she limited their canine performances on the man's desk to, "at the most, a couple of times a month," I started to get a sense that Stephanie Trimble didn't really need me nor anybody else to come to her aid.

And by the time she completed her answer by adding that she knew she should have cut them out completely but, "They were a nice way to break up the day," I kind of understood that Stephanie pretty much knew how to look out for herself.

Over the following year the "affair" I had with Stephanie Trimble was followed by several other similar liaisons. Nothing too bizarre – all were brief, inconsequential dalliances that caused neither party any real harm, other than the odd moment of embarrassment such liaisons often invite. Usually right around the time somebody starts to sober up.

Yet as brief and inconsequential as these encounters might have been, each one was a real eye-opener to me. At least, at first they were anyway. While the thrill of it all didn't last long, at the point in my life when I met Stephanie Trimble, not only had I never experienced gratuitous, guilt-free sex before, I didn't even know such a thing existed.

However, by the fall of 82, not only did I know of its existence, it was "existing" in my apartment on a fairly regular basis. And while the majority of these affairs lasted only a single night, or perhaps a week or two, each of them lasted long enough for me to eventually form what I thought was an awfully worldly outlook on sex. It was a nice way to break up the day.

Looking back on it, I cringe when I think about my whole act during most of '82. I must have looked like such a dork. My standard attire - black jeans, Harris tweed jacket, and tan coloured cowboy boots, a look I once thought reeked of sophistication, now seems almost as asinine as the pastel jump-suits and white disco three-piecers men humiliated themselves with in the late seventies.

Still, as embarrassing as it may be to contemplate, and for all the times I acted like an asshole, I don't view this period of my life with any great sense of shame. Yeah, there are a few things I'd like to take back – like the night I got drunk and within five minutes of meeting her, tried to kiss Julie Newton's cousin. (Causing the cousin to wallop me right in the eye, which hurt like hell, but not nearly so much as when Julie stepped forward and told me I was acting like "a real jerk".)

However, such occasions aside, and there were many of them, the whole time I was cruising through this kingdom of the jerks I also knew that I was getting a lot out of it. Even while being plastered for almost all of 1982, I understood the whole time that all of the bad behaviour – all the drinking, and partying and sleeping around had very little to do with enjoying the pleasures of a hedonistic lifestyle. That wasn't what it had all been about at all.

It had all been about confronting my own fears and hang-ups.

Just because Julie Newton didn't see them didn't mean they weren't there. And not just about sex, and women and intimacy. There were others as well. It was about striking out on my own, and looking at the world from a wider set of parameters. It was about just generally loosening up and learning how not to be afraid to take a chance or to make a mistake for that matter. It was about pushing back. Pushing back against the walls of convention, behind which I had always lived so safely.

I guess what it was mostly all about was growing up. And even if my notion as to how I should go about doing this was often misguided – for the first time in my life at least I was trying.

So, if the price I had to pay to for pushing too hard against what I had always seen as the limitations of my life was that sometimes I acted like a jerk, it was a small price to pay.

I got more out of this sex and drugs (liquor) and rock and roll phase than it cost me. A lot more. And on top of all that it taught me, one night, – I think it was after a Halloween Party – I even got to sleep with twins. And that was pretty cool.

Chapter Nine
CHAPTER NINE

THE SOCIAL AND EDUCATIONAL advantages of my days as a courier aside, I always knew that on the surface it probably appeared to others that, as a university graduate, and a business grad at that, I was underachieving at this point of my life. And they were probably right.

At the time I took the job, I told myself it would only be for a year and then I'd move on. But by the time the first year was up I was having such a good time at AMB I was able to convince myself that the money was good enough to stick it out for a little while longer.

However, by the time 1983 rolled around the economy was starting to heat up and I knew the time had come to move on. There were opportunities "out there" now. So in April I started sending out résumés.

The interview process began shortly thereafter, and in May, after considering three different offers, I accepted a sales position with a medical supply company. On June the 15th my career at AMB would officially come to a close.

I would then start a six-week training program, before taking on a twelve-hospital territory where I would be selling what I had been assured were the world's most advanced inner-ocular lenses.

As the middle of June approached I was having little or no regrets about leaving AMB. In fact if anything I was starting to count the days. My time there had been great but I was looking forward to getting out. I had a real job now, and it was one that actually might lead somewhere.

That had been the only disheartening part of being a courier. The money was good, the parties were great, and the friends I made were for life, but the whole time I was there I always knew the job couldn't lead anywhere. And over the course of my two years in the business, never once, and not for a second, did I ever conceive that my job at AMB courier could springboard me into a career.

And but for a small twist of fate, I'm sure it never would have.

It happened on the Tuesday of my final week on the job. I had driven down to the Bank of Montreal building in order to pick up some computer equipment that had to be taken out to the airport. The name of the customer was Tezco Consultants, an American company that offered specific engineering services to the Canadian mining industry. The firm had fallen on hard times and the American parent had decided to pull the plug. Tezco Consultants of Canada was shutting down.

After arriving at the Tezco offices I was apologetically informed by a Mr Peter Drohan that there was no need to take the waiting equipment out to the airport. He didn't have the proper paper work on hand that would allow the computers into the United States.

As I looked at the state of their office, it seemed to me that Tezco had leased everything, including paper clips, from the building's property management. Even as a maintenance man was removing its name from the wall of the office's foyer, the only items that looked like they were going anywhere were the six computers stacked by the main door. They were packed in the blue and white boxes, and clearly marked IBM XTs.

Drohan was a real personable guy, and even if not tipped off by his southern drawl it was easy to tell he was not from Toronto. He was too friendly. He seemed genuinely concerned that he had called me down there for nothing and promised to "make it worth my while" if I would meet him back there in an hour. He further explained that he was booked on a 2:30 flight to Dallas and that if I would meet him back there in an hour he would have everything in order.

Hiding my disappointment at this turn of events I assured Mr Drohan that this was no problem and that I would be happy to return in one hour.

With some time to kill I decided to head downstairs and grab a late breakfast. And on the way down it suddenly occurred to me that the previous day, in this very building, while picking up some résumés at some placement agency, I heard the owner of the company screaming into the phone about the whereabouts of his back-ordered computer equipment.

What company was that? What was that guy's name? Didn't he cancel that order?

For as long as I could remember Jack had spoken about this theory he had as to why some people just had a knack for making money, while others remained relatively poor their entire lives. Nothing was ever blind or random to Jack, there was a reason for everything, and he surmised that throughout the course of a lifetime each of us would be presented with a number of opportunities to improve our fortunes. And it was the ability to recognize these opportunities that determined just how far we would go in life.

I remember stepping off the elevator into the building's main lobby, surprised that I could recall Jack's theory with such clarity. It really wasn't something I had ever given much thought to prior to this particular day. But some of the theory must have sunk in, because less than ten minutes after leaving the offices of Tezco Consultants, convinced that opportunity had come knocking, I found myself sitting in front of Mr Jonathon Spik, President of Spik Search Group.

"Mr Spik, I hope you'll pardon my casual attire, but it's actually my day off. I was gathering some preliminary information for a job I will be starting on Monday and I came across something I felt I should bring to your attention."

"No sweat, we're actually just getting set up around here anyway. We won't be up to speed for a couple of days ourselves, if we're lucky. So, what can I do for you?" Spik responded in a curious and well-mannered tone.

"Well, it's more what I hope I can do for you. Until yesterday I was a courier for AMB and on my last day I was picking up some papers in this office, and I heard you on the telephone. I gather you're having some trouble taking delivery of some computers?"

"You might say that. I've got about four days of orders, résumés, invoices and candidate info just stacking up on my desk. What does that have to do with you?"

"I'm starting work on Monday for a company called New Venture Leasing. You may have heard of us?" I bluffed.

"No, sorry, I haven't."

Having just dreamed up the company New Venture Leasing in the past five minutes I was well aware that Mr Spik would not know of "our" existence. But feeling that the notion he might have heard of "us" lent credibility to my story, I pressed on.

"Anyway, I'm just getting acquainted with some equipment we have on lease to a company in this building. They're going out of business and they want to break their existing leases. So I'm checking out the physical state of the equipment, determining residual values, that kind of thing."

"Uh huh."

At this point I could see that Mr Spik was getting a sense of where I was going with my little story, so I dropped the hook.

"Well it seems to me that if you need a computer ASAP, I may be able to provide you with exactly what you need by this afternoon and I may be able to do it for a heck of a price."

"How old is the equipment?"

"Between six and nine months," I speculated (lied), figuring that I had nothing to lose. "Believe me, the condition of the equipment won't be a problem, it looks brand new. I'm just not sure if it's configured to meet your needs. What exactly are you looking for?"

"I don't need much. XT's, 2 disc drives, with maybe a twenty meg hard drive, basic screen, fast printer… preferably IBM." Spik answered guardedly.

"Are you going to be in this afternoon?"

"I can be… uh… what kind of dollars are we talking here?"

"Well, these units were valued at about five grand a piece earlier this year. Of course they were new then. Is that about what you're paying? How many do you need?

"It's a little high. We were looking at paying about $4200 and we need about twelve, maybe fourteen." The pace of our conversation began to quicken.

"Forty two hundred, that's a good price... well, let's see if you like the equipment first, but I'm hoping to get 'em to you for about $2200. Maybe even $2000."

"You get me something that I like for $2000, and I'll buy one today. No, I'll buy two today."

Nodding casually, I stood up to shake Mr Spik's hand and in my best "super easy to talk to" voice assured him, "I'll be back around 1:30."

When I had gone in to meet Jonathon Spik I didn't really think things would go as well as they did. I had no reason to expect anything would come out of my little performance and was surprised to have made the sale - if I could get my hands on the equipment and if the equipment was properly configured.

But with the prospect of success now a real possibility I nervously hopped on the elevator for the eleven-story flight down to Tezco Consultants, wondering how I could get Peter Drohan to release two computers to my care? Or maybe even all six? There had to be a way. And in my mind I could hear Jack talking.

"The winners are separated from the losers by their ability to capitalize on their opportunities."

Entering the Tezco offices I was anxiously drilling three words into my head, over and over again, *be a winner... be a winner... come on Hannibal... be a winner.*

Once inside the lobby, Peter Drohan saw me and immediately came over.

"I'm sorry there young fella, I still haven't gotten anything straightened out with Head Office. I don't know what I'm gonna do with all this stuff. This should have been sorted out weeks ago... I just don't know."

The stage was mine.

"Actually I was giving it some thought downstairs while having breakfast."

Come on Hannibal... take your time... be a winner.

"It seems to me there are two things we know for sure. Number one, we have to get these six units out of this building. Number two, you've got a plane to catch."

ALAN BEATON

"Six units, hell, there are another twelve of these things in that office over yonder," Drohan answered almost sheepishly.

"So, we've got 18 units to get out. Man, I'm gonna have one full van. Maybe we should have a fire sale? Do you know how these things are configured? Any idea what they're worth?"

"Well if you're interested, they're XT's, two ports, thirty meg hard drives with modems. I'd say they're probably worth about $3,000 a piece... but under the circumstances I could maybe take $2,000."

The units were more than good enough for Jonathon Spik... come on Hannibal... be cool.

"Huh, $2000. Oh well, maybe we should move to Plan B. Is there anywhere I can take them for you?"

"Sheeeeit... I don't have a clue what to do with these damn things, and I've got to get going... Do you have anything specific in mind?"

Okay, here's your big chance.

"Well it occurs to me that I'm walking into fifty, sixty offices every day and it would only take a second to see if anyone needed a computer. So, if you can't get them into the U.S. maybe I could sell them for you up here. I phoned my boss and he might be interested in one."

"You think you can get me $2,000 apiece for them?" Drohan inquired hopefully.

"I doubt it. These are IBM's so I know they cost you a lot of money. But most companies today are buying clones at half the price. But I'll bet I could sell all eighteen of them within two weeks for $1,200 a piece - that's $1,000 for Tezco and $200 for me."

"I don't think I can sell them for $1,000."

Come on... take your time... he's thinking about it.

"I'll tell you what, and don't get me wrong, because I'll be happy to just drive them to a warehouse for you, if that's what you want. But listen, my boss will take one for $1,200. Let me take another one on consignment to show around the building... you know, to solicit offers. Who knows, maybe they are worth more than a $1,000. But if someone takes it for $1,200 then I'm free to sell at least the one I have on consignment. It's not like I can offer it to people without having a price. In return I'll take the other sixteen back to our warehouse, free of charge. It's the least my boss could do since he's getting such a great deal on a computer. In the meantime, once you get back to Dallas, if your people decide they don't want to sell the remaining equipment for $1,000 apiece, just straighten out the paperwork with customs, tell me where to deliver the final sixteen units, and I'll drop them off - free of charge, of course. The worst case scenario for Tezco is that you sold me two computers for less than you might have gotten elsewhere, and this shortfall will be mostly offset by the free cartage and storage services I'm offering. And for now your problem as to what to do with this stuff is all taken care of - free of charge."

My fate in his hands, Drohan scratched his head before speaking.

"There is some sense in what your saying, but what assurances can you give me that you're not just gonna run off with these things?"

"The first thing I can do is write you a cheque for eleven hundred dollars. It's all the money I have in the world. We can call my bank to confirm the funds are there if you wish. I'll give it to you and my boss will take care of me when I get back to the office. I'll write you a promissory note for nine hundred dollars, on condition that the second computer sells. Beyond that I'll sign for the other sixteen units as a bonded carrier for AMB. We'll assign them an insurance value of $1,000 each and I'll keep them out at our warehouse - pending further instructions from your company."

After a long pause Drohan finally said, "Fill out the paperwork and leave the cheque with it. Here's my card, call me first thing Monday morning. Now start moving these things out of here. I've got a plane to catch."

I didn't get home that night until after eleven. Jonathon Spik was so happy with his two computers that he took me out for a few drinks to discuss future business.

In the end Spik offered to take an additional twelve computers if he could get the modems and extra memory contained in these units at no extra charge. He further expected to get all fourteen units for $1,995.00 per and that the remaining twelve had to be delivered by Friday.

After showing what I gauged to be a proper amount of concern over his low-ball offer, I agreed to it with one proviso. For such a great deal, payment would have to be due on delivery. His reaction was simple.

"Done."

Sitting in my Roehampton Street apartment that evening, I couldn't stop staring at the cheque Jonathon Spik had given me. Payable to New Venture Leasing - $4,269.30 ($3,990.00 + P.S.T). It was truly amazing to see such an amount. The eleven hundred-dollar cheque I had written to Tezco represented the highest balance I had ever accumulated to that point in my life. Now I had $4,269.30 right in the palm of my hand, with another $25,615 possibly due on Friday. It seemed like a dream come true.

In order to deposit the money into any bank, I knew that it would be necessary to register a trade name with the appropriate branch of government. So, first thing the next morning, I drove down to the Wellesley Street offices of The Ministry of Consumer Affairs and at a cost of ten dollars registered a sole proprietorship in the name of New Venture Leasing.

My next order of business was to open a New Venture Leasing bank account. With government certification in hand I accomplished this at a local bank, and by ten-thirty that morning I, as President and sole signing officer of New Venture Leasing, was free to disburse the sum of $4,269.30 in any manner I saw fit.

The next move in my very busy day was to contact Peter Drohan. Prior to making the call I knew that, irrespective of Tezco's instructions, I would be selling Jonathon Spik the additional twelve computers he had requested. I did hope that this move would not be contrary to Tezco's wishes, but if it was, I had decided that I would carry out the transaction anyway. I figured worst case I could tell Peter Drohan that his goods had been damaged in transit and then send him a cheque for their insured value of $1000 per unit.

I didn't relish the idea of lying to Peter Drohan. He seemed like a decent man, and the last thing I wanted to do was get him in trouble with his boss. But this was business. This was my golden opportunity to get ahead of the game. I couldn't be sure that such an opportunity would ever present itself again. The sale of twelve additional units would net me a minimum of $12,000.

There was no way I could let this chance pass. If I had to lie to complete the deal, I was fully prepared to do so. After all it wouldn't be like I was stealing the equipment. I would send Tezco the "insurance money", so it wasn't even really a lie. It was just commerce.

In the end my concerns over any moral dilemma I might have encountered over the sale of the Tezco computers were without foundation. Despite my daily calls to his office, I never actually spoke to Peter Drohan until about two weeks after his return to Texas. He was a very busy man, and once he had abandoned them, his Canadian computers became a low priority item.

My deal with Jonathon Spik closed without even a hint of a problem. The first ever customer of my entrepreneurial career was a very happy one indeed. Although Mr Spik's satisfaction could only have been a fraction of my own.

By the end of its third day of operation, New Venture Leasing had a closing bank balance of $29,885. Not bad for a couple of days' work. And as it turned out, even more profitable than I had originally calculated.

So indifferent was Tezco Consultants to the fate of its consigned equipment, it was as though they forgot about the machines altogether. Finally, in February of 1984, I told them that I had had no luck in disposing of these units individually, but that a dealer in Montreal had offered me $6000 for the whole lot.

Tezco told me to take a thousand dollars for myself and send them the rest. My answer was direct and simple.

"Done."

In addition to this, a man by the name of Sam Wakim, a close colleague of Jonathon Spik, contacted me on my home line to see if I might be able to furnish him with any similar equipment.

At the increased price of $2,395, I sold him three of the four remaining Tezco computers, and promised to provide him another five units within thirty days.

So, within the first week of operation, I had over $37,000 in the bank, a computer at home, and an order for more equipment. All this from an initial $1,100 outlay, and what turned out to be a $5000 payable to Tezco Consultants. I was onto a very good thing.

Having set up the final Tezco computer at home, I immediately ordered letterhead, envelopes and business cards for New

Venture Leasing. I also found a suburban office building that leased New Venture a "corporate identity". While I maintained no office in this building, the New Venture name was placed on the directory in the main lobby, and building management answered a phone line, accepted and sorted mail, and provided secretarial services as needed. For $135 a month I created the illusion that a company by the name of New Venture Leasing was operating within this prestigious looking building.

While the creation of a corporate identity was a common and accepted business practice, I am not sure how common the creation of "real life" employees may have been. When ordering business cards for New Venture Leasing, I ordered a set for myself and for a fictitious character I had created named Michael Armstrong. Michael's title was Vice President, and while he didn't actually exist in the real world, he was a mighty important part of New Venture Leasing. He was the voice on the phone for any potential customers who may have known me as a courier.

During the day I would search buildings for any sign of a new tenant entering, or current one closing down, or any other scenario where there might be a turnover in any computer hardware. I would follow up any potential leads by phone or by letter under the name Michael Armstrong – Executive V.P. New Accounts.

During the evening hours I sent out flyers to companies all across the city, informing them of the services provided by New Venture Leasing. "We buy and sell used personal computers - please call Michael Armstrong if we can be of service to you."

As time went on I expanded my mailings to cover large parts of the north-eastern and central United States, as well as all of Canada. I never actually tried to sell anything into the States, but there was an inexhaustible amount of available hardware to be found down there. Many weekends I would travel to such places as Ashtabulo, Ohio, Muncie, Indiana or Decatur, Illinois, and fill up my van with a load of cheap equipment that had been deemed expendable by some American company.

It wasn't as if deals came up every day, but when they did come up, the profit margin on each unit sold bordered on obscene. What might cost me $100, I routinely sold for $1,000, and by March of 1984, I had accumulated over $76,000 in savings.

One week in the spring of '84, two letters arrived in the New Venture mailbox within a couple of days of each other. The first was from Patriot Leasing, an Illinois financial services company. The letter outlined the configuration of twenty IBM Series One computers the company was trying to liquidate. The other was from a major Canadian bank inquiring as to whether I could provide them with an unmentioned quantity of IBM Series Ones.

While at the time I could not have recognized a Series One to save my life, I can say that as I studied these two letters I did so acutely aware of the fact that, once again, opportunity was knocking at my door.

The fact that I had no idea what a Series One was, or what it did, was of little or no consequence. The IBM documentation enclosed with the leasing company's letter was a perfect match to the configuration of the equipment requested by the bank. That was all I needed to know.

After several discussions with both parties it was agreed that New Venture would purchase six Series Ones along with several pieces of requisite peripheral equipment for $61,500 Canadian. This amount, added to shipping charges and applicable import taxes, brought my costs on the deal to over $74,000.

The import taxes and shipping costs would have to be absorbed up front. The balance owing to the leasing company had to be secured by a letter of credit, prior to shipping, and was payable immediately after my customer had a chance to inspect the equipment. Once the equipment passed inspection, the $61,500 purchase price would be transferred to an account in Rosemont, Illinois.

In early May of 1984 the computers arrived at the bank's data processing centre. Each one was clean, undamaged and fully functional. As documented, it was a perfect match. And with the stroke of a pen, bank information systems manager Scott Duco transferred ownership of the equipment from Patriot Leasing to New Venture Leasing to the Monarch Bank of Canada. Bang - bang – bang, it was over.

The $61,500 transferred as planned, leaving New Venture Leasing with only fifteen hundred dollars in cash, and one very large receivable. Which the bank made good on exactly nine days later.

Ten minutes after receiving payment for the Series Ones I arrived at my bank and nervously handed the teller a deposit slip filled out with such haste that even I could only barely read it. Looking side to side as the girl tried to decipher the number I almost missed the way she raised her eyebrows as she began to key in the amount. The deposit slip read $211,614.82.

I was rich.

The day I deposited this cheque was also the day I retired as a courier. The payoff on the Series One deal provided me with all the security I needed to become a full time entrepreneur, and the mailings I'd sent out had generated enough leads and contacts to keep me busy fourteen hours a day. The time to move on had finally arrived.

After leaving AMB I immediately rented some office space in the building where I had established a corporate identity, as well as a large warehouse in the northeast corner of the city. The warehouse was an essential part of my plan.

My dealings with Tezco had taught me there was an enormously favourable shift in my negotiating position if I somehow were to have physical control of the equipment I was trying to buy. The key to success was in the purchase of inventory. If purchased at a low enough price, anything could be sold at a profit.

If I were to make a low-ball offer for some equipment while it was still in its owner's possession, more often than not the offer would be refused. People would rather leave equipment sitting unused than accept a low offer, because they never factored in the hidden costs of their inaction.

If, however, I were to low-ball a company for equipment I was already warehousing for them, they were much more likely to accept the offer. Not to accept meant they might have to take some action on their own to explore other avenues of liquidation. And rather than actively pursue other options, most large companies were inclined to passively accept a loss on their outgoing equipment and simply leave it up to the bean-counters to deal with the shortfall.

The psychology of this scenario was unmistakable. Once equipment left a company's physical possession, perceived value dropped by at least fifty percent.

In order to implement this strategy my company offered to pick-up and warehouse any form of computer equipment, free of charge, for ninety days, during which time I would attempt to sell the equipment for a straight twenty percent commission. If I were unable to sell the equipment within the ninety-day period, its owners were then free to pick it up or start paying warehousing charges.

In the end most companies avoided paying warehouse charges on "unsold" equipment by simply relinquishing ownership, or accepting an offer for it that was well below market value. And once the ownership was transferred to New Venture, the equipment usually sold within the week.

While this strategy might sound like a scam, it really wasn't. I never held a gun to anyone's head to get them to abandon or undersell equipment. Companies just kept doing it. If consigned equipment in the care of New Venture Leasing no longer fit their plans, companies decided on their own not to pay warehousing charges on outdated assets. So, many took the path of least resistance and turned the equipment over to me.

Well, once companies literally started to *give* me inventory, was I supposed to sell equipment from my consigned inventory and keep twenty percent of the revenue? Or sell equipment that I owned outright and keep one hundred percent of the revenue? You didn't have to be a business grad to figure this one out.

During the first year following my departure from AMB Courier the North American economy was surging and New Venture Leasing certainly caught the full wave. Things couldn't have been going better, and by February of 1985 I was able to buy a nice home in a fashionable Don Mills neighbourhood.

The price of my new house was $355,000, and it was purchased with $115,000 of my own cash, and $240,000 of borrowed money. The cash I used was taken out of New Venture Leasing Inc. in the form of salary, dividends and a shareholder's loan - the details of which were worked out by Joseph Friedman, my new accountant.

The specifics of this monetary breakdown were unimportant to me. These were Joe's problems. The only thing I cared about was that I was a homeowner. And not only was I a homeowner, I still had over $214,000 in the bank, and guaranteed lease revenue that would pay New Venture $9,150 per month for the next five years. Life was very good.

Just prior to buying the house, I had decided to seek out the services of an accountant, and I wound up choosing a personable middle aged gent by the name of Joe Friedman.

After retaining him, Joe's first order of business was to transform New Venture Leasing, into New Venture Leasing *Inc.* The transformation from a sole proprietorship to a limited corporation being an essential move because as Joe explained it, "To generate such revenues as a sole proprietorship is to subject the money to the highest tax rate possible... your personal rate. But, by incorporating New Venture, while subjecting your money to two tax rates, corporate and personal, given the differences in marginal rates, and when and how we declare the money, you'll end up thousands of dollars ahead."

And I couldn't really argue with that.

The next thing Joe did was to set up another incorporated company called Compu Manufacturers. The lowest corporate tax rates in this country are paid by manufacturers and since New Venture routinely upgraded much of the equipment it sold, it technically was a manufacturing company. Even though the upgrading consisted of removing one memory board from used Machine A and placing it in used Machine B, this process, for tax purposes at least, "manufactured" new Machine C. After setting up Compu Manufactures Corp (CMC), any equipment New Venture's sold or leased was first purchased from CMC at greatly inflated prices. The effect of this was to keep the bulk of the profits in the "manufacturing" company, thereby reducing my overall tax burden to its lowest possible level.

The late eighties were a time when even the greatest of individual fortunes seemed to grow exponentially. The world economy was steaming along. Fuelled by inflation, junk bonds, and government deficits, all sectors of every western economy seemed to be growing in leaps that defied fiscal gravity.

With my own financial strategy firmly in place, New Venture Leasing and Compu Manufacturers boldly moved forward into the province's grossly overheated economy. From my minuscule corner, in the midst of this global binge, I continued to generate revenues that went far beyond even my most optimistic projections.

By March of 1989, still several months shy of my thirty-second birthday, I had accumulated approximately five million dollars in assets. I was, or at least I had come to believe that I was, as Tom Wolfe put it, a "master of the universe".

Included in this five million dollar asset base was the house I had purchased in 1985 for $335,000. The realty boom, along with several renovations, had raised the value of my home to more than one million dollars. There was also the cottage on Lake Rosseau which, though heavily mortgaged, still represented over $300,000 in equity. There was over nine hundred thousand dollars of personal and corporate cash, as well as stocks, bonds, automobiles, RSPs, and most importantly of all - an offer.

In January of 1989, Patriot Leasing offered to purchase my corporate empire. In formulating its offer, Patriot factored in the dollar value of all lease revenues ($41,250 per month), the residual value of the equipment on lease, and in inventory, plus the value of "goodwill" these companies carried with their established customers and tabled on offer of $2,250,000 (US). All cash.

My response to their unsolicited offer was not only simple, it was delivered with the arrogance of a fool who had begun to believe in his own myth. It's not that the offer wasn't fair. On the contrary, while I didn't acknowledge it to them it seemed to be a very generous offer. But this was 1989, and what was a "master of the universe" going to do with a mere three million dollars during these high-powered times? Besides, I had a plan that would make me at least three million over the next couple of years, and I would still have my companies.

"Offer rejected,... nice try guys."

On April the 14th, 1912 the greatest ship of its day struck an iceberg while steaming across the North Atlantic. It is said that at the moment of impact, few if any of the passengers on board even noticed the collision that had sealed their fate. Those who were sleeping - slept, those who were eating - ate, those who were dancing - danced. All on board that fateful night carried on with life, completely unaware that the events necessary to end the lives of so many on board had already taken place. The ship sank in less than three hours.

In April of 1989, exactly seventy seven years after the downing of the RMS *Titanic*, I walked out of Joe Friedman's office holding the corporate seal of the newly formed Hannibal Investments Corporation. I had decided to become a real estate mogul and Hannibal Investments Corp was to be my flagship company.

A couple of years earlier, Caroline and I had made a little over $200,000 when we sold a parcel of land I had purchased shortly after we were married. And while I have never forgotten the look on Caroline's face when our lawyer handed us the cheque, it was me that never got over the significance of the transaction.

I came to believe that, given enough capital, dealing in Toronto real estate was a no-lose proposition. And now that I had the capital, once again I could hear opportunity knocking loud and clear. Hannibal Investments was just the vehicle I needed to rocket myself into the outer stratosphere.

It was a Friday, and I was on my way to meet Caroline. We had arranged for a babysitter and had decided to spend the weekend hanging out downtown. We checked into a hotel and spent the next two days dining, dancing, shopping and fooling around like a couple of teenagers. And somewhere along the way I took the time to confidently lay out my plan for the coming years.

The five million dollars we had amassed to that point would soon look like petty cash. I reasoned that with the capital we had to work with, my own particular brand of cunning, and the "can't miss" nature of Toronto real estate, we would be worth fifty million by the time I was forty. Fifty million, I actually said that.

I recall that weekend as one of the happiest of my life. There was a taste and feel about it that was different from other times. It was better. I felt I had the world at my feet. And I'm sure that even as I made love to my wife, my performance was enhanced by the vision of $50,000,000 that was mixed in with my every thought. I couldn't get the money out of my head. It was as if I had already earned it.

Yet, as I basked in the glory of that opulent weekend, happily dreaming of ways to spend my forthcoming $50,000,000, I did so completely unaware of the fact that from the moment I'd registered Hannibal Investments Corp, my fate, much like those on board the famous ocean liner of 1912, had been sealed. The events that would lead to my downfall had already taken place.

A BETTER PLACE

The RMS *Hannibal Rankin* had struck an iceberg, and its captain hadn't felt a thing. It was amazing how quickly it would all be over.

Chapter Ten
CHAPTER TEN

THE MORNING SUN WAS NOW an orange fireball that shone brightly over the tall hedge on the yard's east side. And as if charged by the sun's growing intensity, not only had the muted thumping beneath my left temple begun to pound relentlessly, it had also spread to both sides of my head.

Lying prone in the lounger, I knew from experience that getting on my feet was the first step to recovery. I had to get up and take a walk, or get some food into my system - anything to get my body moving. But it was useless, I simply could not move.

Stretched out in the blinding sun, I grew angrier with myself over the previous night's drinking binge.

I had not accompanied my wife and children to the cottage because I had too much work to do in preparation for an upcoming court appearance. And now I was too hung over to prepare for anything.

I couldn't even put my arm over my eyes to shield them from the sun. I tried, but the arm draped so heavily across my face that as soon as I put it there I began to feel sick. All I could do was lie there, and wonder just how much worse the day was going to get.

By instinct I reached into my shirt pocket, hoping to find my sunglasses. They were my last chance for any comfort at all. But alas, even this small mercy was not to be found. There were no glasses in my slightly torn pocket - only two small pieces of paper.

I was definitely going to have to get up.

Drawing energy from the growing futility of my situation, I blocked out all sense of thought, and lurched up to a sitting position. It was a move I had assumed would make me feel better. But as the bulk of my two hundred-pound mass dropped crudely into the pit of my stomach, I wasn't so sure the move had helped anything at all.

Jumping up, I stumbled awkwardly, as my weight redistributed itself once again – this time dropping to the soles of my feet. My sense of equilibrium almost totally gone, I stepped shakily towards the back door, uncertain as to whether or not my legs would carry me that far.

Pausing at a nearby railing, I could feel the sweat pouring off me as I stopped for a moment to collect myself.

How could I have gotten so drunk last night, on this of all weekends? This is a disaster.

Three short days away from a court appearance which, should it not go my way, might finish me off completely, I was far too fucked up to study any of the legal files I was supposed to review this weekend.

The case involves a $160,000 overdraft left over from a company I had formed with two minority partners that owned and managed a small strip-mall north of the city. Several months after the partnership began to unravel the bank came-a-knocking. And since I was the only one foolish enough to personally guarantee the company's line of credit, the bank chose me, and only me, to sue for the balance of the outstanding funds.

Which it has proceeded to do, and will do successfully according to my lawyer if we don't win the Motion that is set to be heard on Tuesday morning.

The Motion we have filed is a long shot. My lawyer sees only one razor-thin strain of legal logic, which, if he can get the judge to recognize it would prevent the bank from taking any action against me personally. But, while he does not completely rule out the possibility of success, he also isn't overly optimistic about my chances.

So, that's why I had remained at home – to study those files.

Over the counsel of my wife (let the lawyer handle it) and protests of my lawyer (there's nothing you can do at this point) I decided to stay behind and see if there was anything I could do to improve my chances of winning. I'd had to really. I couldn't afford to lose this one. A loss would set the final dominoes in motion that could topple me within a matter of months.

Swaying involuntarily against the railing, the searing pain in my head was a constant reminder of just how big a mistake I'd made in ignoring my wife and lawyer. Not only was I feeling like I'd fallen off a tall building. I also had three days of legal study ahead of me in which I was supposed to gain some useful insight into the law's most complex nuances so I could solve a sophisticated legal riddle that my lawyer hadn't been able to crack in over two years. And I was going to have to undertake this task at a time when my mind couldn't properly process the subtle intricacies of a game of Go-Fish.

No wonder I felt like I might throw up.

And it wasn't like this excursion to the cottage wasn't an important one.

On July the 15th the cottage was scheduled to become the property of Mr Sammy Tsang. I had insisted on that date, (even though I could have used the money a month earlier) over Mr Tsang's protests, so that my kids could have one last hoorah at their beloved Muskoka retreat. It was killing me to let the place go, but there was nothing I could do about it. I couldn't carry the mortgage any longer.

Over the previous three years I had lost control of a considerable number of assets. There were two strip-malls, an office building, six commercial condominiums, four waterfront residential condominiums, and a couple of undeveloped parcels of land that had all slipped through my fingers one way or another. And while all of it had hurt, even as an aggregate all of these losses didn't cut through me like the thought of losing the cottage.

The cottage would be the first item I would lose that I truly cared about. And other than my house, the one I most feared having to part with. And not just because I was going to have to explain to my children why we couldn't go there anymore. It also hurt like hell to lose it under such circumstances - selling it one week before the bank would have listed it under Power of Sale. It made it seem like the whole experience of owning the damn thing was nothing more than a huge mistake.

The night I signed the papers to sell the place was the same night I started making my humiliating appearances on *The Oprah Winfrey Show.*

Weakly stumbling across the deck, trying to bring some feeling to my moribund legs, I now had two battles to fight. While each breath brought a new wave of pain shooting through my head, I now also had to contend with the anger I felt whenever I thought about losing the cottage.

I knew I didn't have time to be angry about the cottage, or anything else for that matter. Being angry wasn't going to help me get through the next few days. But I couldn't help it. Damn it, I was pissed off.

How did you fuck everything up so badly?

Trying to fight back, I used the energy the anger had created to propel myself towards the entrance of the house. But even the anger could only drive me so far. God, I was feeling like hell. I didn't have a leg under me. And just because I had to get into the house and get some things done, did nothing to change that. Even before I reached the doorway, I had to grab onto the family barbecue for support.

Resting against the barbecue, my grip on its unfinished wooden handle growing less reliable with each passing moment, I caught sight of something I hadn't yet noticed. Ever since I'd jumped up from the lounger, I had been holding the two pieces of paper I'd found in my shirt pocket.

The first one was an American Express receipt. The total was $192.67, $157.67 plus a $35.00 tip. One hundred and ninety two dollars. That certainly explained the hangover.

The second was a plain white piece of paper. It read,

Thanks for your help. See you Monday.
Love Barb 493-4487

The sight of Barb's note must have caused my heart to pick it up a notch because within seconds of seeing it the pounding in my head got even worse.

Looking at the note, I couldn't really make much sense of it.

Barb? Barb? – "Thanks for your help?" What could I possibly have helped her with? And "See you on Monday" – what were we doing on Monday? Is that what we were talking about down by my car, and *were* we making out?

The way I was feeling, I knew the last thing I wanted to do was think about Barb. But there didn't seem to be anything I could do to shake her image from my mind. And it was while I was standing there, clinging to the barbecue handle that I had my first real memory of kissing Barb – hard – the previous night.

Fuck! Had I really done that?

Reliving these lost moments from the previous evening I released my grip on the barbecue and dropped my face into the palms of my clammy hands. However this remorseful posture did nothing to drive Barb from my thoughts, and immediately after assuming it, I began to see her even more clearly than before.

Even through the darkness of closed eyes, Barb kept coming more clearly into focus. Until finally, not only could I see myself kissing her the night before, I could also feel my hands roaming freely over the outer regions of her clothing.

Christ Hannibal! Are you out of your fucking mind?

Further distressed by the thought of Barb and I pawing away at one another like a couple of school kids (which I suppose she was), I tried to drop to my knees, but before I reached the ground, my ass clipped the front of the barbecue and down I went. Toppling in a heap onto the deck below.

My recollections of Barb already had me feeling like a Grade-A loser, but as I crashed onto the cedar deck, I reached a conclusion right around the moment of impact that made almost everything else (except maybe the pounding in my head) seem quite trivial.

Rolling onto my back, my ability to rise debatable at best, it suddenly became so clear that on a day I had purposefully set aside to tackle a couple of serious issues I had managed to hit yet another all time low and it wasn't even 7:00 am.

As this truth sunk in I couldn't help but wonder – even if I could get to my feet, what was the point?

All the businesses were gone – the real estate, the cash, the cottage, one of the cars, the Lexus and the house would be next (even winning the Motion on Tuesday would only delay this outcome for a few months at best). I had three other lawsuits pending, no current prospects, and perhaps worse than all of this I couldn't even see how I was employable at this point in my life.

So, what was the point of getting up, anyway?

I'm not sure how long I remained down on the deck pondering all of this but there did come a time when I could hear the phone ringing.

While my first reaction was to ignore it, little by little it occurred to me that it was probably Caroline trying to get through. Who else would be calling at 7:00 am, let alone let it ring forty or fifty times?

So, while still in a dispirited haze, I started to make my way inside the den to the impatiently ringing phone.

"Hello?"

"Hello, Hannibal... Hannibal?"

"Jack?"

"Hannibal, Jesus man... where have you been. I've been calling for over half an hour?"

"Jack, is that you? What the... Oh sorry... I was outside, I guess I didn't hear it ringing. Jack, what the...?"

"Hannibal, are you awake?... You sound all fucked up."

"Yeah, yeah, I've been up for over an hour. Jack, what...?"

"Hannibal, listen... listen carefully. Bruce Thatcher is dead... Hannibal? Hannibal? Did you hear me? Thatch is dead."

Though I heard what Jack had said, when I first tried to respond, nothing would come out.

"Hannibal, you okay?... Did you hear me?"

"Jack, you gotta be... I mean that can't be right."

"I just got off the phone with his wife. She called. I gotta go pick her up... We have to get down to Niagara Falls. Listen, that credit card you gave me last night, can I use it?"

"Credit card?... Oh... yeah, of course," I answered, unable to recall giving it to him. "Go right ahead. What are you going down to Niagara for? I can't believe what you're telling me? Are you sure?"

"It's what his wife told me. I can't believe it either... I'll call you from down there. When I know more."

"Jack, wait. How? I mean… how?"

"I don't know any of the details, but it looks like he threw himself over the Falls."

Chapter Eleven

CHAPTER ELEVEN

IT WAS NINE O'CLOCK ON A QUIET summer morning and Bruce Thatcher was running well behind his normal Friday schedule. Throughout his working career at D. C. Investments, rare were the days when Bruce did not arrive at his desk by seven. Yet this was just such a day, and it marked the second time in less than a week that Bruce had wavered from his normal routine.

At D. C. Investments there was nothing uncommon about an individual being late for work twice in one week. In fact, the whole notion of "being late" was almost indefinable since few of the employees had designated hours. A time clock is seldom observed in such a sales environment. People work the hours required to keep their desks clear and their commissions in-line with their respective lifestyles. Punctuality and discipline are not common traits among your typical investment brokers.

But this was not the case with Bruce Thatcher. It was almost unthinkable for him to be late at all, and for it to happen twice in one week was without precedent. Despite his preferred status with the company Bruce was always at his desk long before anyone else arrived.

As well as being the first to arrive, Bruce was usually the last man out the door in the evening. Even on Fridays during the summer, when the city's financial district was deserted by the lunch-hour, Bruce would remain at his desk until at least 5:00 p.m. It may seem a little anal, but that's just the kind of guy he was.

On this particular Friday morning Bruce Thatcher had decided on a very different course of action. The task of opening up the offices of D. C. Investments would fall to somebody else this day, probably Brett Sadler or Scott Cotton. Brett or Scott were usually the first to arrive after Bruce, normally showing up about fifteen or twenty minutes behind him.

As he pondered who was more likely to show up first at his place of employment, he thought it would be better for those working that day if Brett Sadler arrived first. For, of the two, Brett made better coffee - almost as good as his own.

Regardless of who made the coffee at work that morning, by now it would already be done. After showering, and carefully picking through his closet, Bruce Thatcher selected a navy blue Nino Danieli suit to wear on this, his final day on earth.

The suit he chose was one of his favourites. While still maintaining the conservative appearance on which he insisted, its green and red pin stripes were woven into it in such a way that it gave the suit a real touch of panache. Matched with the proper tie, the suit took on an unmistakable aura of power. Just the look required to win the confidence of a potential investor.

If the truth were known, the grey Hugo Boss hanging beside the Danieli was Bruce's all time favourite. Despite its sporty cut, the suit's understated grey colouring afforded its wearer a truly dignified manner. It was a respectful and deferential look, and may have been more appropriate for the action he was about to take. Though for those same reasons Bruce determined the Boss would be more proper for his burial.

In accenting the crisply pressed suit, Bruce went with an older Stefano Ricci tie. It was no longer in style, but its muted blue colouring had the kind of subdued look he felt would be more fitting for the day he had planned. Most of his more recent ties were too flamboyant, sporting designer colours that gave off an almost festive look. And that wouldn't be right. After all, it wasn't like he was going to a party.

After donning a pair of black brogues, Bruce crept downstairs to his desk in the main floor den. Although the house was empty, he unlocked the top drawer as quietly as possible and took out a blue envelope. Slipping it into his jacket pocket, Bruce noticed three additional envelopes on top of the desk. These envelopes contained cheques to American Express, Bell Canada and Maclean's. He had written them out the night before, and reaching into a side drawer, he removed three stamps and attached them to the envelopes.

Resisting the impulse to go out to the backyard where he knew his wife and infant son were playing, Bruce dropped the three stamped envelopes on the small table by the front door and walked out into the morning sunlight. As he reached the front step he instinctively opened the side entrance to the garage. It was Friday, garbage day, and as he did every Friday morning Bruce Thatcher awkwardly dragged two large plastic pails down to the end of his driveway.

And from there Bruce took one final look at the street that had been "his" street for the past six years.

The neighbourhood was about twelve years old, and the trees and gardens that adorned each home had finally reached a point where they gave the street a decidedly established look. It was a look the street had lacked at the time Bruce and Jennifer Thatcher first moved into 43 Lanturn Lane.

Ever mindful of his plan, Bruce suddenly felt a little sad. What a shame to be leaving this neighbourhood, when it finally looked so good. However, this brief moment of sadness gave him no pause for second thoughts. He'd had second thoughts before, but would entertain no such notions today. The day's events would unfold as planned. It was definitely time to go.

Opening the door of his 1990 Maxima GXE, Bruce took a deep breath as he looked up into the bedroom window of four-month-old Andrew Thatcher. He squinted to focus in on the multi-coloured animal mobile that was suspended above his son's crib. It had been a gift to the yet to be born Andrew. Presented to his mother at a shower held just three weeks prior to his birth. What a happy day that had been, February the 8th, 1993.

With an involuntary shrug of his shoulders, Bruce slipped into the Nissan and without looking back made his final exit from 43 Lanturn Lane.

Travelling west across Highway 7, he opened the car's sunroof. In all the time he had owned the car, he had never once opened the roof while dressed for work. Rather than risk having the wind ravage his perfectly styled hair, Bruce had always relied on the car's meticulously set climate control feature to comfort him on his way to and from work. But this day was different, and since he wasn't going to the office, he allowed his hair to blow about in the soothing summer breeze. It made him feel so free.

Heading south on Highway 404, Bruce grunted derisively as he saw the line of cars backed up on the Don Valley Parkway at Highway 401. It was unbelievable to him that even at ten-thirty people were still lined up trying to get downtown. On a normal day he would have continued south, heading into the snarled mass of cars before him. Of course on a normal day he would have arrived at this intersection at about 6:30 a.m., when traffic was at least moving a little bit. Grateful that he was pulling off onto the westbound 401, Bruce felt genuinely relieved that he would never again have to deal with the vehicular congestion he faced each morning.

Driving across the 401, Bruce looked south in the direction of the Genuine Deli. It was only yesterday that he had told his closest friend, Jack MacDonald, that he would meet him and his cousin Hannibal, on the Deli Patio this very evening. He worried that perhaps he owed his friends an explanation for the course of action he had mapped out for himself. But then reasoned that such an explanation would serve no purpose. They could never understand what his life had become. Even Jack wouldn't understand, and Jack knew the reasons behind Bruce's unhappiness.

Life is such a paradox. In spite of the reservations he had for all the loose ends his suicide would leave behind, Bruce Thatcher felt great. Speeding along towards Highway 403, knowing full well that his life would soon be over, he felt as if he were soaring with eagles. The heaviness in his heart and mind had lifted. He felt as light as a feather, he felt young, and soon, soon he would be free.

It was the same carefree feeling that had come over him as he drove to the Niagara Peninsula just four days earlier. Except this time he felt even happier, for this time he would not allow himself to be fooled.

Driving to the same location earlier in the week, Bruce had become so happy that the demons which had haunted him in recent times would finally be put to rest, that he mistook these feelings of happiness as a sign he had conquered the dark forces of his life. He then reasoned that, with the demons conquered, there was no longer any reason to kill himself. Convinced that everything was going to be okay, Bruce had turned the car around in St Catharines, and driven back to Lanturn Lane the happiest man in Canada.

But alas, the following morning, the demons returned, stronger than ever. He had not conquered them at all. And as each day passed his sorrow grew deeper and deeper, further convincing Bruce that he could never again be a happy man.

On February the 14th, Bruce Thatcher had been dealt a fatal blow. The depression that set in afterwards was so dark, and so relentless, that it gutted the very core of his existence. From that point in time he saw himself as nothing more than the outer shell of a human being and he believed that no force on earth could restore his soul to its previous state of existence. It was too late. What was done, was done.

As the grey Nissan sped across the QEW, its destination nearing with each passing second, there was not even a trace of the depression that had dogged Bruce Thatcher these past few months. However, as he crossed the Burlington Bridge he understood that this absence of gloom and sorrow was only an illusion. He would not again abort his mission because he was seduced by a temporary lightness in his heart.

The plan he would execute this day offered him the only shelter he could see since being caught in this personal storm of misery. Peace and tranquillity would soon be his. There would be no second thoughts today. Perpetual happiness was less than an hour away.

Arriving in the vicinity of Niagara Falls, Bruce Thatcher parked in front of a restaurant located not more than three hundred yards from the top of nature's mightiest wonder.

Pressing a button to close the car's roof, he smiled as he noticed in the rear-view mirror how well his hair had held together. With the roof open, his journey had been made all the more pleasant by the feel of the sun and the wind on his face. It made him think he should have started using that roof years ago.

Running his hand through the back of his dark locks, Bruce went through a very short mental checklist. He reached inside his jacket to make sure the blue envelope was in place. Then, opening the car's glove compartment, he removed his wallet.

After making sure that the wallet contained only his identification, he placed it inside his jacket pocket, next to the envelope. Check. Reaching into his shirt pocket, he then felt the twenty-dollar bill he had placed there that morning. Check.

His list complete, Bruce took one last look in the rear-view mirror, dropped the keys into the console beside him and stepped out of the car.

Looking toward the water's edge as he exited the Maxima for the last time, the sound of crashing water sent adrenaline racing through his entire body. And moving across the parking lot Bruce started to tremble as the magnificence of his surroundings began to take hold.

It had been over twenty years since he had been to the Falls and he had forgotten what a powerful visual force they really were. But today, as the first speckles of mist began to settle on his face and hands, Bruce Thatcher was awestruck.

In making his way to a nearby restaurant, Bruce knew that he was too excited to eat. The sound of surging water was calling him to the edge of the mighty gorge, and he was anxious to fully absorb the miraculous setting in which he would play his final card.

Still, he contained his excitement until he was able to grab a cup of coffee. The coffee was not a stall tactic. Bruce knew he would be implementing his plan in very short order. It was just that, as in all circumstances of his life, Bruce Thatcher was not going to carry out his plan in a rash or barbaric manner. There was a definite methodology to be followed here, and he wanted to enjoy his coffee while he searched the area for a favourable point of entrance.

The cheerful girl working the counter looked stunned when Bruce told her to "keep it", referring to the eighteen dollars change he had coming after purchasing a large butter pecan coffee. He had never treated himself to a specialty coffee before, but he had always wanted to try the butter pecan version.

Making his way to a railing that overlooked the full expanse of Niagara Falls, Bruce was very proud of the large tip he had left the girl working the lunch counter. Her eyes had positively beamed as she realized the size of his gratuity.

"Geez, Mister, thanks a lot... are you sure?"

Never before had Bruce left such an outrageous tip, and for a moment he had second thoughts about having been so reckless. Then, confidently assuming that he had made the young girl's day, he just let it go. It would be his last act of human kindness, and he had truly been touched by her reluctant acceptance of his gracious offering.

Looking across the two great waterfalls before him, Bruce was once again blown away by their physical beauty. There was not a cloud in the sky, and the midday sun shimmered without obstruction off the river's emerald surface. Flowing ribbons of rushing water cascaded effortlessly around the jagged rock formations that jutted up from the river's floor, and then seemed to collide with the unbroken wall of raging white water that continuously crashed over the gorge's horseshoe shaped edge. What a perfect place to die.

Sipping lightly on his coffee as he continued to scan the river, Bruce noticed a rusted old barge lodged against some rocks a short way up from the Falls. The sight of this caused him a great deal of concern. He had never once considered the possibility he might get smashed against a rock on his way downriver. He wanted to be alive and conscious when he went over the top.

Prior to selecting the falls, Bruce had considered a high-dive from the Bloor Street viaduct or perhaps a well-timed collision with a TTC subway as a means of ending his life. But then decided that either of these methods might be a little gruesome. The Falls he had gauged as a much more dignified exit, though not if he were to be impaled against a rock. He would have to be careful.

Spinning around, Bruce Thatcher began to walk hurriedly upstream, along a path that ran parallel to the river. His heart was pounding. This was it. The end was now very close at hand.

As he walked, in lieu of a prayer, Bruce said a short goodbye to his mother and his three sisters, and even to his brother, Richard. To young Andrew Thatcher, whom he realized was probably enjoying his afternoon nap he simply sighed, once again horrified at the cruel charade that had been played on both of them.

Thinking of his wife Jennifer, he reached nervously into his jacket pocket and fingered the blue envelope resting beside his wallet. Once again reassured that the wallet and envelope were in place, Bruce focused in on two elderly tourists walking towards him on the same path.

As the two old sightseers were about to pass, Bruce calmly slipped off his jacket, and offering it to them, said,

"Excuse me, could you please hold this for a second?"

Before either of them had a chance to answer, Bruce thrust the jacket into the woman's hands and without another word hopped over a nearby guard rail.

As the tourists holding his jacket watched in horror, Bruce did a quick little step as he reached the river's edge and then hurled himself out as far as he could.

He entered the river feet-first. This surprised him, because each time he had visualized his entry he had gone in headfirst. But at the moment of truth, some involuntary survival instinct would not allow him to enter unfamiliar waters headfirst. After all, he didn't want to break his neck.

The stunned tourists never saw Bruce come up. The icy temperature of the water had shocked him so, his whole body simply locked-up. As he was pulled downriver he warily held his hands out in front of his body hoping to fend off any large rocks that might be looming in his path. As determined as he was to be alive and conscious when he went over the Falls, nothing was a certainty in these unforgiving waters.

But according to eyewitnesses, at approximately one-thirty five, Bruce Thatcher popped up about twenty feet from the crest of the Falls. They said he had his fist clenched high in the air and even seemed to be smiling as he struggled to catch one final breath. Then, as quickly as he popped up, Bruce was sucked under, never to be seen alive again.

As he popped up in the water, just seconds before going over the top, Bruce thrust his right arm up in the air in celebration of his victory over the mighty river. He knew that his death was only an instant away, and he was a happy man. There was no bitterness in his heart. He had no fear of the fate that was about to befall him, and no regrets about having chosen such a fate. As he thrashed about in the freezing waters that swirled around him, all

Bruce could feel was the warm glow of salvation.

He had purposely avoided saying a prayer before entering the water. Bruce knew that if the priests of his youth were right his actions on this day would damn him to eternal hell. Suicide was not to be tolerated, and prayers would not help.

But in his final second of life, Bruce Thatcher saw that the priests of his past had been wrong. In the face of the raging waters before him, he knew that his God, an all-merciful and ever-loving God, would never let one of his children suffer in eternal damnation. He knew that his God, God the Almighty, was just now preparing to receive him. Secure in this knowledge, Bruce smiled without shame, as eternal peace enveloped him.

There are storms that some men are simply not meant to weather, and it was Bruce Thatcher's fate to have been caught in just such a storm. There was no way to heal the wounds that had been inflicted on him. He accepted that. He knew long before he actually died that Friday afternoon that his life was already over. It had ended exactly one hundred and forty-three days prior to his stepping into the Niagara River. The events that had sealed his fate had taken place several months, and possibly years before that. This act of suicide was merely a formality.

Chapter Twelve

CHAPTER TWELVE

Soon AFTER SPEAKING WITH JACK, I began pacing the floors while I tried to make some sense of his early morning call. But it wasn't easy. The news he had delivered about Bruce was a lot to take in, especially at a moment when I wasn't exactly operating at full capacity to begin with. Yet, it wasn't my precarious state of mind, or the day's early hour that made understanding his news damn near impossible. It was the fact that almost from the moment I'd first heard it, I hadn't been able to catch my breath.

For several minutes after hanging up the phone the only way I could breathe was in deep, calculated gasps. It was like the act of inhaling had become a voluntary act, and each new breath was something I could no longer take for granted. It was a strange feeling, and one that further blurred the reality of Jack's news.

Bruce Thatcher – dead – and by his own hand – impossible.

I didn't know Bruce nearly as well as Jack did. But I had known the guy for almost thirty years. And he was about the last person I'd ever expect to commit suicide. Bruce was one of the most rational people I'd ever met. For someone like him to even consider killing himself was unthinkable. He just wasn't the type.

And besides, I'd seen him the previous week and he seemed fine. If he had something like this on his mind, I'm sure I would have - or certainly Jack would have - spotted a warning signal. A person does not simply walk out of his house one day and throw himself over Niagara Falls. Something had to be wrong with this picture.

Walking restlessly from one room to the next, I stopped in the kitchen and swallowed a small handful of Tylenols before continuing on. The pacing was helping to bring my breathing back to normal, leaving my mind free to search out a plausible explanation as to why the news of Bruce's death could not be true.

Lost in this thought, I barely noticed when I stepped into a marble pedestal near the front door and sent a large crystal elephant plummeting to the hardwood floor below. But even the sound of exploding crystal wasn't enough to interrupt my train of thought.

I was too close to convincing myself an error had been made about Bruce to concern myself with some damn piece of crystal, or its eighteen hundred-dollar replacement value. After all, by his own admission Jack had been awfully short on detail. And he was dealing with second or third-hand information. So there was no way he could be certain that anything had happened to Bruce.

Though somewhat buoyed by the reasonableness of the conclusion, I was still too restless to sit down. And rather than risk walking through the sea of glass the main floor was now awash in, I moved upstairs to continue my pacing on safer ground.

I'm not sure how many times I browsed through each of the bedrooms speculating about Bruce, but shortly after moving upstairs I did start to become quite conscious of something that had nothing to do with why I had gone up there in the first place.

Several times during my impromptu tour I was struck by what a nice house I lived in. It was something I suppose I'd always been aware of but had never given much thought. And even after thoroughly examining eleven of its twelve rooms, (I didn't go into my office because… well… because I almost never go in there) it was impossible to detect a significant design or decorative flaw. The place was pretty close to perfect.

Between 1986 and 1989 Caroline and I spent about $360,000 in reconstructing and remodelling the place. Together, we overlooked no detail as we unwittingly indulged ourselves in rebuilding the dreary structure I had purchased in 1985. (I say unwittingly because in 1989 spending $42,000 to remodel a single room - the kitchen - did not seem overly indulgent).

Two exterior walls had been knocked down in order to expand the house to almost twice its original size. A pool, jacuzzi and stand-up bar had been built in the backyard. Three separate skylights were installed on a newly constructed roof. And each tree, plant and bush on the grounds had been ripped out and replaced, along with every window, door, and patio stone.

Looking back on it, I don't know how we got so carried away. It all started with the notion that we might like a bigger kitchen, and before either of us knew it we were throwing the old house out one garbage bin at a time.

It became a sickness, and by the time we were finished with the property's interior, not a square inch of it had been left unchanged. Everything was redone, and not just the wall and floor areas. We're talking the works here, including ceilings, light fixtures, cupboards, sinks, faucets, tubs, and toilets. We were out of control, and in hindsight I guess I should be grateful we never found roaches in the place. Because I'm sure our reaction at the time would have been to replace them with bigger ones.

I suppose the time and effort we put into rebuilding the house is part of the reason I'd spent so much time lately worrying that I might eventually have to surrender it to creditors. However, as I ended my tour and found myself in my daughter's bedroom staring at the hand-painted 'Little Mermaid' character my wife had sketched onto her wall, for the first time in a long while I wasn't overly worried about the future of my home.

After putting on some shoes, I moved back downstairs to clean up the elephant I had trashed earlier. Having convinced myself that the news about Bruce was probably not true, I decided to carry on with the day until I heard something a little more concrete from Jack. I was still feeling uneasy about the initial reports of Bruce's death, but the whole thing struck me as too bizarre to have actually happened. That combined with the knowledge that speculating about what might have happened wasn't helping anything anyway, I concluded that the only thing I could do at this point was wait.

Come on Bruce – hang in there – I know you're okay.

After sweeping the remains of the elephant into a box, I ruled out sorting through the legal files I was suppose to be studying, opting instead for a different course of action.

Prior to selling the cottage, I had considered any possible avenue I might have for raising cash, including the sale of some personal items from the house.

In the end it was an idea I had passed on for a number of reasons. First, it struck me as a humiliating thing to do. Second, for all the money we had spent remodelling, there was precious little in the place I could unload quickly. (It's not like I could run an ad and try to sell the pool, or the kitchen cupboards, or anything like that.) And finally, for all there was that I could unload quickly, it wouldn't have come close to raising the cash it would have taken to save the cottage.

But this was a different day, and these were different circumstances. And for some reason I became bound and determined to sell – something. Even if it was just enough to get the $8500 Jack needed.

I don't know what set if off. Maybe it was the fact that I had trashed an eighteen hundred piece of crystal and had watched it disintegrate without an iota of regret. (How bad was I supposed to feel about breaking a gift from a former partner who'd left me high and dry after a real estate deal went bad?) Or maybe I was just looking to do something to get my mind off Bruce. But whatever it was that got me motivated, it proved to be extremely effective. Because by eleven o'clock I had re-appraised every item in the house and was ready to make a call.

Over the years my wife and I had accumulated a number of limited edition prints by Canadian wildlife artist Robert Bateman. There were six of them in all, and some of them were Bateman's finest. At retail, Caroline and I had paid a downtown art dealer a total of thirteen thousand dollars for all six pieces.

Sitting on the floor in the den I felt an unfamiliar calm as I started to check the phone book for the number of Masse Art Gallery. This was very unlike the previous occasion I had contemplated making this exact call.

Picking up the phone and dialing, I felt no shame, or guilt, about what I was about to do.

"Good afternoon, Masse Art Gallery."

"Yes, Sean Masse please."

"This is Sean."

"Sean, I thought it was you," I lied. "John Rankin here... do you remember me?"

Not having been to his store in over three years I felt pretty sure Sean Masse would not know who I was, but I was hopeful that talking to him in such a familiar way might help him to recall that I was once a wealthy and faithful customer.

"John Rankin... John Rankin... the name sounds fam... Oh yes, Mr Rankin, the Bateman collector. How are you? It's been quite some time since you dropped by to see us."

This guy either had one hell of a memory or he was awfully fast on the roll-a-dex.

"Yes it has and I'm fine, thank you. Yourself?"

"Never better. And how's our friend Jack doing?"

This guy was good. Even I had forgotten it was actually Jack who had introduced me to Masse Art Gallery.

"Oh, he's great. You know Jack, always miles ahead of the rest of us."

"Yes that definitely sounds like our boy. So what can I do for you today? Is there anything specific you were looking for?"

"Well to be truthful I'm not looking for anything."

Now don't sound desperate.

"The reason you haven't seen me in a while is that I spend most of my time in Vancouver."

"Oh, really."

"Yeah, just busy as hell with a bunch of Pacific Rim companies. Anyway, my wife and I have finally decided to move out there. We're leaving in about a month," I casually explained.

"I see. Well, that sounds very exciting."

"Yes, I think so too. But we're moving into a condo on the waterfront that's about half the size of our house, so there's going to be a lot of stuff we won't be taking with us."

"Uh huh."

"Yeah, well I was going to put an ad in the paper for these prints we own, but then I thought, maybe I should run it by Sean first," I said, trying to sound like Masse and I were close friends.

"Well that's very kind of you. I'll be happy to help you out," Masse responded, sensing a major windfall for himself.

"Yes, I thought you would be. I'll fax you a listing of what we have. I want $8500 for myself. Whatever you get over that is your business. I'm going to Vancouver Monday evening, so I'll hold off until four before placing the ad. Let me know before then if you can hit that price. Fair enough?"

"Yeah, sure, but I can't promise anything."

Hanging up the phone, I leaned back against the couch and tried to gauge how plausible my story might have sounded to Sean Masse. There was a time when I could tell within the first few minutes of a conversation if I was going to be successful in completing a deal. It was a sort of sixth sense I had developed through constant wheeling and dealing over the phone. I could hear meaning in people's words that went far beyond what they were actually trying to say.

However, because I hadn't successfully completed a deal of any sort in almost two years, my ability to read another person's intentions was something I could no longer trust. I couldn't tell if Masse had seen through my little charade about moving to Vancouver or not. I thought my story had sounded credible, but I wouldn't know for sure until he tendered his offer. The price I had set for the prints was a fair one, but if the wily art dealer were sharp enough to detect any desperation in my call, he wouldn't offer anything close to the $8500 asking price.

Chapter Thirteen
CHAPTER THIRTEEN

IT WAS ABOUT ONE IN THE AFTERNOON before I heard back from Jack, and after talking to him any false hope I had clung to about Bruce Thatcher quickly disappeared. It was clear from a number of credible witnesses that a man had gone over the Falls, and in the absence of a body, all indications pointed towards Bruce.

According to at least two witnesses the man had entered the water voluntarily. The couple claimed that someone matching Bruce's description had approached them at approximately 1:30 p.m. and asked them to hold a blue sports jacket. After dumping-off the jacket, the man then ran over to the edge of the river and jumped in.

The jacket contained Bruce's wallet, as well as an envelope for his wife, and had been identified by Jennifer Thatcher as her husband's. His car was found near a restaurant in the area, and an employee there was certain that she hold sold him a coffee shortly after one o'clock. In the face of all of this evidence, it didn't seem likely that an error had been made. Bruce Thatcher was dead.

Jack was obviously upset as he gave me all the grim details. And after listening to his account of things, the whole picture came clearly into focus. Now that the news was officially true, the reality of it all began to hit home. Someone I knew quite well had become so disenchanted with his life that he chose to end it in this most frightful of manners.

After Jack had finished telling all that he knew, I asked him almost rhetorically, "How could Bruce have done such a thing, it just doesn't make sense," and was surprised to find that Jack did know something about what had sent Bruce over the Falls.

"I dunno Hannibal, I certainly didn't see this coming. Although I can't help thinking maybe I should have. Bruce was dealing with some pretty difficult stuff lately... he always had been really," Jack started to say, before his voice trailed off into silence.

"What do you mean, was Bruce sick? That's the only reason I can think of. Was he dying or something?"

There was a long pause on the other end of the line before Jack commented on my speculative question.

"Look Hannibal, I don't really want to get into this over the phone. It's been a long day, and it's not even half over, so..."

"Yeah, I'm sorry," I cut in, wishing I hadn't asked the question in the first place.

"Just wait till I get home and I'll tell you everything I know," Jack replied in a raspy whisper.

"Sure, no problem. You doing okay?"

"To be honest with you, it's all so creepy I don't know how I feel. I just stand out there looking at those Falls and I can't believe it happened. What an awful way to go. A cop down here told me a body will usually surface within the first three days, but they're not sure when, or where, or even if Bruce will ever come up at all."

"Jesus, that's scary. This whole thing sounds like something out of a Stephen King book. But I know what you mean about not knowing how to feel. All morning I thought you'd be calling back to tell me everything was okay. And now that it's not, I'm just sort of numb."

"Me too." Jack answered, before carrying on after a brief pause. "Listen, I can't stay down here any later than tomorrow night. Whether they find Bruce or not I've got to be home for Monday. There's some things I need to take care of, so, if you don't hear from me before then, I'll call you first thing Monday morning and we'll see what we can get going."

"Sure. Just take care of things down there and don't worry, we'll raise the $8500," I chimed in confidently, not sure if I was trying to bolster Jack's spirits or my own.

"I hope so. Anyway I appreciate you trying to help me. I knew you would, but I still appreciate it."

"No sweat. You know I can't believe Michael Kilroy is putting the screws to you."

"Yeah, I can't either. But the old bastard probably needs the money. I'm sure he's got his own problems to worry about," Jack answered reflectively.

"Maybe, but no matter how badly he needs the cash, I'd never have thought he'd try to squeeze it out of you. I mean, he was like a father to you."

"Yeah, well, it's a strange world out there these days old buddy. You just never know what's going to happen next."

"I suppose, but..." I began before Jack cut me off with a surprising interjection.

"Speaking of which, what the fuck was with you last night?"

"What do you mean, what was with me?"

"With you and Barb for chrissakes. I thought I was going to have to turn a hose on the two of you."

Ouch. At this point in the day I could clearly remember fooling around with Barb the previous night, but I wasn't sure how indiscreet it all might have been. (Apparently I had my answer now.) I also couldn't remember anything about a possible date on Monday.

"Yeah, well, like you said it's a strange world," I started trying to explain, before throwing in the towel and ending my response with, "Ahh shit, I don't know how it started... but obviously things got out of hand. To tell you the truth I don't really remember too many of the details."

"You were pretty loaded by closing time. So was Barb. She must have downed at least a dozen B-52's on top of whatever else she had during the night."

"So how bad did it get?"

"I'm not sure I know it all, but around last call you disappeared somewhere, so I went over to have a drink with my doctor pals. And around one-thirty or so, after I'm finished with these guys, you're still missing. So I figured you must have fucked-off home. Anyway, I stumble out to the parking to grab a cab that's sitting there and I look over to see if your car is still where you left it and not only is it there - you and Barb are leaning up against it trying to devour one another."

I was already feeling like a heel before Jack started recounting the story and listening to his version of the details wasn't making me feel any better.

"Well, seeing you and Barb together like that I wasn't really sure what I was supposed to do about it. But I figured if you were going to start something with her – which I'd strongly advise against by the way - you'd be better off doing it when you were sober. So I jumped in the cab, and told the guy to drive over to your car. Then I tried to figure out an excuse that would pry you two apart."

"Yeah, so what did you come up with?"

"I acted as if I was staying at your place and that I needed you to get in."

Listening to Jack tell the story brought a lot if it back to me. And for the first time that day I could (much to my horror) recall telling Barb a couple of pretty intimate details of my life. Like my incurable fascination with lingerie and how much I'd like to see her dressed up in some nasty silks and satins. It was an idea she had eagerly embraced.

"And how did Barb and I react to the intrusion?"

"At first you growled something at me. Then you and Barb started whispering to each other. I couldn't hear what you were saying but I think Barb wanted you to give me your house keys and send me on my way. But you didn't. You just talked to her for another minute or so, and that was about it."

"That was it – nothing else?" I inquired tentatively, embarrassed about all Jack had told me, but still hoping he might know something about the date I had arranged for Monday.

"Yep, pretty much. Before she left, she wrote you a note. Then you jumped in the cab with me."

"I had a feeling I had acted like an asshole, but I didn't... Man, what in the fuck was I thinking?"

"Yeah, well that's sort of what I was wondering. I mean she's a nice looking girl and all that, but Christ, Hannibal."

Christ, Hannibal – I guess that about says it all.

121

"I don't know what to say," I started out like it was a preamble to an apology. But Jack cut me off again.

"I think the best thing here is to say – nothing. Not to me, or to anybody else if you know what I mean. There's nothing you can do about it now. So just be cool and let it blow over. In the end nothing happened."

"You think nothing happened?"

"No, obviously something happened. But let's face it, you could have tossed me your house key and left with Barb. But you didn't. You did the right thing. You went home. And I'd focus on that part of it if I were you."

"I suppose, but that's a little different than saying nothing happened."

"Hannibal, supposing anything about last night is only going to get you into more trouble. You could have gone home with her, but you didn't. Leave it at that. What's done is done. There's no point in being *too* hard on yourself. I mean, you've never done anything like that before – right?"

"No, never," I answered truthfully.

"Then write it off. If after seven years of marriage the worst thing you've ever done is a little drunken smooching, you're not doing too bad. So just let it go. Anything you do now to try and fix it will only make things worse."

Sitting quietly, I tried to absorb Jack's logic. There was some merit to what he was saying. Technically, I had not cheated on my wife. And it was the first time I had ever stepped out of line. So part of me could see where he was coming from.

On the other hand, knowing that another part of me was wishing Jack had just minded his own business the previous night I understood that the depths of my indiscretion went several steps beyond what Jack was aware of. And then of course there was the matter of the date I had arranged for myself.

"You're right. Especially about making things worse if I try to fix it. But ahhh, I seem to have made a date with Barb for Monday. Do you know anything about that?" I finally had to ask.

"Maybe. Inside the cab you told me Barb had inherited some money from her grandmother. Apparently after taxes, she'll be getting almost two hundred grand. Does that sound right to you?"

"Yeah," I responded quietly, surprised to find that it did.

"Well, right now she's living in some condo at the top of the city. The place was her grandmother's. Anyway, it was appraised last week at $185,000, but all of the others mentioned in the Will have agreed to let Barb have the place for $160,000. And Barb knows you own a few condos, so she wants you to take a look at the place, I presume to give her your opinion on the property from an investment point of view."

While not recalling all of the specifics of what Jack was telling me, this part of my conversation with Barb was coming back to me.

"Oh yeah, I met her in the restaurant on my way back from the men's room and she was telling all this. I guess *that's* why I'm seeing her on Monday. She wants a second opinion on the condo," I answered as the final pieces of the puzzle dropped into place.

"Well, I think Monday might have become the back-up plan after I arrived in the cab. Because according to you, Barb wanted you to go back to her place last night so that you could take a look at it. And after your expert inspection of the premises, Barb had assured you that the liquor cabinet was full, and that you were then free to do anything you wanted… anything."

"That's what she said? I was free to do anything I wanted?"

"That's what you said, she said."

"Holy shit. And I was going to go for it. Like I haven't fucked up enough things this year. Now I'm ready to toss my marriage away for a cabinet full of liquor and a night with a beautiful girl."

"Come on now, we just went through this. Put it behind you. Half the guys I know would have tossed their marriage away just for the cabinet full of liquor. So stop overreacting. Just remember two words – nothing happened."

"Yeah right. Nothing happened."

"That's right – and nothing will happen so long as you stay away from her on Monday."

"Don't worry, that's one appointment I'll be cancelling."

"You better – because if you think you feel bad now about last night, imagine how you'd feel if you had actually gone home with her?"

As he was predisposed to do, Jack had analyzed the situation and throughout the course of our conversation had framed it within perfectly logical parameters. And of course he was right.

There was nothing I could do about what had already happened. So maybe the thing to do was to minimize the damage and move on. Even if I weren't thrilled about it.

"Listen, I've got to get going. I told Jennifer I'd meet her at her hotel before two," Jack started to say as he began to bring our conversation to an end.

"How's she holding up?"

"About like you'd expect. I'll fill you in when I see you. And Hannibal, remember, the sooner you deal with Barb the better off you'll be."

"Don't worry, I'll be cancelling. Everything's under control here. Call me when you get some news on Bruce."

Chapter Fourteen
CHAPTER FOURTEEN

As YOUNGSTERS, GROWING UP on the same street in the Beaches district of Toronto, Bruce Thatcher, Jack and I were practically inseparable. Or more properly put, Bruce and I followed Jack around wherever he went.

We all lived within half a block of one another in an older working class neighbourhood that had been built not long after the turn of the century. The houses were solid brick, three-storey, semi-detached units that, while blessed with an unmistakable touch of character, would only barely qualify as middle-class.

Being a modest neighbourhood, it was often the case that many of the houses actually served as a home to more than one family. With the majority of households being supported by a single working-class wage, many families needed to rent out the top floor of their house just to make ends meet.

Neither my home, nor Jack's was an exception to this common rental practice. It was often the case that a room, or even a floor in either home would be occupied by a tenant - though usually only by a single person or childless couple. My place wasn't big enough to accommodate a family with children, and Jack's father wouldn't tolerate having kids around.

The Thatcher household on the other hand did not rent out

---

space. With the exception of an uncle who lived with them for a while the Thatcher's never had a tenant in their home – nor many guests for that matter. But for the short time that he was there, Bruce's Uncle Fred, or Fog as he was known to all the kids on the street, was a great guy to have around. He was like everyone's big brother.

He always had time for us, no matter what we were doing. Whether it was playing hockey, or baseball, or taking us to the pool for a swim (where he'd jump off the ten metre diving board as many times as requested), or even for a spin on his motorcycle – Uncle Fog was up for just about anything.

Until one day he was suddenly gone. Packed up and moved on without so much as a goodbye.

The inevitable result of so many homes renting out rooms was to fill the neighbourhood with an improbable number of children. Which was a great thing, especially when you're a child yourself. Because while our over-populated street may have been an equal mix of Protestants and Catholics, the children of each household practised only one religion - road hockey.

Services started each year around Labour Day, and would carry on without interruption through the long weekend in May.

On most days there would be two or three separate games going on at the same time. And each game ended only through attrition as one child after the next would eventually yield to his mother's exasperated calls to dinner.

The neighbourhood's main game was always centred at the street's only four-way intersection. While playing through an intersection may have doubled the number of stoppages in play due to oncoming traffic, intersections were also the only break we could find in the endless line of parked cars that permanently lined the street.

The community had been built at a time when there were virtually no cars in Toronto. Therefore very few of its homes had been designed to accommodate a family vehicle. There were no garages or carports, and only a few of the houses had driveways running along the unattached side. There was however, the street, and fathers parked in any available space, untroubled by the inconvenience this caused their children.

The intersection that had become the preferred site for all major games while free of parked cars did present a couple of other problems. Aside from the extra traffic this locale invited, drainage holes were built right into the curbs at this part of the street. And several times throughout the course of a game play would have to stop while one of the bigger kids lifted the small manhole cover above the drainage basin in order to retrieve a lost ball.

The other problem with the intersection was that Phillip Watson's home sat on its southeast corner. And 'old man Watson' was by any measurable definition of human character assessment - a real prick. He lived only with a mangy German Shepherd named Oggy, and neither dog nor owner had any love or patience for children.

Every weeknight, and each weekend morning, old man Watson would chain Oggy to a post located a few feet from his front step. While the chain may have prevented Oggy from leaving the yard, it did not prevent the vicious beast from claiming any ball that was mistakenly directed onto the Watson property.

The hazard of Oggy Watson and the drainage holes notwithstanding, the intersection was still the site of choice for any major game. These games began every night after school and carried on throughout the weekend. And every game started the same way, with team captains Paul Hillman and my cousin Jack selecting players for their respective teams.

Regardless of who picked first, Paul Hillman always took his brother Neil, while Jack always picked me. The fact that I was an early selection in this draft process had very little to do with my ability to play the game. It was an obvious case of nepotism, plain and simple. Given that I was at least two years younger than any of the other participants I was not really first selection material. However, given that I was also the cousin of the game's best player, no one ever questioned the wisdom of Jack's biased selection.

With the Hillman brothers on one side, and Jack and me on the other, the rest of the players were divided up strictly on the basis of ability. Which did not bode well for one of the game's most constant participants, Bruce Thatcher.

Bruce was the worst road hockey player anyone had ever seen. He couldn't shoot. He couldn't pass. He couldn't run. He couldn't play goal. In point of fact, even in situations when it was most called for, Bruce Thatcher couldn't even get out of the way. Yet every day without fail he would show up, and to the best of his cruelly limited ability, would play his heart out. And always for our side.

In the same way it was accepted that Neil Hillman and I would be the first players taken, everyone also knew that Jack would use his final selection to bring Bruce Thatcher onto our team. As bad as Bruce was, Jack would never leave him to the predatory elements he would face as a member of the Hillman team.

Once the teams were selected, the games were played on a daily winner-take-all basis. This was very serious stuff, and there were no prisoners taken. While Jack was the best player, it was by no means a given that our side would emerge victorious. To the best of my recollection we did win more often than not, but there were also many days on which Jack, Bruce and I were forced to walk home with our heads bowed in defeat.

Losing was brutal. There wasn't a worse feeling in the world than watching the other team fire the winning goal into your net. It could turn friend against friend, and brother against brother, though usually only for the remainder of the day. Grudges and hard feelings seldom lasted very long, even after the toughest of defeats. Because in road hockey there was always the next day – when you might just win. And winning a big game was something that could stay with you for a very long time - sometimes forever.

It was a sunny day in the spring of 1965. The NHL play-offs were drawing to a close, which meant the significance of our street games was at its annual high-water mark. And on this particular Sunday, it had been decided that the undisputed championship of all road hockey would be decided once and for all.

The game was of such importance that the Hillman brothers brought in a ringer. It was Paul Hillman's turn to make the first selection as the teams were chosen, and just by coincidence his cousin, Victor Arceneaux, had shown up to play that day. Victor was a big, fat, mean-spirited son of a bitch who lived one block south of us. His participation in our games had ended abruptly the previous year after Jack had beat the hell out of him in retaliation to several slashing violations.

The ease of the beating that Jack had put on him was quite surprising, given that Jack was a year younger and at least twenty pounds smaller than Victor Arceneaux. Yet beat him with ease he did and there was no question that a strong element of bad blood still existed between them. Even though Victor's immense size and nasty playing habits ensured that he would score a good number of goals that day, Paul Hillman knew that Jack would never select Victor to play on his team.

Secure in this knowledge, Hillman immediately selected his brother Neil, and waited for Jack to make his move. The move should have been obvious. Pick Victor Arceneaux. If Arceneaux were teamed with both Hillman brothers, there simply wasn't enough talent left in the remaining pool of players to beat them.

Yet Jack, as if oblivious to Paul Hillman's plan, calmly nodded towards me. Jack's selection made, the Hillman's gleefully selected their cousin Victor, and almost certain victory.

Jack's next move was a little bit unexpected. He chose Steve Hutchison, the street's best goalie. This was unexpected because goalies were always left outside the draft until the end. In choosing his goalie Jack had bypassed Jim Scott, who was by far the best of the remaining players.

Paul Hillman should have chosen Jim Scott next, but instead opted for Blair Malone, the street's second best goaltender. As soon as he made the selection, Hillman realized that Jack had duped him. If he had chosen Jim Scott instead, the Hillmans, Arceneaux and Jim could have beaten us without using a goalie.

Paul Hillman had figured that Jack would have taken Jim Scott right after he had chosen me. Jim was an excellent player, who could run like hell, and Jack would need him to have any chance of winning. With Jim gone, Hillman had then figured on taking Steve Hutchison, thus giving his side a decided advantage in goal, as well as the edge his fat cousin brought to their side.

By crossing Hillman up, Jack wound up not only with Jim Scott, but the better of the two goalies as well. We would still be heavy underdogs but thanks to Jack's trickery at least we had a chance - even with Bruce Thatcher playing left wing.

The game that followed was a childhood classic. Jack had decided to play defence in order to keep Victor Arceneaux's slash and hack attack methods to a minimum. But not even Jack could contain Victor completely. As big as Victor had been the previous year, he was even bigger this year. He was also a pretty damn good player. He was particularly adept at shooting the ball, and his bullying style often ensured that he had enough room to get a shot off at the net. He had managed to zing four such shots past Steve Hutchison.

In spite of Victor's four goals, and five others by various other attackers, Steve Hutchison had played brilliantly for our side. He made some of the best saves I'd seen since my uncle Talbot had played net for Jack and me on Christmas Day a couple of years earlier. And if not for his nifty manoeuvring, the game would have been a fairly one-sided affair. But thanks to Steve, along with five goals by Jack, three by Jim Scott, and one by myself, after several hours of high-speed play the game was tied at nine. The next goal would be the winner.

With the game tied, I misdirected a clearing pass that bounced up onto old man Watson's lawn. As custom dictated, Oggy Watson grabbed the ball and snarled at any one who dared to try and retrieve it. It was Oggy's third such claim of the day, and he showed no signs of any willingness to part with any of the balls.

With two others floating peacefully in separate sewer basins on the opposite side of the street, it became clear that the game would have to stop while we reclaimed one of the lost balls. But just as Paul Hillman and Jack reached one of the manhole's, Bruce Thatcher reached into his pocket and pulled out a ball.

I could never recall Bruce offering a ball to any past game, and certainly the one he offered that day looked like it had never been used before. In fact the ball looked like it had never even touched the pavement. It was still bright green, very fuzzy, and was much bouncier than any of the five others we had used that day.

Once put into play the ball looked and handled so differently than any of its predecessors it seemed to quicken the pace of the game.

Anyway, about five minutes after play had resumed Neil Hillman clanged the green ball off the crossbar of our net, almost ending the game. The ball ricocheted off the bar and bounced past both Hillman brothers. Jack grabbed it and went streaking past me, with Neil and Paul Hillman in hot pursuit. Up ahead of the play, Jim Scott was on open road and was flying towards the other team's goal. With both defencemen and fat Victor Arce-neaux converging on Jim Scott at the left side of the net, Jack lowered his head and blasted the ball.

The goalie made a great save on Jack's shot and unfortunately the defencemen had Jim Scott too well tied up for him to take a second whack at the ball. The play should have ended right then and there, and would have, had it not been for Victor Arceneaux.

A split second after Blair Malone had made the initial save, Victor came crashing into the pile of players at the left side of the net. Everybody went flying, and when the dust settled, Victor, Jim Scott, the goalie, and both defenceman were all sprawled together behind the net. The ball itself had been knocked loose and was sitting motionless about three feet in front of the unpro-tected goal.

It was a moment that will be forever frozen in my mind. After four hours of non-stop war, it had come down to this, a tap-in.

I was too far behind the play to be of any consequence, but my position did offer me an excellent view of the game-winning goal.

Both Hillman brothers had run to Jack as he fired the ball and were now standing beside him, watching helplessly. Jim Scott, Victor Arceneaux, and the rest of the Hillman team were scrambled on the ground, staring in disbelief. How could the ball have remained in front of the net?

For the Hillman team, all hope of victory had been lost in an instant. As the ball was positioned, it presented an unmissable opportunity for the next player to arrive. And from the right side, methodically steaming towards the net, was none other than the ball's owner, Bruce Thatcher.

Bruce had of course been hopelessly out of position as the play unfolded. However with everybody having gone for a tum-ble behind the net, he was suddenly poised to score not only the first goal of his road hockey career, but the most important goal of 1965.

No player present that day had ever seen Bruce actually get a shot on net, let alone score a goal. But in his dreams Bruce must have scored a thousand times, because as he reached the ball, he simply tapped it in on his backhand side, like he had been doing it all his life.

The game was over. We had won. History had been written, and there was nothing the Hillman brothers could do about it. Well, nothing except berate the man they perceived as the architect of their misfortune. In the lexicon of Foster Hewitt, Danny Gallivan or any other sportscaster in history, Victor Arceneaux had earned himself a major set of goat horns, and his cousins were going to let him hear about it.

Paul and Neil Hillman swooped down on their cousin with all the mercy of a pack of starving jackals. And the verbal assault that followed was long, vicious, and foul.

"You fat fucking bastard… you asshole… you blew the whole fucking game!"

"How could you run over your own fucking goalie?"

"Look what you have done. Christ Almighty you let a reject like Thatcher score the winning goal."

"You useless piece of shit!… I knew we never should have let you play… you fucking stink!"

On and on the brothers continued with their rapid-fire attack until finally, after a minute or so of non-stop abuse, a wild-eyed Victor Arceneaux rose to his feet. The look on his face told the Hillmans that it would be in their best interests to immediately halt their disparaging remarks. A point Victor accented by picking up his hockey stick and splintering it within inches of his two cousins.

Then, after retrieving the ball that was still lying in the net beside him, Victor began marching directly towards our team. His head was beet red as he approached us, stomping his feet harder and harder into the ground as he drew closer.

If this theatrical approach was meant to intimidate, it didn't work on all of us.

As Victor approached Jack calmly dropped his stick and stepped directly into his path. He didn't say a word, nor did he assume a fighting position. Just dropping the stick was message enough and Victor caught its meaning.

He passed by with tears rolling down his face, and while he wasn't prepared to fight with Jack, he did have a message for Bruce.

"You lucky little prick, I'll fix you."

Bruce, being half English and half German, was not one to let an insult go without some sort of reply.

"Say it when you don't have snot all running down your face."

I'm sure that if Jack hadn't been with us, Victor would have taken Bruce Thatcher apart for such an impertinent remark. But, since Jack was there, Victor merely continued on through the intersection and began his ignominious journey home, completing his departure by deliberately tossing Bruce's ball to a surprised Oggy Watson.

Well, what can you say, Victor's performance was not going to win him any awards for sportsmanship, but he was always entertaining.

Over twenty-eight years have passed since that spring day of long ago and I can still see Bruce's green ball crossing the goal line like it happened only yesterday.

Looking back on it, I think I remember it all so well not just because we won, but because of the justice that was served in the way we won. The Hillman's had tried to stack the deck, and it blew up in their faces. Victor Arceneaux's dubious playing methods did earn him some gains, yet in the end he was the biggest loser of all. And Bruce, Bruce Thatcher, after all those years of trying, after all of the disappointment and failure, his efforts were finally rewarded with the greatest single shining moment of them all.

However, all lessons and morals aside, what I remember most clearly about that day was the look on Bruce Thatcher's face as Jim Scott and Jack hoisted him onto their shoulders and marched him triumphantly back to our end of the street. He was as happy as a ten-year-old can get.

Looking up at him from my lowly vantage point Bruce Thatcher was the undisputed king of the mountain.

And now the king is dead.

Reliving the moment I couldn't help but wonder if the gods had known when they granted him this brief moment of immortality that Bruce Thatcher would one day take his own life. As I see the young boy who so happily rode my cousin's shoulders home that spring day, I can see no hint of doom in his happy face. Yet I couldn't help but wonder if, at his happiest moment - was his fate already sealed?

I was once told by an old Jesuit priest that life is a game, and once we are in it, we are subject to many arbitrary rules, some of which we may never understand. Which I took to mean that life never stops and sometimes - shit happens.

Somewhere over the past twenty-eight years a lot of shit must have happened to Bruce Thatcher. But in remembering him that sunny day in 1965, his smiling, laughing face turned directly up towards God's heaven, twenty-eight years suddenly seemed like such an insufficient period of time to have felled such a mighty king.

Chapter Fifteen

CHAPTER FIFTEEN

BY NIGHTFALL THE DEN'S total darkness was broken only by a small overhead light that shone down on the room's lone picture. Lying back on the couch, cradled in these hushed surroundings, I basked in this friendly setting, patiently studying Robert Bateman's *Northern Reflections*. It was a peaceful evening, and I felt a growing sense of ease with myself as I breathed in the warm night air.

I didn't know what time it was, but I knew that it was late. It had been several hours since I had ordered a cab to the house and used it to retrieve my car from the Genuine Deli.

Having returned home I moved into the den and after pouring myself a double-shot of Drambuie started trying to sort through all that had happened the previous day.

Bruce Thatcher had killed himself. Jack had revealed to me that he was broke and desperate. I had tried to cheat on my wife.

Yet as I pondered these events, for all the misfortune I could see in each of them, what troubled me most was why I wasn't feeling a whole lot worse about all of it than I actually did.

It wasn't that I felt great or anything close to it. On the one hand I did feel bad, especially about Bruce. But on the other, for the first time in recent memory I was also conscious of the fact that a lot of the anxiety that had plagued me in recent times was gone. And in the calm of the evening's late hour, I couldn't get over the feeling that something about the night - just felt right.

My first reaction to this sense of peace was one of denial. I didn't want to believe that I could start feeling better about my life on a day filled with such tragedy for others. It made me think that perhaps I had reached such a low point myself that I was now taking comfort in the knowledge that other people had screwed up worse than I had.

Unable to understand this paradox, and having grown tired of trying to figure it out, I decided to interrupt my train of thought by listening to some music.

Hearing the disc and laser engaged, it was a little exciting to realize that I was going to hear music without first having to do some major negotiating with one of my children. As a general rule, anytime I move near the stereo I am met with frantic and often teary eyed pleas from at least one of them (usually my daughter), insisting that I replace whatever it is I have just put on with some medley of children's songs they all want to hear. Hence for the last year or so the only artist I have listened to with any regularity is that brilliant existentialist Barney the Dinosaur. There are no words to describe how much I hate that fucking dinosaur.

Settling back onto the couch, I waited for the first pulses of the beating heart that would soon pour from the room's four built-in speakers. Though more upbeat than I should have been, the night's late hour had left me a bit weary, and trying to wind down further, I closed my eyes and listened.

As the slow, rhythmic beat of a solitary heart started to give way to the sound of ticking clocks and shrill screams, I found myself thinking about Caroline. I had wanted to talk to her all day, and now that I was feeling a little better about things I was just dying to speak with her. Yet, as was the case earlier in the day, I knew that I still wasn't quite ready to give her a call. I mean, what could I really say?

"Oh, hi honey, sorry to wake you. Just wanted to let you know I think I have some of my marbles back in the bag and that from here on in everything is going to be fine. Oh, by the way, Bruce Thatcher has killed himself, Jack is virtually destitute, and as for me, well nothing new, except, ahhh, I think I might have a new girlfriend. Yeah, her name is Barb, she's almost twenty, she's very attractive and is one hell of a waitress. I tried to screw her on Friday night, but things just didn't work out. Not to worry though, I'll be taking another crack at her on Monday. Well, I'll let you go now. See you on Tuesday… sleep tight."

No, somehow I knew such a conversation with my wife was not going to happen. I didn't know what I was going say to her when I did get around to giving her a call. But I knew that none of it was going to revolve around my recent trip to the Genuine Deli.

There have never been many secrets between my wife and I but this little situation with Barb was something I'd be taking to my grave.

"Breathe, breathe in the air…"

As the first words of Pink Floyd's journey to the 'Dark Side of the Moon' began to fill the room, I tried to clear my mind of everything. I didn't want to think anymore. I just wanted to ride the mystical rhymes and sounds of rock's most famous album to that point in my brain where nothing exists.

But soon after I began to search my mind for this point of nothingness, I began to drift back. Back many years, to a day I had all but forgotten. And by the time the band's lead singer had warned…

"All you touch and all you see
Is all your life will ever be…"

my thoughts had locked on to a hauntingly clear image of a young schoolboy named Ed Flanagan.

It had been a long time since I had thought about that spring morning in 1972, when Father Brisebois informed my ninth grade class that one of our fellow students had passed away. And in returning to that fateful day, it seemed as though I could suddenly understand it in ways I never could before.

On the day Ed died, I was not quite fifteen years old. Which at the time did not seem so terribly young. At that point in my life, fifteen years seemed like the entire history of the world. But looking back on it all from the age of thirty-five, I could now see what none of the students present that day could possibly understand. Ed Flanagan was a mere babe when he passed away.

It's no wonder his death had such a moving effect on Father Brisebois.

In considering this day for the first time not only as an adult, but also as a father, I began to remember Ed's father. The vision of him enduring Father Mancini's sermon in the St Ignatius Chapel was so clear it seemed impossible that over two decades had passed since all this happened.

I had never heard any news of Ed's parents since the day their son was buried and I began to question how they were doing. I wondered if they had ever gotten over such an inexplicable loss. Had the reasons for such a loss ever become clear to them?

In remembering Ed, and his family, I also found myself becoming a little angry with Bruce Thatcher. I didn't want to be angry with him, but I couldn't help it. The selfishness I attached to his actions seemed to magnify the injustice of Ed Flanagan's death.

It seemed so unfair that Ed could be randomly taken from this world through no fault of his own, while Bruce simply decided to toss it all away.

What was it that Bruce wanted out of life that he didn't feel he was getting? He certainly seemed to have a lot to be thankful for. How could he have decided that he wanted to die?

Bruce Thatcher was as an extremely logical human being. I'd never known anyone so even tempered. Everything he did was so well thought out, it just didn't add up that he would throw himself over Niagara Falls.

No matter what reaction a situation called for, Bruce would not lower himself to emotional or thoughtless behaviour. His response to all emotions, even anger, would be well planned, and carried out only on his terms. As our former nemesis, old man Watson found out one day.

After scoring the winning goal in what had been the mother of all road hockey games, the euphoria of Bruce's triumphant ride home was quickly dampened by a problem that had arisen at the game's conclusion. The ball, the virginal green ball Bruce had scored with, was now the property of Oggy Watson. Victor Arceneaux had tossed it to Oggy as he began walking home.

While at the time we didn't realize it, the ball Bruce had brought into the game's final moments was actually the property of his brother Richard. Now, if old man Watson was our street's version of Boo Radley, Richard Thatcher was Norman Bates, minus the good manners.

He was the strangest kid any of us had ever known. He was friendless, charmless and demonstratively cruel, and you didn't have to know him long to realize it.

My first memory of him was the day he called Bruce and I into the Thatcher's backyard to show us some mice he had captured. Richard had the mice pegged to the clothesline by their tails, and had doused each of them with lighter fluid. The moment Bruce and I arrived in the yard, Richard grabbed Bruce and started twisting his arm. Then, after forcing a lighter into his younger brother's hand, Richard began to apply greater pressure on the arm until Bruce finally set the squealing rodents ablaze.

It was the most frightening thing I'd ever seen. And as Bruce and I trembled, Richard Thatcher simply laughed. Well, he laughed until he released the mice from their pegs, then he became quite intense as he began to run the furry little torches over with the family lawn mower. Yeah, no mental problems there, right?

Richard Thatcher was bad news, pure and simple. And the only recreation he engaged in beyond the murder of defenceless animals, and the odd motorcycle ride with Uncle Fog, was his participation in the church-sponsored tennis tournaments he so frequently won. The lost ball was one of his match balls, and Bruce knew that it would mean a savage beating for him if he didn't get it back.

Returning to the scene of the crime, Jack, Bruce and I spent the next half-hour acting as human bait hoping to lure Oggy far enough away from the ball so that one of the others might grab it. But it was hopeless. Oggy proved to be a master strategist. He knew that front lawn and could not be fooled on his home turf. Nothing we tried got us even close to the green ball.

Finally, as the sun was going down, old man Watson came out to bring Oggy in for the night and as the miserable prick began rounding up the balls Bruce Thatcher stepped forward and bravely tried to plead his case.

"Excuse me sir,... Mister Watson, could we please have back the green one? It's my…"

Old man Watson didn't even break stride. It was as if the three kids standing on the perimeter of his lawn didn't exist. He collected the balls, and his dog, and returned to the house without any response to Bruce's request. And as Oggy's ass disappeared behind the front door, we all knew that Bruce was in deep, deep shit.

Richard Thatcher was five years older than Bruce and over the years had beaten his younger brother up so many times that Bruce had come to accept the beatings as an almost normal event. Most everybody on the street had, at one time or another, seen Richard attack his much smaller brother with anything from a golf club to a metal pipe, and never once did anybody ever try to intervene. The only adult that had ever raised a voice in protest to Richard Thatcher's behaviour was an elderly man by the name of George Downs and not only did the neighbours regard his protests as meddling and intrusive, but three days later the old man's cat disappeared. Richard was a busy boy.

After Watson closed his front door we all stood in stunned silence before turning to walk home. But we didn't get very far before Jack spun around and, after instructing Bruce and me to stay where we were, trotted over to Watson's veranda and began hopping up the steps.

Neither Bruce nor I could believe it. Nobody had ever confronted Watson in his home before. What did Jack think he was doing? Either Watson or Oggy would surely kill him.

It wasn't until Jack's third series of raps that the door finally opened, and with Watson's leg as the only restraint between Jack and the snarling Oggy, my cousin began to make his case for the ball. From the street, it appeared more like a monologue than a discussion, but after a few minutes old man Watson finally said something, before shrugging and closing the door.

At first we thought Jack had failed, but seconds later the door reopened and an instant later Jack was racing down from the veranda with the green ball held tightly in his right hand.

Bruce and I were amazed that Jack had won back the ball. But before we got too deeply into our questions, Jack tempered our enthusiasm with a bit of bad news.

"Don't get too excited. We gotta take care of the old bastard's lawn for the next four weeks."

"We gotta ... What?"

Phillip Watson was not only something less than a prince as a human being, he was also an unqualified pig as a homeowner. While he washed, waxed and vacuumed his big black Oldsmobile every Sunday morning from April through October, during that same period he cut his lawn no more than twice. And the semi-annual clipping of his lawn represented old man Watson's full range of gardening activities. The lawn was so covered with weeds and dog shit that it more resembled a farmer's field than the front yard of a family residence.

Nevertheless, over the next four weeks, Bruce, Jack and I held up our end of the bargain. And in spite of the limited quality we had to work with, by the end of May old man Watson's lawn was not only trimmed to a very respectable level, it was also totally free of weeds and excrement. Our deal with the devil was complete.

It had been a hellish price to pay, but we had the ball back, the street was a prettier place, and never for a second did Richard Thatcher ever suspect that one of his beloved tennis balls had been compromised by his younger brother. Bruce was off the hook, and that was the end of it. Or so Jack and I thought.

Bruce Thatcher on the other hand didn't regard his business with old man Watson as quite yet done. While Jack and I may not have liked the way Phil Watson had gained the upper hand in forcing us to do his lawn work, to our way of thinking it was us who had approached him about the deal. So in the end we had nothing to complain about.

However Bruce did not share this point of view. I don't know if it was the British or the German blood in him but to Bruce the advantage seized by Watson in stealing his ball amounted to extortion and therefore the gains he made had to be negated. To that end, ever since Jack had negotiated the return of the green ball, Bruce Thatcher had been plotting a well-measured retaliatory strike on the unsuspecting Phillip Watson.

It was the fourth Saturday in May when we finished our yard duties at the Watson home and immediately upon completion Bruce offered Jack and me a very short directive.

"Follow me, I've got something to show you."

Walking at a military pace, Bruce passed Jack and me and reached the front of his house several yards ahead of us. Stepping to his right, our fearless leader then dropped to his hands and knees and pushing back the fragile wooden lattice that covered the side of the front steps, disappeared under the veranda.

As Jack and I reached the side of the steps we heard Bruce's voice from deep inside our onetime secret hiding place.

"Hurry up... get in here."

Without hesitating, Jack and I both dropped to our stomachs and squirmed into the dirt-covered underbelly of the Thatcher household. It had been a couple of years since we had abandoned this locale as our private headquarters and neither Jack nor I had any idea why Bruce had led us back to our former hideaway.

As soon as we had righted ourselves, and assumed a comfortable sitting position, Bruce produced a large plastic bag. Inside the bag was another plastic bag, which was wrapped around a large Tupperware container. As Bruce started to unwrap the second plastic bag the foulest of odours began to seep into the air around us. It was the most powerful smell I had ever encountered, and that was saying a lot, considering I had just spent the morning shovelling hot dog shit into a paper bag.

The smell coming from Bruce's package went far beyond the foulness of an Oggy Watson turd. This stuff was deadly. And just when you thought it couldn't get any worse, Bruce cracked the seal on the Tupperware container and all hell broke loose. Jack did an infantry-style crawl right through the flimsy wooden entrance of our secret hideaway, while I fell in line behind him, gasping for air.

While Jack and I were outside trying to recover, from underneath the veranda we could hear Bruce shuffling around, repacking and restoring his unearthly package.

"What the fuck is that?" Jack tersely whispered through a crack in the staircase.

Amid the commotion coming from the darkness under the Thatcher's front step, came no response to Jack's furious inquiry. So Jack, being pissed off, and in no mood to wait for an answer, again leaned into the staircase to demand an explanation.

"Bruce, what the hell are you doing in there. Bruce... Bruce, I'm gonna..."

A BETTER PLACE

Just as Jack was about to threaten him further, Bruce's head popped out from underneath the staircase, his cheeks pressing out so far from his face that he almost looked like he was about to explode. Seeing he was in some trouble Jack grabbed Bruce by both shoulders and pulled him up into the outside world.

Even though Bruce was badly winded, Jack could not hold back the anger in his voice.

"Bruce, what was that all about? What do you have in there, a dead cat?"

Although he could see the anger in Jack's face, Bruce began to smile as he sat back in order to more easily catch his breath.

"Isn't the stuff unbelievable? I almost didn't make it out of there."

Stepping forward, trying to be the voice of reason, I sat down beside Bruce and asked, "What's going on?"

"It's Limburger cheese."

"It's what?"

"Limburger cheese," Bruce repeated, as he began to lay out his plan. "I've been letting it rot in there for about three weeks now and tonight we're going to put it to good use. We're going to cheese his car."

"We're going to what? Cheese a car? What are you talking about, cheese whose car?"

"Old man Watson's of course. I've got the stuff rolled into little balls. I'm going to put it in the basement freezer this afternoon so it won't be so smelly to work with. Then, tonight we're going to break into that bastard's car and drop little balls of frozen cheese down into every crevice, into the seats, the air vents, - everywhere. And when it thaws out, he'll have to take the whole car apart to clean it, and it'll still stink for a month. Pretty good, eh?"

Listening to the details of Bruce's plan I felt pretty certain that Jack would veto it. Until, from behind me, I heard, "When Watson opens those doors to wash his car tomorrow – BAM - he's not going to know what hit 'im."

Apparently we were going to go for it.

Talk about a master schemer. During the time we were working on Phil Watson's front lawn, Bruce Thatcher had not shown one trace of resentment in carrying out the task at hand. In fact, quite to the contrary, as was his nature, Bruce was much more thorough in his gardening duties than either Jack or I had been. At times it almost seemed as though he even enjoyed tending the Watson lawn. Yet the whole time we were working Bruce had been secretly plotting his revenge.

Jack and I were both surprised when Bruce laid out the plan, but we shouldn't have been. Bruce was a planner. That's what he was, and if there was one act in his life that defined Bruce Thatcher it was the cheesing of Phillip Watson's car.

He wasn't mad at Watson. He just felt that the old man had gone too far. If Watson had made us do his lawn once, maybe even twice Bruce might have let it go. But four times - for one tennis ball? No, that was too much, and the injustice of it demanded a response.

That night, with the aid of a coat hanger, Jack broke into the black Oldsmobile and while I stood guard he and Bruce hid little balls of frozen Limburger cheese throughout the pristine F-85. The purpose of the exercise was not to smear the cheese all over the interior. It was to put the cheese in places where it would be difficult to find, and even more difficult to remove.

As Bruce and Jack entered the car, I watched from a nearby corner. Jack had insisted that I stand lookout, reasoning that two people could work faster than three within the confines of the car. However, I knew he had insisted on this only to protect me in case the plan should go awry, and was a little saddened at my lack of direct involvement in *The Great Limburger Ambush*. But as I watched my two gloved co-conspirators at work, it became clear that it was a two-man job. With Jack in the front seat and Bruce in the back, both worked quickly but carefully to ensure that the cheese was left in only the most inaccessible places.

In the end, Jack's concern about keeping me from any direct involvement was a well intentioned but unnecessary precaution. The cheesing of old man Watson's car went off without a hitch. After five minutes of non-stop work, Bruce and Jack checked for my signal, then calmly slipped out of the car. The gloves they wore during the caper were then buried underneath the Thatcher's front step, while the Tupperware container was transported a few blocks south where it was tossed on to the grounds of Greenwood Race Track.

With all physical evidence properly disposed of, the only thing left to do was wait.

The following morning was a memorable one. It was hot and within the dark interior of the 1964 Oldsmobile the sun baked the rotten cheese to a point where it could be smelled from a block away. It was as if the black Olds had captured all of the world's foot odour and then somehow made it nuclear.

The smell was unbelievable. So bad that Watson could not bring himself to enter the vehicle. All he could do was take very quick peeks in one of the windows as he tried to find the source of the incomprehensible stench.

To this day I have no idea if old man Watson ever figured out exactly what had been so deviously placed in his beloved automobile. The rumour around the neighbourhood was that Richard Thatcher had distributed the remains of a dead racoon throughout the car. But nobody was really sure.

The only thing everybody knew for sure was that for several weeks a masked Phillip Watson could be seen carrying a bucket of water, a can of air freshener, and several towels out to the side of the road in order to wage battle against the rancid evil that had possessed his automobile. He was a determined old bastard, and would spend hours each day trying to return the car to its former state of cleanliness.

But alas, in the end, all his efforts were in vain and one day in late June a new Pontiac turned up in front of the Watson home. Phillip had given up. The F-85 was history.

I remember that first morning after the cheesing how hard Jack and I laughed at the sight of old man Watson. The cloth he was holding over his face as he peeked inside the car was no match for the unstoppable smell of the cheese. And several times he had to dash away from it like the car had somehow just bitten him.

The sight of him standing in the middle of the street gasping for air left both Jack and I on the verge of pissing ourselves with laughter. But while Jack and I laughed, Bruce Thatcher barely cracked a smile.

He was pleased that his plan had worked so well, but to him, it wasn't meant to be funny. It was meant to be punitive. Bruce saw it only as a counterbalance to what old man Watson had done to us. And that's the way he was throughout all of his life – perfectly symmetrical. Every action had a logical reaction.

It was understanding Bruce's analytical nature that made the thought of his suicide such a frightening one. I knew that his decision to end his life would not have been born out of hatred or anger, and that the manner he chose to do it had not been a rash, nor an impulsive decision. He hadn't arrived at Niagara Falls by chance, and he didn't throw himself over in a moment of weakness or sorrow. No, Bruce's trip over the Falls was a well-thought-out response to some God-awful circumstance that had crept into his life. And while I couldn't imagine what chain of events could have knocked him so off kilter that his response would be suicide, I knew that whatever it was it must have been pretty goddam bad. Bruce didn't do what he did because he was having a bad hair day.

Chapter Sixteen
CHAPTER SIXTEEN

"Hello?"

"Hi, how ya doing?"

"Oh, well hello, so you finally decided to give us a call, I was beginning to think you had forgotten all about us."

"Hey, sorry about that, things have been pretty hectic around here, but believe me, I've been thinking about you," I answered, pleased by how good it felt to hear Caroline's voice.

"Don't worry about it, I was just kidding. Things are fine up here. Everyone's getting along and it's been such a beautiful weekend... so, how are things?"

"Things are moving along..."

"Oh yeah, did you find the magic loophole you've been looking for?"

"Sort of."

"Sort of. You're starting to sound like your lawyer," Caroline teased playfully.

"Whoa, honey... that's a little cruel for this time of day. Where are the kids?" I asked, knowing that I didn't want them to be around when I told her about Bruce Thatcher.

"They're out on the front lawn, still in their P J's. I had to call a late game of croquet on account of bedtime. So the boys have been out there since the crack of dawn finishing it up. I can't even get them in here for breakfast."

"Who's winning?"

"Shane, same as always… but Michael's been getting a little creative with the rules, so most games end up fairly even. Whitney just got up a little while ago, and I'm making the boys let her play."

"In other words the boys will break up the game two minutes after she arrives. You're pretty sharp, honey."

"Well, it's the easiest way to get them in for breakfast. So are you still coming up after court on Tuesday?"

"Maybe sooner, I'm hoping to get away tomorrow. Listen Caroline, something has happened down here, are the kids still outside?"

"Yeah, I can see the boys chasing Whitney down… she seems to have run off with Shane's ball. Hold on a sec SHANE!… SHANE!… I'M WATCHING YOU!… YOU BE GENTLE WITH HER!" Listening to my wife police the situation, I tried to think of the best way to tell her about Bruce, but before anything appropriate came to mind she was back on the line. "Hannibal what is it, what happened?"

"Well, it's ahhh…" As soon as I tried to answer Caroline's question I started to stumble. It wasn't that I was overly worried about her reaction (she didn't really know Bruce all that well) but never having had to articulate a death notice before I had no idea how hard it would be to find the right words.

"Listen, I don't know how to… uhhhh," I continued, until finally I just blurted it out. "Bruce Thatcher killed himself on Friday."

"Noooo!… My God! No," Caroline responded, sounding more hurt than I thought she would.

"Yeah, that's why I wanted to tell you when the kids weren't around."

"What happened?"

"He threw himself over Niagara Falls."

"He what!"

"Yeah, tell me about it," I answered, now thinking that maybe I should have gone up to the cottage and told her this news in person.

"Do you have any idea why?"

"Not a clue. I was completely blown away when I first heard it. Jack seems to know something about it though."

"Why, what did he say?"

"I haven't really had a chance to talk to him. He's been down at the Falls. He says he'll be home either tonight or tomorrow morning, so I'll find out what he knows then. But for now I'm completely in the dark. All I know is what I just told you."

"Well, my God, that is just awful - how are you doing with it?" Caroline asked, now sounding noticeably calmer.

"I don't really know how I'm doing. It's such a shock. At first I didn't believe it. Then I was mad. And right now I don't know what to feel. It's really strange."

"I'm sure it is. Have you been able to sleep?"

"Yeah, not bad. I just got up − and what is it now, about eight?" I neglected to mention that I hadn't dropped off until sometime after four.

"That's pretty good − any sign of Oprah?"

"No, nothing. Under the circumstances I'd say I did pretty well."

"It's a step in the right direction," Caroline offered, before shifting the conversation back to Bruce Thatcher. "So, is there anything I should do? Should we come home? Or should…"

"I don't know what anyone can do," I interrupted, before allowing Caroline to get too far into her questions. "At this point there is no body, no funeral, no nothing. I don't see how either of us can do anything. So I'm going to head up to see you guys tomorrow. Even if it's only for a couple of days."

"Well that would be great if you think you can swing it. The kids would love it. But what about court?"

"I'm just going to leave that up to the lawyer. If I lose,… I'll deal with it. Either way, nothing is going to change because of some brilliant legal discovery I'm likely to make in the next forty-eight hours," I answered, still not sure why I had adopted this outlook on the case.

"Well you know I'm not going to argue with you?"

"No, I had a feeling you wouldn't. You know I should have let this thing go a long time ago… I was just so determined not to lose that I… I don't know − somewhere along the way this whole thing got the better of me. Anyway, the hell with it. It's all water under the bridge now," I continued on, feeling more and more unshackled from the millstone that this legal battle had become.

"Well it's nice to hear you talk that way stranger. So listen, if you're not going to court on Tuesday, why don't you just jump in the car and come up right now?"

"Huh, good question. Actually I would except I've got to see if I can get a couple of things done for Jack."

"Jack? What in the world do you have to do for him?"

"I'll tell you about it when I see you, but the long and the short of it is that Jack is in even bigger trouble than I am."

"Jack, yeah right," Caroline replied, not taking me seriously.

"No, I'm not kidding, he's in trouble."

"I can't believe that."

"Neither can I."

"Well, is there anything *you* can do to help? I mean..."

Before finishing her question Caroline suddenly stopped short after realizing there was no diplomatic way of suggesting that I was hardly the man to be helping anybody out of a financial jam.

Stepping into the pause she left, I finished her thought for her. "Yeah, I know what you mean. The chances of me helping anybody right now are about as likely as Elvis showing up at Jimmy Hoffa's next birthday party. But I've got to try something."

"Well of course, yes, do whatever you can. How bad are things for him?"

"I saw him on Friday and I've seen road kills that were having better days," I stated regretfully.

"That doesn't sound too promising. Did you know he was in trouble?"

"No, not at all. I'm sure he'll be okay though. He'll certainly be a lot better off than Bruce anyway."

"That goes without saying. Boy, what a shock it is to hear all of this. I see what you mean when you say it's been pretty hectic down there. Did anything else go wrong?"

Although I understood Caroline's question to be largely rhetorical, as soon as I heard it much of the comfort I had taken from the sound of her voice quickly vanished.

My thoughts returned to the Genuine Deli and the image of Barb and me pressed up against the side of the Lexus. And even as I tried to escape the image by picking up the conversation right away, I could still feel my hands roaming freely over each of Barb's breasts.

Jesus, why did I ever go there?

"Did anything else go wrong?... No I don't think so. That about covers my weekend," I replied unsteadily. "Although I have to tell you, I wish I had gone up with you and the kids on Friday"

"Well that wouldn't have changed anything. Things with Jack and Bruce would still be the same regardless of what you did on Friday. So try not to worry about it, and see if you can get up here for tomorrow."

"I know, everything would be exactly the same," I answered quietly, before recalling Jack's advice to just forget about what happened with Barb, and "move on". At which point I added, with slightly more enthusiasm, "Listen, I'm really going to try to get out of here ASAP. I'll be up there tomorrow - you can count on it".

"Hannibal, are you sure you're okay? Because we can always..."

"No, I'm fine. I'll see you tomorrow"

"Okay,... well, then bring up some wine and I'll make the trip worth your while."

"You got yourself a deal. I'll be there by dinnertime."

"See ya then... love ya," my wife replied as she hung up the phone.

"I love you too," I answered after the line had gone dead - never meaning it more.

* * *

It's strange how relationships evolve in ways that could never be imagined in their early stages. In our first days together, the reasons I loved Caroline were so tangible to me that I lived and breathed them every waking second. To me, she was not only the most interesting woman in the world she was also the most beautiful. I was curious about every aspect of her personality, and craved her company and companionship constantly. She became my life, so much so that if anything had ever caused us to part back then, I probably would have become one of those guys who ends up on a water tower shooting at passing cars.

I met her at a party at Julie Newton's place in the fall of 1985. A seemingly random event that I later found out was actually more of an arrangement than a chance encounter.

It would not be completely truthful to suggest that it was love at first sight. For while I became interested in her the night we met, I did not approach her in response to an immediate physical attraction. She was dressed far too conservatively for a man of my uncomplicated tastes to notice right away.

But as the night wore on I became more and more interested in the dark eyed beauty whose name, I had learned through a less than subtle inquiry, was Caroline Hall.

I found myself continually watching her, eavesdropping on her conversations, and even anticipating traffic flows so that I might "accidentally" bump into her. But she never moved. She was content to stand against the doorway of the kitchen and the dining room and cheerfully engage in casual conversation with any passerby who chose to approach her. She never went to the bar or to the washroom and worse than all of this, she seemed to be becoming more and more intrigued with the frequent and, in my view, amateurish advances of some jerk named Owen Naismith.

There did however come a point, sometime late in the party, when I realized my own date for the evening, Tracy Fielding, was not only hammered, she had slipped outside to smoke a joint. (Something I never discouraged because getting high seemed to enhance Tracy's natural inclination towards performing oral sex in a moving automobile.) Which left me free to rather uncharacteristically act on an impulse. While still not knowing exactly what I was going to say, I excused myself from the guy I was talking to and went over to where Owen and Caroline were standing.

Stopping beside Owen Naismith, my heart was pounding as I put my hand on his shoulder and untruthfully informed him that Julie Newton was looking for him in the backyard.

After thanking me Owen left for the yard, where he would find any number of potheads but not Julie, whom I knew had left the house a few minutes earlier to pick up a bag of ice.

"Hello, my name is John Rankin."

The words came out smoothly enough but not having contemplated a second line, I was forced to improvise and did so by taking an unprovoked cheap shot at Owen Naismith.

"Sorry about Owen,... I guess he's living proof of why cousins shouldn't marry."

"What?"

"Owen, well you know, it happens in the best of families," I said smugly, confident that I was being ever so amusing.

"Owen is my cousin," Caroline responded coldly.

Holy shit - great opening line you idiot.

Caroline held her icy stare, and just as I was about to be swept away in a tidal wave of panic, I tried to maintain my composure for one further moment while my mind searched for a conversational lifeline.

"I know he's your cousin. I was just kidding around... I must confess that I made some inquiries about you and Julie Newton told me you had a great sense of humour."

I had seen Caroline talking amicably with Julie earlier in the evening and had decided to place my last hope in the possibility that they were friends.

"She did, did she? Well she's right, I do have a pretty good sense of humour... except, well... Owen Naismith is not my cousin,.." Caroline replied with a hint of a smile.

Uh oh... you've been had, stay calm.

"Ah, not your cousin,... well, maybe she said he was your uncle."

"No."

"In-law."

"Uh uh."

"Pet."

That did it. Her smile broadened, slightly.

"So Owen's not a relative of yours, now why would Julie have lied to me about such a thing? You just can't trust anybody these days."

Believing that I had brought things back to square one, I decided to breeze over my earlier faux pas.

"Listen, I've been watching you from over there, and I noticed that you didn't have a drink, or any food, and I just wanted you to know that if you need something, anything at all, like a drink, or a tour around the grounds, or maybe someone to paint your apartment tomorrow, I'll be standing right over there. Just let me know and I'll take care of it."

"Well that's very kind of you," she offered, saying nothing more until I started to fade away from her as if retreating into the shadows of defeat.

"Tell me something Hannibal, does your companion object to you offering such personalized service to the other female guests?"

Hannibal? I knew that I had used my proper name in introducing myself, so I was caught a little bit off guard when Caroline called me Hannibal.

Seeing that I was slightly confused, Caroline continued, "Yes Hannibal, that's what people call you, isn't it?... What? Did you think you were the only one who could make an inquiry?"

She was making inquiries about me. I like that. To whom would she have made an inquiry about me? Don't worry about it, just stay calm.

"No, not at all. I think we all have a right to inquire, I'm sure it's in the Constitution, and as for my dinner companion, well what can I tell you... she's my cousin? But I have a feeling I'm not going to be seeing her any more after tonight."

"Well I hope not," Caroline said sweetly, flashing a smile that shot right through me.

And that, as they say, was that. My bumbling approach had been well received, and Caroline and I went on talking to one another, each feeling that something really great might be happening between us. She confessed to me that Julie Newton had told her several nice things about her friend Hannibal, and that she had come to the party to check me out. I told her, in an obviously untruthful manner, that I knew she was there to meet me, and that I had waited until the end of the evening to introduce myself because I wanted to make her sweat.

It wasn't exactly the kind of first encounter people make movies about, but it was a nice moment for the two of us and it was amazing how quickly we connected. Within minutes Caroline and I were carrying on like old friends. And by the time Owen Naismith made his way back to the kitchen, it was apparent even to him that the ship he had hoped to sail home that night had already left the harbour.

The party, for me, ended shortly after midnight. At twelve o'clock, Caroline's ride and roommate, Liz MacAndrew, decided it was time for them to go. Having brought a date to the party, I was in no position to offer an alternative ride, so I bid Caroline good-bye, disappointed that she was leaving but happy in the knowledge that we had arranged for a lunch date the following day.

With Caroline gone, there was no reason for me to hang around the party, so I quickly rounded up the fortuitously stoned Tracy Fielding and headed for the car.

I remember driving home that night feeling strangely enchanted by the memory of Caroline's dark eyes and her breath-taking smile. It was a real high. And I was so excited about the lunch date we had arranged for the following day that I could barely keep the car on the road. And Tracy Fielding certainly wasn't helping.

So focused were my thoughts on Caroline that when Tracy dropped her head below the seat line to engage in that certain vehicular exercise which, when she was high, would be initiated by simply turning the ignition key, my first reaction was to resist. In light of what happened at the party, the act that I had eagerly anticipated as the highlight of my night now seemed somewhat unseemly. And while my resistance to Tracy's oral advances was a first, I remained quite resolute in my opposition, and did almost manage to fend her off completely. Until I realized that there are certain things that men are not meant to resist. So eventually I did relent, though I didn't feel very good about it.

The next day I took Caroline down to Harbourfront for lunch and we spent the day doing all the dorky things that most couples on the brink of a relationship do, including, I am embarrassed to say, going on a horse and buggy ride.

We walked along the water's edge and discussed our respective outlooks on life, while I tossed stones into the lake like I was little Opie Taylor. I was genuinely fascinated by Caroline's interest in areas where my own experiences had left me with a complete void of awareness, and I felt both enlightened and interested as she shared her knowledge of books, the arts, travel and history with me.

Two weeks to the day after that first date, a period in which we spent every available second together, I made Caroline dinner in my home. I had gone to great lengths to prepare a proper meal, even though we both knew the dinner was largely a ceremonial prerequisite for what was to follow.

What followed of course was our first night together, a night that started unbelievably badly when a premature outburst of my intended affection brought our first attempt at intercourse to an abrupt halt, just as it was about to begin. A sense of over-eagerness, coupled with a momentary lapse in concentration, caused me to fall victim to nature's second cruellest form of sexual non-performance.

Nonetheless, undaunted by my dubious beginning, in a short time, and I mean to say a very short time, the batteries did recharge, and long about 9:30 p.m., on a cold Saturday night in mid November '85, the earth beneath Caroline Hall and Hannibal Rankin did move. And again at eleven, and once more sometime in the middle of the night. It was great, and if my opening misfire is what we most often kid about, it was that last one, the one in the middle of the night that we most often remember - we were smokin'.

The kids had definitely found a rhythm and over the next few days we imaginatively christened every room in that house, along with some of its more secluded outdoor locales. From that weekend forward Caroline and I have been, for the most part, inseparable. We really fell for each other. And what a time we had.

Life's most pressing problems evolved around ordering theatre tickets, deciding which restaurant to check out, and trying to figure out how to get together for a nooner. We were two people endowed with life's greatest gifts - youth and health, who had found its greatest rewards - love and money. It was as close to having it "all" as I ever could have imagined

Three months after we became a couple Caroline and I moved in together and six months after that, in the summer of 1986, we were married. Married after only nine months together, and we'd 'a done it after nine days had the opportunity presented itself.

Eight years later and I think we're still in love. Though it's not as easy to tell as it once was. A lot has changed since that first night we spent together. Not the least of which is the likelihood that we'll ever again make love three times in one night (and it was actually four times for me). A night such as that is not going to happen again. And the same is true of many other things.

Much of the mutual fascination we once found in one another has been gradually replaced by something far less dramatic.

The days when our top priority was planning a new recreational activity or making ourselves available for a nooner are long gone. They were gone even before the kids arrived.

But if the passage of time has robbed us of something we once had, it has replaced it with something of equal, if not greater value. Closeness. And from the moment Caroline answered my early morning call, all I could hear coming from the other end of the line was the sound of my life.

No matter what other conclusions I might reach, even on the days when I'd like to be standing alone in a bar, free of all family baggage, with a drink in one hand and an unfiltered cigarette in the other, in the back of my mind I know the only thing that matters to me is Caroline and the kids.

I could see them all now. Even while away from them I knew what they'd be doing. Caroline would be hustling around the kitchen making enough pancakes to feed eight hungry adults.

Shane, my second born, and the spitting image of his mother, would be soundly defeating his older brother in yet another game of skill, and would be taunting him every step of the way.

Michael, my oldest, and the one most like me, would be negotiating new rules at every possible opportunity in order to compensate for his general lack of co-ordination, and would most certainly assault his smaller brother as his prospects for victory slipped away once again.

And Whitney, my youngest and possibly smartest child, who prior to turning one already knew she had me wrapped around her little finger. Poor little Whitney would be incessantly chattering while burning up every ounce of energy an eighteen-month-old is blessed with just trying to fit in somewhere.

It was another typical Sunday morning at the cottage, except that it would all be happening without me. My life, and everything that is important to it, was a mere two hours away and I felt a growing urge to jump in the car and race up north to surprise them. And if not for the fact that I was certain I would be joining them the next day anyway, I surely would have.

Chapter Seventeen

CHAPTER SEVENTEEN

JACK MACDONALD STOOD QUIETLY against the same railing Bruce Thatcher had leaned against two days earlier, and under a tranquil morning sun, while purposefully averting his eyes from the search vessels scouring the waters below, he fired up an American cigarette.

While as a general rule Jack seldom smoked unless he was drinking, he didn't *have* to be drinking to take a cigarette. There were other times when he'd partake. Sometimes when he was extremely bored he'd light one up, assuming he was offered one, or the odd time after sex he'd try one, although considering he hadn't had sex in almost a year, his post-coital smoking habits could hardly be qualified as problematic.

Still, these exceptions aside, Jack essentially only smoked when he drank, and therefore, albeit illogically, had always considered himself a non-smoker. Even during recent times, times when the days on which he smoked far outnumbered those on which he didn't, Jack had written off this statistical anomaly as more of a drinking problem than a smoking problem, and still considered himself to be a non-smoker.

However, after considering this additional exception to his rule, smoking on days when he had to witness an official search for the body of a life-long friend, Jack wearily began to suspect that his status as a non-smoker had become like so many other things in his life. Simply no longer true. And as he pondered this fact he exhaled another lungful of poisons into the air around him without fear of consequence.

Until recently the aspects of his life that were no longer true hadn't caused Jack a great deal of concern. He wasn't happy about a lot of what had been going on lately. Especially those aspects of his life that had hit all-time lows. Like his financial condition, or his lack of a social life, or the health scare he'd been dealing with since the beginning of the year when a polyp had to be surgically removed from his small intestine. But to say he felt any of these matters had ruined his life simply would not be true.

Jack never saw anything as being ruined - especially his own life. It just wasn't in his nature. As bad as things had gotten, he didn't see anything as being so bad he couldn't fix it. He knew he had messed up a few things, and that he had some ground to make up. But that this would cause him to see his life as ruined? The thought never entered his mind.

In his heart of hearts, Jack MacDonald was an unqualified optimist and as recently as five days earlier had set a plan in motion that he figured would give him enough breathing room to solve his current dilemma.

After securing the job with Flynn and Gunn, Jack knew that he was going to need some cash in order to hold the wolves at bay until his commission cheques starting rolling in.

So, after carefully perusing his old contact list from his days in the business, Jack determined that Terry Donnelly was his best chance for help. Donnelly was a banker, a man who had risen through the ranks on the strength of his ability to put bank money to work – safely. And no one had helped him more (by arranging investment loans for clients) than Jack MacDonald.

Jack had put millions to work for The People's Bank, and Donnelly had been his main contact.

So Jack had targeted him as the perfect man to approach. He was senior enough to get a relatively small ($10,000) loan put through without much scrutiny, and not so senior that he wouldn't realize the short-sightedness of turning Jack down.

And on the previous Tuesday morning, even though it had

159

been over four years since they had last spoken, Jack MacDonald leaned on Terry Donnelly – hard. Jack knew bankers and he had pushed every button as masterfully as a man without a pot to piss in possibly could.

He spelled it out for him. He let him know that it was unlikely he would qualify for the loan on paper. But if Donnelly helped him out, Jack assured him that his bank would see more loan business from Flynn & Gunn this year than it had seen in the previous three.

Prior to ending the call, a call he thought had gone extremely well, Jack also let Terry Donnelly know that it would be "helpful" if Donnelly could have an answer for him by Thursday. But as he hung up the phone, Jack was confident he'd be hearing back from Terry Donnelly within the hour.

However that was not to be the case. And not only did he not hear back from Terry Donnelly within the hour, he didn't hear back from him that entire day. Nor did he hear from him the next day, nor the next as well. Which was why Jack was so badly out of sorts when he met Hannibal at the Genuine Deli.

It hurt him that he had formulated a plan and led with his ace, only to find that his best card wasn't good enough to warrant so much as a return phone call.

Talk about a fall from grace.

Rolling a slightly crumpled Malboro between his thumb and mid-finger, Jack knew that smoking was the last thing he should be doing. The polyp his doctor had cut out of him earlier in the year may not have been cancerous "this time", still, an absolute ban on tobacco products, along with a healthier diet, were the two "precautionary" medical recommendations his doctor had been most forceful about.

However, his doctor's admonishments aside, in the face of his friend's death, and the snubbing he had received from Terry Donnelly, Jack was having a hard time giving much of a fuck about some raisin-sized growth that had been plucked out of his ass almost six months earlier.

Pondering his next move, Jack MacDonald inhaled delicately on the nearly spent butt, before dropping it over the side of the gorge, and turning his attention to the search below.

Jack had known Bruce Thatcher since the first grade, although they didn't become friends until halfway through grade four. It would have been tough to become friends with Bruce anytime prior to the fourth grade, and it wasn't just because that was the first year his mother stopped forcing him to wear Lederhosen shorts to school everyday.

Even at the best of times Bruce didn't really mix well with other people, and whether it was at school or at home on his street, Bruce Thatcher just always seemed to be the odd man out. It was a reality that couldn't be denied. Bruce himself seemed to recognize it even as a small child. And perhaps for that reason, prior to aligning himself with Jack, young Bruce Thatcher kept pretty much to himself.

He saw himself as his peers did. He was the strange boy, from the odd family, with the enormous teeth and continually runny nose, who cried easily, dressed in weird clothes, and couldn't run, pass, shoot, hit, punt, hide, seek, nor - and perhaps cruellest of all given the natural target his other shortcomings made him - fight.

As a child Bruce Thatcher really was the underdog's underdog. While Jack MacDonald, naturally blessed with all the random virtues a child could wish for, lived at the opposite end of the social spectrum. On the face of it, it seems unlikely that two boys who had drawn such opposite lots in life could ever become friends. Or perhaps it was their differences that made their friendship inevitable.

It started one morning as they came to a field each would have to pass in order to get to school. It was here that Bruce, after waiting for Jack to arrive, offered him ten cents (half his milk money), if Jack would accompany him through the field.

Jack, who had been walking to school with his younger cousin Hannibal, looked across the field and understood in an instant why Bruce Thatcher had made the request. And though only in grade one – so did Hannibal.

Every student of Corpus Christi had at one time or another seen Bruce Thatcher arrive at school beaten, bloodied, dishevelled and light on milk money. And all knew that his most constant antagonists were a pair of no-good brothers named Ronnie and Roman Cook – renegade Protestants from a nearby public school.

On this particular Tuesday morning it was ten-year-old Ronnie Cook, the larger of the two brothers, who had staked Bruce out. And as the three boys surveyed the field, Ronnie was making no attempt to add an element of stealth to his criminal activities. There he was, sitting like a big-ass bird on a large rock in the middle of the field, puffing on a home-made cigarette, waiting patiently for Bruce, or any other of a number of potential victims.

While contemplating Bruce's request, Jack didn't take his eyes off young Mister Cook. He had seen him there the day before, and passed by without incident. Though he'd had a feeling Ronnie had sized him up. Jack wasn't sure if Ronnie knew who he was or not, but after yesterday's pass-through he suspected that Ronnie knew now. Which would make both of the boys perfectly aware that he was the Jack MacDonald who had pounded the living daylights out of Ronnie's brother, Roman, the previous weekend.

Looking over to Bruce Thatcher, Jack had every intention of turning him down. It wasn't that he was afraid to fight Ronnie Cook. Quite to the contrary, Jack figured Ronnie was waiting there for him, rather than Bruce. So a fight was inevitable. It was really just a matter that while he had never been a party to the cruel treatment Bruce routinely endured throughout the course of a week - neither the larcenous attacks by the Cook brothers, nor the less criminal assaults (gotchy, or pink belly treatments) people like the Hillman brothers routinely put him through - it wasn't exactly like Jack needed a guy like Thatcher for a friend either.

But as he turned to decline Bruce's request, Bruce hopefully suggested, "I thought I'd just give you the money to hold, that way if he tries to take it, well, nobody could say you started it."

It was the thoughtfulness of the suggestion that Jack took note of first. He had been in trouble for fighting before and it touched him that Thatcher had thought far enough ahead to think of this and was in his own way actually trying to protect Jack.

Still Jack followed his first instinct and turned Bruce down. But not before explaining to him that Ronnie Cook was there to fight him, and therefore Bruce was in no danger.

After Jack declined Bruce's offer, he handed his books to Hannibal and was instructing his cousin to bypass the field on his way to school when Bruce walked directly in front of him and offered another suggestion.

"You know Jack, if he's here to fight you, maybe I could

help… I mean no matter why he's there, he'll certainly still go for my money if I got there first. And then if you were to arrive while he was stealing from me, like I said before, nobody could say you started it."

Listening patiently, Jack still had no intention of accepting Bruce Thatcher's "help". He thought it was nice of him to offer, kind of brave, too. And he even figured Bruce must be a smart little guy to come up with such a clever plan so quickly. Still, he saw no reason to take Bruce up on his offer. After all, it wasn't like Jack was going to get into trouble for punching out a lout like Ronnie Cook.

But there was something about the look on Bruce's face as he waited for an answer that somehow got to Jack. And he knew as soon as he saw it that, almost against his will, he was going to accede to Bruce Thatcher's wishes.

He didn't know what it was, and wasn't really sure he fully understood it to this day. But there was something about looking down at a nine-year-old boy, the neighbourhood leper, who was wearing eyeglasses that were held together by more tape than your average hockey stick, holding books that had the covers torn off them in the first week of school, and knowing that he was friendless, and would likely remain that way throughout his school days, that somehow made Jack understand, even at age nine, that befriending this boy was simply the right thing to do.

The right thing to do. It was a lesson Jack learned for the first time in his life that day at the field crossing. And if the pounding he put on Ronnie Cook was any indication, it was one he learned rather well.

Still perched against the railing, Jack's mind was a long way from the day he beat the hell out of Ronnie Cook. But three decades later he was still trying to figure out what to do about Bruce Thatcher.

Jack knew more about Bruce Thatcher than anyone else on the planet. And he certainly knew where all the skeletons were buried. He knew about the abuse in his past. He knew about the bouts of depression and associated problems that had plagued Bruce since his teenage years. He even knew about the unconventional fertility program Bruce and Jennifer Thatcher had followed in order to conceive a child – and of the ugly turn that program had taken. In the private matters of Bruce Thatcher's life, Jack MacDonald knew it all. And now he had to figure out what to do with all of this knowledge.

Given the circumstances of Bruce's death, Jack couldn't figure out if it was his responsibility to speak out on his friend's behalf – to try to explain the unexplainable – and let people know how hard Bruce had tried to hold things together. Or was it his duty as a friend to hold the secrets of Bruce's life to himself – as he had done for so many years already? And let them die with Bruce.

Did his friend not deserve a dignity in death he was never afforded in life?

Reaching for another cigarette Jack knew that deciding what to say about Bruce was going to be a tough call – no matter which way he decided to address it. It was a problem he had been contemplating ever since Jennifer Thatcher had called to tell him about Bruce. And one he probably would have spent the rest of the day pondering had it not been for the smartly dressed woman who was now tentatively tapping him on the right shoulder.

Chapter Eighteen

CHAPTER EIGHTEEN

PERCHED ATOP THE SHORT diving board of the back-yard's kidney-shaped pool, contemplating a full swan dive into its cool waters, I soaked in the elements around me. By 9:00 a.m. the final Sunday of June was already shaping up to be another mas-terpiece in the Creator's week-long celebration of summer. The sun was bright, the sky was blue, and the clouds were well spaced, majestic masses of undiluted whiteness, that hung like moored freighters across the morning sky.

It had been almost three years since I'd last found the inspira-tion to jump in the pool and surveying the grounds from this unfa-miliar vantage point I took a moment to enjoy my surroundings.

The spectacular beginning of summer had graced the city with such seasonal kindness that the lawn, as well as each tree, plant, and flower in the yard were standing tall and strong, proud-ly basking in the kind of near perfect conditions in which each was meant to flourish.

After my telephone conversation with Caroline, I knew that I should have gone up to bed and forced myself to rest. However, after speaking with her and making tentative plans to join the family as early as the following afternoon I was too charged up to consider even a short nap.

There was too much to do before I would be free to leave for the cottage. I had to call Barb and cancel our date. I had to call my lawyer and inform him that I wouldn't be attending the Courthouse with him on Tuesday. I had to close my proposed art deal with Sean Masse. And finally, I had to bring some order to the gloom-filled upper bedroom that had served as my so-called office for the past two years. A task that I could have begun immediately, but didn't.

Having been drawn outside by the splendour of the morning sun, I decided that a vigorous swim would be the perfect way to begin a new day. I had been promising myself for quite some time that I would start using the pool regularly, and had decided to finally honour that pledge.

After changing into a pair of black trunks, I made my way to the pool and bravely hopped up onto the diving board. I had purposely avoided dipping a toe in the water to gauge its temperature. I knew what the temperature would be. It would be bloody cold. We had been late in opening the pool this year, missing our annual target date of Victoria Day weekend by over a month. There wasn't any point in opening it earlier. The heater was broken, and while the $600 required to fix it was not out of reach, it certainly was not a priority expenditure. So we delayed the opening to a point when we believed a stronger sun would more quickly warm the frigid, thirty-six-hour flow of tap water that was required to fill the pool. A thirty-six-hour flow that ended only five days ago.

Bouncing ever so slightly on the middle of the board, waiting for the necessary shot of courage that would send me into the water, I once again caught myself admiring the yard's many garden areas. All around me, in clusters, columns and rows, flowers of every colour stretched towards the heavens.

In a setting where everything seemed so healthy, and so alive, it was impossible not to draw on the positive energy such surroundings create. And as I stepped to the end of the diving board I was once again becoming very conscious of the same sense of contentment I had experienced the night before.

Even as I threw my arms up to augment the two-footed thrust that would send me off the end of the board, there was an unfamiliar grace and rhythm in my movements. I just seemed to be in sync, an unusual state for me, even during my glory years.

While not exactly being a complete lummox, I had lost a good deal of physical co-ordination during my sixteenth year, a year in which I had endured a nine-inch growth spurt. It wasn't like I couldn't walk and chew gum at the same time, it's just that I was also not likely to be mistaken for Baryshnikov any time soon. And the awkwardness that has plagued me since that year of precipitous growth could turn an attempt at even a simple acrobatic feat into the unkindest of misadventures.

It didn't happen all the time, but whenever I sprung off the diving board anything was possible. And certainly more than one poolside guest had gasped in disbelief as a miscommunication within my internal electrical system inexplicably transformed a simple swan dive into an organ splattering belly flop. But not on this day.

Planting my feet and pushing off towards the heavens, I hit that dive like I was an Olympic athlete. A deep virile cracking sound escaped from the board as it launched me into uncharted space, high above the grounds of the home I had been so desperately afraid of losing.

It was a beautiful feeling, and for a moment it almost seemed as though I was flying. Not in the way that one might imagine an airborne Superman powering his way across the sky. This sensation of flight was more like an effortless gliding feeling that went on and on. And as I flew across my backyard in apparent defiance of the laws of physics, I felt as though everything that seemed to have been so wrong in my life, was going to be all right.

Of course at no time did I hear voices, or sense that any unearthly presence had possessed me. It was just a feeling, a sudden premonition of better things to come. And for whatever reason, I believed it.

Stretching my arms out and falling without fear towards the liquid plain beneath me, I closed my eyes and revelled in the sweetness of inner peace. It was a perfect moment, on a perfect day, and in a life that had found such moments so recently elusive, it didn't seem as though anything could dim the richness of my new-found optimism.

Though as I cracked the pool's calm surface I did find myself wishing I had fixed the water heater when I had the chance. Moment of perfection or not, this was going to be cold.

And holy shit, was I ever right about that. The water was *freezing*, and anybody that heard my high-pitched screams as I emerged gasping from its depths, must have thought I'd landed in a pool of sharks.

In spite of the water's unpleasant condition, I was determined to enjoy at least a short swim. However, my good intentions aside, after only a couple of rigid strokes, I quickly aborted the mission and frantically began to search for the nearest point of exit. The water was far too cold to possibly enjoy a swim, and by the time I finished my first crossing, it was all I could do to drag my shivering carcass over the side of the pool's shallow end.

Once safely out of the water, I remained stationary until my breathing returned to normal, and my heart rate dropped below that of a mating humming bird. Though disappointed at my swim's slight duration and aware that my short dash across the pool had turned my skin a noticeable shade of blue, I felt fully vindicated in my decision to attempt this frosty adventure, as my body began to respond to the cold water's invigorating qualities.

My impromptu dip had definitely recharged the old batteries. Leaning back into the sun's brilliant light, I smiled at the realization that I was once again enjoying my house without any fear that someone was going to come and take it away from me.

Determined to take advantage of my heightened energy level, I pulled myself up and started getting on with the day. Returning to the house, I stopped in the laundry room to grab a box of garbage bags, before bouncing up the fourteen steps that led to my bedroom. Entering the tan coloured room I quickly wrestled off my bathing suit and dropped it into the clothes hamper parked outside the ensuite bathroom.

Standing naked, I hesitated for a second after catching a glimpse of my reflection in Caroline's dressing mirror. Studying myself carefully, I couldn't deny that for a man on the verge of thirty-six, I really didn't look all that bad. The fairly strict work-out schedule I'd adhered to over the past decade had left me in better physical condition than most my age. I was by no means a hard body, but I still appeared to be strong and healthy. Yeah, there was clear evidence of a middle-aged spread, and it did seem as though my ass had dropped down an inch or two. But overall - I didn't look half bad.

Though I had never been a pretty boy, my face and neck were taut and largely unwrinkled. My hair was full and ungreyed. My shoulders, arms and back were still substantial and well defined. And while I could easily afford to shed a few pounds, at six foot one I was of a height that more than reasonably carried my two hundred-pound weight.

No, I really couldn't complain too much about the way the calendar had treated me. In fact, if not for the miniaturizing effect the pool's cold water had on the barely visible mushroom cap that was masquerading as my penis, if I sucked in the gut, and flexed real hard, I'd almost look like a stud.

Spinning away from the mirror, I moved purposefully through the bedroom. Fishing through a drawer, I grabbed a pair of white cotton underwear, and pulled them on, along with a blue tracksuit. Then, exiting the room, garbage bags in hand, I raced down the hall towards the small bedroom that served as my in-house office.

Approaching the closed door at the end of the hallway, I felt none of the fear and hopelessness that had so often possessed me on even a short visit to my office. And, as I confidently pushed into the room that housed the final remains of my corporate empire, there was not even a hint of hesitation in my stride. I felt like I was nine feet tall and bullet proof.

However, once inside the doorway, not even my cocky entrance could lessen the embarrassment I felt at the room's shameful appearance. It had been over a year since I had banned all others from entering my office and at least three months since I had found the courage to peek in myself, and the uninterrupted neglect of the room had taken a disastrous toll.

The place was such a quagmire of mis-arranged junk that it was difficult to tell if, beyond the dust, it was the thousands of files lying among various clothing items on the floor, or the room's lavish assortment of used coffee mugs, that would qualify as its most offensive feature. An argument that became moot after my eyes focused on the disassembled bicycle that was spread across my desk.

Yet, while the room's piteous state was embarrassing, and it did accurately depict the futile nature of my recent business agenda, it did nothing to spoil my pleasant mood. Yes, it hurt a bit to see that all that remained from several years of hard work were some outdated furnishings and a roomful of superfluous files. But whatever regrets I felt in this realization were short lived. For I knew that this was not a day to get bogged down in the past. It was a day to finally let the past go.

Chapter Nineteen

CHAPTER NINETEEN

AT THE TIME I FOUNDED Hannibal Investments in April of 1989, I'd grown tired of watching the $41,000 monthly profit being earned by New Venture Leasing do nothing more than accumulate in a bank account. So I began devising an investment plan that I felt certain would pay enormous dividends in the short, medium and long run.

In implementing this plan, my newly formed real estate company went on a six month buying spree, acquiring two strip-malls, a four-storey office building, eight industrial condos, and six residential condos. While I had partners in most of these new acquisitions, with the exception of the office building, I held a majority position in all of the properties.

My total stake in all of this real estate came to almost five million dollars. Hannibal Investments Corp was up and running and the good times were set to roll.

By October of 1989, the same $41,000 was still rolling into the New Venture's bank account each month, but now part of it was being offset by the expenses incurred by Hannibal Investments Corp.

The four million dollars in mortgages I had assumed in purchasing the properties, along with other related expenses, brought my carrying costs on these projects to $46,000 per month. This amount was offset by rental income, which lessened my burden by $28,000. Leaving me with a fully deductible, negative monthly cash flow of $18,000.

Having projected that the value of my new properties would grow from five to six million dollars within the first year, I figured to "earn" one million dollars in growth, simply by carrying $216,000 (12 x $18,000) in tax write-offs. Now, how could you beat that?

It was so simple. The $18,000 in monthly losses could be expensed from my $41,000 lease revenues, without impacting my personal lifestyle at all. The net profit of $23,000 that New Venture would still take in each month was more than enough money on which to survive. The plan seemed foolproof.

However, in spite of my belief that the only possible downside of this strategy was that I might have to learn to live on $23,000 per month, within a very short period of time, my flagship company started taking on water.

In January of 1990, Builders Insurance Group decided not to exercise its purchase option on an assortment of IBM equipment I had leased to them five years earlier. Of course at the time I set up Hannibal Investments, I was fully aware that the $9,150 monthly payment I had been receiving from B.I.G. would be coming to an end, but I had not considered the possibility that the buyout option on this lease would not be exercised.

Still, though I was caught a little off guard by this turn of events, I wasn't the least bit worried. Yes, I had been expecting a buyout cheque from B.I.G. in the amount of $50,000 on the last day of January, but the fact that I wasn't getting it was not a problem. The equipment B.I.G. was passing on could easily be sold for $75,000. It would just take a little more time.

However, much to my surprise, after marketing this hardware to several faithful customers, the only offer I was able to generate came from a third-party service company in Tennessee. The equipment I'd believed to be so valuable had become almost obsolete over the past couple of years, and nobody really needed this stuff anymore. The company that did want these pieces only wanted them for parts, as was reflected in its $8,000 offer.

Refusing to panic, I turned down the $8,000 and simply left

the B.I.G. equipment sitting in the warehouse. There was nothing to worry about. I could sell these units for more than $8,000, and even with the loss of $9,150 in revenue, I was still clearing over $14,000 a month.

In May of that same year a chain of convenience stores, tenants in the two strip-malls I had invested in, went out of business.

In August, a small retail clothing chain also went out of business, causing the two strip-malls, which had yet to fill the vacancies brought on by the last bankruptcy, to lose their largest tenant. And perhaps even worse than this additional loss of revenue was the fact that the second bankruptcy touched off the first round of squabbling amongst the partners.

Letters started going out from various legal firms across the city. People were starting to cover their asses.

The result of these two bankruptcies was to raise the net monthly carrying costs of Hannibal Investments from $18,000 to $26,500. All this at a time when New Venture Leasing was only generating $32,000. All of a sudden I was being forced to make ends meet on about $5000 a month.

In November of 1990 I set up a meeting with Bill Ferguson, my lawyer. The continued defection of partners in various projects had left me feeling a little bit uneasy, and I wanted to know the full extent of my liabilities in these properties.

The outcome of my meeting with Bill left me somewhat reassured in my belief that this was no time to panic. We both felt that an upturn in the real estate market was just around the corner. The various holdings of Hannibal Investments would start to perform better any day now. The best thing to do was hang tight.

However, as our meeting ended, Bill did say something that caught me by surprise.

"One thing you might want to do… just to be safe… is transfer the house into your wife's name."

Transfer the house… what is he talking about… I thought we just agreed that everything was going to be fine.

Lawyers, they're always so cautious.

Unenthusiastically telling Bill I'd give the idea some thought, he responded in a way that sort of stung a bit.

"It would be foolish not to."

Did he just call me a fool?

By the early part of 1991 the real estate market was showing no signs of picking up and as bad as it had been performing, things at New Venture Leasing and Compu Manufacturing were going no better. Almost all of my customers had cut way back on major capital expenditures, and even when I could put a deal together, it had to be done at rock bottom prices.

Trying anything and everything in order to fight back, I called Techno Services in Nashville Tennessee and let it be known that I was now willing to accept its $8,000 offer for the equipment I had removed from B.I.G.

Techno Services refused, and then offered $4,000.

I couldn't believe it. Losing at real estate was one thing, but now I was getting beat at my own game.

"Done." What else could I do?

In March of 1991, just around the time I'd come to believe that my situation couldn't get much worse, it did. Northern Development Corporation, the majority owner and main tenant of the office building in which I had invested, filed for bankruptcy. NDC was gone, and with it not only did I lose the $300,000 I had put into its building (without a tenant, the value of the building dropped to less than half the amount for which it was mortgaged), but New Venture Leasing also lost its biggest customer. Northern Development Corp was in the third year of a five-year lease that was paying me $8,200 a month, and now that was gone too. Talk about a shitty day.

The second I heard the news of NDC's demise I called Bill Ferguson.

"We gotta talk - immediately. Get the paperwork ready to flip the house into Caroline's name, ASAP… along with the two condos. Please Bill, right away."

Panic had set in.

If there was a moment in my life that I could clearly define as its worst, it happened the night NDC went bust. It was late and I couldn't sleep. Sitting alone in my office, trying to figure out how I had turned my previously carefree life into such a nightmare, I became so consumed by feelings of guilt and shame that I began to tremble uncontrollably.

I felt a pain that night that went far beyond any kind of hurt I had ever known, and it was an experience that left me a decidedly different person. At that exact moment, I could feel myself somehow becoming disconnected from everything around me.

By the next day, a depression had set in that was so debilitating I found myself unable to cope with even the simplest of tasks. I knew that there were steps I should have started to take in order to cut my losses, but I just couldn't. I couldn't do anything. I was too shell-shocked, too afraid of making yet another mistake - I couldn't even open my mail.

So complete was the self-doubt that took hold of me, the only way I could respond to any burden of responsibility was to run away. And the more I ran, the easier it became to continue running.

I went through the next year of my life strictly going through the motions, and at no point during this period did I ever feel even remotely like myself. I did get around to finally selling off most of the remaining assets of Hannibal Investments, and I did eventually flip the house and a couple of other assets into Caroline's name, but there was no structure, or intelligent design to anything I was doing. I was lost, and in a very short time came to feel as though I were caught in some sort of free fall.

Chapter Twenty

CHAPTER TWENTY

REACHING INTO THE BOX of garbage bags, it felt strange to feel so little after replaying the highlights of my demise. As recently as the previous week even an involuntary glimpse back to the day NDC went bust would have been tantamount to driving an ice pick into both sides of my head. But, for the first time since my collapse, I could focus very clearly on these matters and feel nothing at all. For some reason the whole sequence of events seemed pretty insignificant. Stepping over an irreparably broken typewriter lying in the middle of the room's only traffic area my eyes were drawn to the three stacks of yellow folders standing tallest in the assortment of junk around me.

Calmly unfolding a large orange garbage bag, I began to smile as I envisioned completing the first step of my cleaning detail.

The yellow folders contained all relevant information pertaining to my court battle with the bank. And while I knew that trashing them would do nothing to weaken the bank's position in this matter, the act of tossing these stacks of legal bullshit was going to add a large dose of satisfaction to my day.

Win, lose or draw on Tuesday, I no longer cared about the upcoming verdict. For me, the case was already over. It had ended the previous night. I was fed up, and was claiming victory, irrespective of what the official outcome might be.

It had been over two years since the bank had issued its original Statement of Claim. And since that time, throughout the process known as Discovery, the Motions, the Affidavits, and all of the other crap associated with this type of proceeding, somewhere throughout all this manoeuvring a case had emerged that I no longer really understood, or cared about.

Long ago, the lawyers on both sides of this matter had turned a relatively simple disagreement into something more complex than a constitutional negotiation. The truth and intent of my original dealings with the bank and my former business partners was now so distorted that I could no longer see which points of the fragmented truth that remained had any legal relevance at all.

However, what I had come to understand was that, regardless of what truth did remain, it was no longer relevant to me.

Dropping the orange bag beside me, I placed my left foot on the first yellow pile, and gently pushed it into the pile in front of it. Turning away to get to my desk, I heard the first and second pile of folders go crashing to the floor. Upon reaching my desk, I was still listening for the sound of one more thud, when I turned and saw that the third stack had not fallen with the other two. Reaching for the phone, I playfully determined that the defiant third stack of legal files would be the first one bagged – right after I made this call.

It has always been my practice when faced with a series of tasks, to start with the one that would be the most unpleasant. In keeping with this strategy, I picked up the phone and began dialing. Having never called the number before, I hit each button with exaggerated care. I also pressed each button firmly and deliberately as if to assure myself that I was in full control of the situation.

Though fully confident when I first picked up the phone, I could feel my sense of resolve decline as each digit was entered. It was a softening of resolve that my dramatic dialing technique failed to bolster, and one that caused me to slam the phone down just as I hit the last number. Damn it, I really didn't want to make this call.

Dumping Barb was something I was not looking forward to doing. Not that I was having any second thoughts about the need to break our date. I was just so embarrassed about having put myself in a position where breaking a date was necessary. After all, what was I supposed to say to her?

"Yeah, sorry about mauling you the other night but you know what? I just remembered that I'm married, so if you don't mind I'll take a pass on appraising your condo. Take care, and ah, thanks for the memories."

Immediately picking up the phone I hit the redial button and sat back in order to review the excuse I had prepared. I could feel my hand trying to slam the phone down yet again, but I held firm. It was time to face the music. And I calmed myself in the realization that no matter how ugly the conversation might get, this call had to be made.

Listening to the end of the first ring, I began reconsidering the idea of using Bruce's death as an excuse for breaking our appointment. In the wake of this tragedy, it would certainly be easy to present Barb with any number of plausible reasons as to why I would be unable to keep our date, all of which she could easily accept without feeling the least bit slighted. So using Bruce's death would be the easiest route to take. *But would it be the right thing to do? Why not just tell her the truth? Tell her you were way out of line the other night, make her aware of your family situation, and apologize for your stupidity. What could be easier, and more final than that?*

As the second ring ended, I started to think, or maybe hope, that perhaps Barb wasn't home. Two rings isn't much, but it should be plenty of time to reach the phone in an apartment.

Three rings. Fantastic, she wasn't home?

Hang up the phone... Hang up the phone... hang up the phone... she's not home... hang it up and next time you see her, just tell her you tried to reach her on Sunday morning, and couldn't. Hang it up you idiot! Ring four. Almost over - great, I'm out of it.

"Hello."

Shhhhiiiitttt. Why didn't you hang up when you had the chance? Okay, don't panic. Just tell her the truth. It'll be all right.

I was just about to return Barb's hello, but she kept right on talking.

"This is Barbara Sutherland, I'm not in right now, however if you leave me a message, I will..."

Perfect. It was an answering machine. I couldn't believe my good fortune. This wasn't going to be too bad after all.

"… be sure to get back to you as soon as possible. Please wait for the tone, and have yourself a great day."

The realization that I had been granted a gimme on my day's most unpleasant task, brought all the anxiety I felt about speaking with Barb to a complete halt. In fact for a second I even started to regret that I wouldn't have the opportunity to talk to her right then and there, so that we might settle this whole misunderstanding on the spot. But, accepting that an answering machine would have to suffice, I quickly formulated a new "plan A" - leave a message letting her know that some unmentioned circumstance had come up, and I would have to miss our appointment. Then maybe even suggest that she contact a real estate agent for the advice she required.

Waiting for the beep, I took note of what a business-like message Barb had left on her recorder. Her voice was almost unrecognizable with so little enthusiasm or inflection in her words. It made her seem much older.

"Hello Barb, it's Hannibal. Sorry I missed you. I just wanted to touch base and let you know… "

"Hello, hello,… Hannibal."

"Barb?"

"Yeah! Hiiiiii, it's great to hear from you, just a sec, okay. I just stepped in the door."

Oh fuck…no. You idiot, why did you try to leave a message? Why didn't you just hang up?

Barb's voice had come bursting on the line so unexpectedly it caught me completely off guard. What to do now?

Don't panic. Go with "plan B" - get this thing over with. Tell her the truth.

An approaching rustling sound alerted me that Barb would soon be picking up the line. And in the amount of time it took for me to clear my drying throat, her sweet voice was once again singing in my ear.

"Hiiii, sorry about that. Whew, what a morning… I just finished a killer aerobics class. I swear I feel like I've just been bent and twisted into positions I had never imagined before. What a way to start…"

Barb was talking to me so casually I couldn't tell if she was unaware of the complications our last meeting had created, or if she didn't care about such complications. I also couldn't tell if discussing her morning's events with me was just an honest recounting of her day, or if she wanted me to start thinking about her bending and twisting around in her aerobics outfit - which is what I was doing.

Whatever was going on in her head, as soon as I saw the first image of Barb stretching out before me in a spandex leotard I quickly switched to "Plan C".

Take the easy out - tell her about Bruce's death, and head for the hills.

"Anyway I guess I'll survive," she was saying. "It was just extra tough today, especially after being so hung over yesterday. So how are you doing, I guess you've had a pretty awful weekend, huh?"

"No, not too bad... I recovered pretty quickly."

"Wow, I wish I was so fortunate. I don't know what happened to me. I didn't think I had all that much, then all of a sudden – Bam! - I felt so drunk. It was terrible. I can't even remember cashing out."

"Yeah well, those liqueurs can really sneak up on you. You've got to be careful," I answered, like I was some sort of responsible citizen.

I started to feel a little safer in our conversation after Barb mentioned that she couldn't really remember cashing out. I'd watched her complete the final tally on her night's work and knew that she had completed the job without incident. But if she couldn't remember cashing out, then maybe she couldn't remember other things as well - like the prolonged groping session that followed. Maybe I was in the clear. Maybe I could break this appointment without embarrassment or rancour.

"Yeah, you're right. But it was all in good fun... and you guys are always a lot of fun."

While feeling safer in our conversation, I was still analyzing every syllable that came out of Barb's mouth. You guys are always a lot of fun. Guys, as in the plural. She had me and Jack lumped together. What a break. Even if she did remember making out with somebody, she probably couldn't remember if it was with me or with Jack. It was all just a simple night of fun to her. *What in the hell was I so worried about? Everything's cool.*

"Well, Jack and I do aim to please."

"You did, you definitely did. It was great. So, anyway, are you still okay for Monday night?"

I was so lulled by the tone of the early part of our conversation that I didn't recognize a possible warning signal when Barb asked me about Monday night. I didn't make the connection that if she remembered setting up a date with me for that night, she sure as hell must have recalled that it was me she had been making out with. But I missed this rather obvious point, and as the conversation continued, I still felt like I was in the clear.

Feeling mostly exonerated from the drunken mischief of Friday night, I leaned back in my chair and prepared to drop the axe. In the clear or not, I still had to cancel.

"Monday night, yeah well that's what I was calling you about."

"Yeah, I hope it's still okay. My family really wants me to decide what I'm going to do with this place, so it would be just great if you could help me out."

"Yeah, well you know I want to help you. It's just that... eh."

After Barb told me that it would be just great if I could help her out, any reason as to why I shouldn't help started leaving my head. I'd listened very closely to every word of our conversation, and had detected no evidence of a hidden agenda in her request for help. So, if the purpose of our meeting was purely innocent, what reason did I have not to help her? I would do it if Barb were a guy. I would also do it if she were unattractive. I would do it for virtually anybody that made such a request. So why wouldn't I do it for her? Just because I had kissed her a little bit the last time I saw her? She didn't even remember that.

Breaking in on the noticeable pause I had left in our conversation, Barb then started to offer me an easy out.

"I was really hoping that we could get together, but if you are having second thoughts, I don't want you to do something you're not comfortable with."

At this point in the conversation I was so intent on analyzing my own thoughts as to why going over to Barb's was such a big deal that I was no longer really listening to what she was saying. Having become fully convinced that I had gauged the innocent nature of our proposed meeting correctly, I just blurted out.

"No, I'm not having any second thoughts. I was just wondering what time you wanted me to meet you. I was thinking maybe sometime in the afternoon… say between four and five.”

But even as the words left my mouth I found myself wishing I had taken a second to rethink what Barb had last said to me. What was it - she was hoping we could get together - but if I was having second thoughts? She wasn't asking if I was too busy to help, she was asking if I was having second thoughts about “getting together”. Why would someone have second thoughts about simply helping out an acquaintance? And why did hoping we could “get together” sound so different than “it would be just great if you could help me out”. Hold on a second here. Are we talking about the same thing?

“Sure, between four and five would be just great. I'm looking forward to it… well, it looks like I've got myself some shopping to do. I'll remember what you told me about what you like your women to wear… See you tomorrow! Byyyyyyye.”

Her sweet and provocative “Byyyyyyyye” was still buzzing around in my head as the line went dead. I couldn't believe what I had just done. Of all the outcomes I had considered before calling Barb, I had never once figured that I wouldn't actually break our date. And now, after less than three minutes of conversation, I had improvised my way into “Plan D”. Whereby, not only was our date now confirmed, but its true purpose had also been clarified, and Barb would be spending part of the next day shopping for erotic lingerie in order to launch the affair I had just agreed to, in style.

Standing up with the phone still in my hand I became furious with this outcome and the broadening scope of my incompetence in dealing with this matter.

How fucking stupid can you be? Why did you call her? Why did you try to read her intentions? It doesn't matter what Barb's intentions are… It doesn't matter… get that through your thick skull… it doesn't matter what she thinks or wants… you are not allowed to go to her apartment, regardless of the danger or innocence of the situation! Why can't you understand that?

I knew that I was going to have to call Barb back immediately, but in light of our first conversation I was understandably fearful that in a second conversation I might try to break our date by volunteering to bring the condoms.

In something close to rage I looked down at the phone, and

once again pressed redial. This was it. My business with Barb was about to come to a very curt finish.

Beep… Beep… Beep.

Goddam it. Busy. Slamming the phone down I stepped around to the middle of the room cursing like a sailor.

Reaching back across my desk, I violently swept the in/out basket off the top, and while its contents scattered around the room, I once again grabbed the phone. Stretching the cord over the desk, I pressed redial and stood impatiently by.

Beep… Beep… Beep.

Shit! Fuck me! Dropping the phone to stop myself from throwing it, I turned into the middle of the room and without thinking kicked the remaining stack of yellow legal files as hard as I possibly could. I don't know why I thought that kicking forty pounds of paper with my bare foot would make me feel better about what had happened with Barb. But immediately upon impact I realized what a mistake I had made.

The pain was like something straight out of hell. While the force of the kick left the neatly stacked files unmoved, it caused my foot to fold up like an old accordion.

Gingerly grabbing the injured foot, I began screaming like a banshee as I hopped around the room, and it was on about the third or fourth hop that my already low fortunes took a considerable turn for the worse.

Landing on the lone foot still supporting me, I came down on a full roll of unsecured fax paper which tossed me backwards like the big time loser of a log rolling contest.

Trying desperately to gain enough body control to prevent a thunderous crash to the floor, I turned around to see if I could grab hold of the bookcase I knew was somewhere behind me, and did so just in time to plant the side of my face on its top corner.

Ricocheting off the book case, as if choreographed to cause maximum damage, I did a delicate half-turn before landing squarely on the back of my head on one of the very few inches of floor area not cushioned by any form of paper product.

Groggy from a lack of sleep, and stunned from the fall, little, bright coloured birdies started fluttering around me, as an endless train whistle blared out from the centre of my brain. I could hear myself laughing, and chattering incomprehensibly. I think I was saying, "Toto, I've got a feeling we're not in Kansas anymore."

And we sure as hell weren't. I felt like I had stepped into a cartoon. Blinding flashes of light were popping off in all directions, and as I tried to get up I suddenly heard a voice.

"Hannibal… Hannibal…" For a second I thought Caroline had come home, but after the voice called out again I realized it wasn't her at all.

It was a voice from the dream. It was Amanda.

I could hear her footsteps, the pointed tips of her long heels piercing the paperwork around me, as she moved closer and closer to the man she had admitted betraying in front of a national television audience.

Closing my eyes, and half wishing she would go away, I desperately tried to listen above the sound of the train whistle to ascertain Amanda's whereabouts. No longer able to hear the sound of her footsteps, I flinched in anticipation as she suddenly beckoned from directly above me.

"Hannibal… Hannibal… when are you coming back to me baby?"

Opening my eyes, I could see Amanda standing directly above me. Her legs were spread wide apart and each foot was planted on opposite sides of my head. Because she wouldn't look down as she spoke to me, I couldn't see her face, but the unmistakable baby-like quality of her voice left no doubt in my scrambled mind that it was she. The long, silk-covered legs that I had so admired on the show, grew right out from beside me, and ran up into the same black dress she had worn while visiting Oprah Winfrey. And while I tried to be a gentleman, and not look, my vantage point confirmed two indisputable facts.

Fact one was a confirmation of an earlier suspicion. I had been correct in my assumption that Amanda preferred wearing stockings and a garter belt to pantyhose. Fact two was that a garter belt and stockings were all that Amanda was wearing under her scandalously short dress.

Lying defenceless on the floor, studying the anatomical perfection of this uninvited hallucination, I did not move a muscle until Amanda reached down and took both of my hands in hers. Unaware of proper protocol when addressing or touching imaginary beings, I tried to resist as Amanda placed her hands over mine.

My hands felt like blocks of stone as Amanda began to pull them across the lower parts of her silk covered legs. But by the time she led them over her knees and up into the softness of her inner thighs, they had regained much of their flexibility, and were now playfully caressing each exotic contour of her well-muscled legs.

Gliding effortlessly still higher, my fingers electrified at each touch of the icy silk on which they journeyed, I began to realize that while my hands were still moving up, Amanda was no longer pulling them. Though still guiding my movements, Amanda was now making me do some of my own dirty work. And I was happily complying.

On reaching the end of the silk covered area, my fingertips burned as they pressed into the alabaster skin that bulged slightly from the top of each stocking. In sharp contrast to the coolness of the silk, Amanda's simmering flesh was warm and clammy, and seemed to get warmer as my fingers danced across its seductive surface.

After several moments of naughtily toying with her searing upper thighs, Amanda released my hands. Having expertly led me to the Promised Land, Amanda leaves it to me to enter heaven's gate on my own. But my hands can move no further. With my shoulders pressed firmly to the floor, and my arms stretched to their maximum vertical limit, I can reach no higher. No matter how hard I try to lift myself in order to extend my reach, I simply cannot.

All I can do is watch in silence as Amanda calmly steps through my outstretched arms and begins to walk away. No longer supported by her willowy legs, my arms drop limply to the ground. As she moves further away, my eyes close. The bright lights and fluttering birds that had accompanied her visit begin to fade into nothingness, and while the sound of her last discernible footstep leaves me feeling both relieved and frustrated, it is only the distant sound of a fading train whistle that escorts me into darkness.

Chapter Twenty-one
CHAPTER TWENTY-ONE

IN WHAT WAS BECOMING a pattern that began with my Saturday morning spill on the back deck, after my Sunday morning trip to never-never land in my second floor office, it was once again the sound of a ringing phone that brought me back to the world where the sky is blue. And once again the caller was Jack.

My eyes opened instantly on what I thought was the first ring and staring straight above me I ran my hand through the space in which my rattled head had conjured up my provocatively attired television wife. Thankfully, she was gone. I was not completely insane. Ignoring both the sight and memory of Amanda's visit, I pulled myself up and with great care slowly hopped through the room's ankle-high trash.

Picking up the phone I could see that it was still very bright outside. I figured it must have been about four o'clock, although subconsciously I believe that I did notice that there was something odd about this Sunday afternoon.

"Hannibal, it's Jack, how ya doing?"

"Good, fine, not much going on down on this end. What's going on with you? Where are you?"

"I'm still down at the Falls and there's quite a bit going on here. Sorry I didn't get back to you sooner, I got tied up last night and Bruce popped up first thing this morning."

"He did, they found him. Well shit, I guess that's something to be thankful for."

"Yeah, I guess so. Anyway, it's over. They're going to run some tests on him to see if he was drunk or stoned or something. He should be home in a day or two."

"What a mess. How's... ahhhh never mind, I'll talk to you when I see you."

"Well that's what I'm calling about. Listen, I'm going back to the hotel to pick up my things and then I'm heading home. I thought I'd see if you wanted to grab a bite to eat?"

"Sure. I'm just sitting around. Spent the day cleaning up my office - just wasting time, waiting for your call."

"Spent the day? What are you talking about?"

"Nothing, I've been in my office since about ten doing a little cleaning up. Why?... What are you talking about?"

"You've been in your office since about ten? It's only eight now."

"It is?"

"Yeah it is. What's going on?"

"Nothing. I was sleeping when you called... I guess I lost track of... Jack eeeeh,... now here's a question you hope you don't need help with too often. What day is it?"

"Its Monday, what's wrong with you?"

"MONDAY! Holy shit."

"Hannibal, you okay?"

"Yeah I'm fine. I may have suffered a concussion, but other than that..."

"A concussion?"

"I'm just kidding, I'm fine. I'll explain it to you when I see you. I'll meet you at the Deli - no, no, not the Deli, I'll meet you at Shantys at one. Okay?"

"Shantys at one, I'll be there."

Hanging up the phone, I hobbled around my desk and sat down in the middle of the floor. Quietly picking up a large garbage bag I grabbed a file marked "Office Supplies" and mindlessly slipped it into the bag. *Monday morning - Jesus... How could I have slept for over twenty hours?*

My head was still quite foggy as I began to sort through the mess, but it didn't take long to separate fact from fiction. Damn it, I had gotten virtually nothing done. I was starting the day no further ahead than I was yesterday, probably even a little behind if I factored in my botched call to Barb.

Talk about one step forward, two steps back.

As frustrating as it was to realize that I had wasted all of Sunday, there was nothing I could do but pick myself up and start all over again. Making it up to the cottage before nightfall was still a possibility, if I caught a few breaks. There was no time to lose. I would have to call my lawyer, meet Jack, recall Barb, close my art deal, and above all, avoid hopping around on one foot while I cleaned this office.

By eleven-thirty I was sitting at the kitchen table sipping a tall glass of orange juice and holding an ice bag against the side of my head. I was also resting my foot in a bucket of hot, salted water. Though why I added salt to the water, I'll never know.

The determined grimace I had worn on my face for the preceding three hours had given way to a Cheshire Cat's grin of accomplishment. There were now thirty-nine garbage bags full of junk from my upstairs office en route to the city dump. With the exception of some pertinent tax returns, and the files containing the contracts of the three small leases that were still active, I threw out everything, including two filing cabinets and a typewriter.

The first several minutes of this whirlwind cleanup had gone quite slowly as I sorted through each file like it was a piece of the Dead Sea Scrolls. It wasn't until I spent five minutes trying to decide whether or not to save the Destiny Media file that I realized that if my office were ever to be saved a new strategy would have to be employed.

Back in 1985 Destiny Media had leased eight computers from New Venture Leasing at a cost of six hundred dollars a month, for twenty-four months. The last payment on this agreement had been received in September of 1987, and since Destiny did not exercise its buy-out option on these units the eight computers were returned to my warehouse that same month.

I knew from memory that these computers had been tossed in a dumpster in 1989. I also knew that Destiny Media had gone out of business in '91 and that its owner, Herb Johnson, had died the following year. Yet I had still spent a full five minutes trying to determine if this obvious piece of junk was worth keeping - just in case. Just in case Mr Johnson were to rise from the dead, revive his old company and decide to exercise a six-year-old purchase option on equipment I had destroyed years ago. What were the chances of that?

After coming to terms with the fact that the Destiny file was junk, and had been for years, my cleaning activities kicked into warp speed. Over the next ten minutes I filled six garbage bags to the breaking point, before stopping to run them out to the side of the road.

This frantic pace continued on without pause until every visible file was bagged and tossed. And at no point in this entire process did I have even a single second thought as to the prudence of my actions. The business, legal, and scholastic value of any of this information was non-existent, and I started feeling better and better as I trashed it, especially the legal files.

It was almost eleven by the time I walked the last bag out the door, just in time to meet a city garbage truck. The quantity of neatly stacked plastic bags at the bottom of the driveway made the front of the house look like an aspiring landfill site. In order to appease the garbage men, I tried to joke about the mess.

"Sorry guys, we had my mother-in-law over for dinner on Saturday night... big eater. You know how it is. Come on, I'll give you a hand."

The tall black man simply raised his hand as he grabbed the first of the bags.

"That's okay man, we'll take care of this." Then, staring at me, he added, "It looks like your mother-in-law is also one hell of a fighter. You better go in and take care of yourself."

I couldn't understand what the guy was talking about, but after the slight Asian kid behind him stepped forward to grab a couple of bags and I saw he was wearing the same look of concern, I sheepishly recalled driving myself into the upstairs bookcase.

Feeling a little uncomfortable as the two trash collectors sized me up, I lifted my hand and started massaging the melon-sized lump on the side of my head.

"Yeah, thanks a lot guys, it was a tough weekend… parachute didn't open. Guess I got off lucky."

Returning to the house I checked myself in a hallway mirror, before going into the kitchen to grab an ice bag and a glass of juice. Once sitting down I refused to let my battered appearance dampen the sense of accomplishment I felt in having removed all that garbage from my life. Black eye or not, at least I was a man of action again.

The next thing I did was call my lawyer. The momentum caused by the success of my early morning cleaning detail had brought me to my second task of the day. I had to inform Bill Ferguson that I would not be accompanying him to court on Tuesday. Then I would be off to meet Jack and work on the $8500 solution.

"Good morning, Marshall, Kellog and Christie."

"Yes, Bill Ferguson, please."

"One moment…………………….. I'm sorry, Mr Ferguson is with a client right now. Can I have him call you back?"

"Yes, have him call John Rankin when he gets a chance."

"Thank you."

There was little surprise in not getting a hold of Bill on my first call. It seems that no matter what the degree of urgency it always takes at least half a day of telephone tag to make contact with my fidgety solicitor. It didn't really matter though. I could just as easily feed him my instructions later on.

Chapter Twenty-two

CHAPTER TWENTY-TWO

AFTER SHAVING, SHOWERING and putting on a freshly cleaned suit, I jumped in the Lexus and began the short drive to Shantys. Before leaving the house I stopped in the front hall and picked up a black pair of Ray Ban sunglasses. The Ray Ban's had bigger lenses and much wider arms than my regular glasses and would more effectively cover my damaged eye.

Leaving the driveway I was having mixed emotions about seeing Jack. On the one hand I was looking forward to our meeting. I had been worried about him ever since he told me about his money problems and was hoping that together again, and both sober, we could come up with a solution that would help him get through the week without losing his home.

I was also looking forward to hearing the details of his trip to Niagara Falls. I wanted to know what "difficult stuff" Bruce had been dealing with, and how it might have led him to take his own life.

On the other hand, as much as I wanted to talk to him, and as much as I wanted to help him, I was also concerned that I might see a different person when I looked across the table at Jack.

Ever since he told me that he was on the verge of tapping

out, the aura of success through which I had always viewed him had disappeared. He was a mere mortal to me now. Flawed like the rest of us, and perhaps even more so. For he had broken the golden rule – he'd run out of gold.

Approaching the restaurant, I was a little nervous about how I might react to seeing him. If Jack ever suspected that I was looking down on him it might tarnish our friendship forever. Which was the last thing in the world I wanted to happen.

Shantys was a restaurant very close in atmosphere to the Genuine Deli. Both were casual establishments, and had similar menus, though Shantys generally drew a younger crowd. Like the Deli, Shantys also had a patio, and since I was a little late in arriving I was hoping Jack had selected an outdoor table so that I might keep my sunglasses on without looking too conspicuous.

Turning into the driveway I stopped to let an old Honda Civic pull out of a small parking space beside the front door. Waiting patiently while a young Oriental girl wrestled the car out of the spot, I nodded politely as she drove past me and out onto the street.

After the Honda was gone I could see that the space it had vacated was actually only half a space, thanks to a poorly parked Jaguar on its left side. Wheeling a few feet past, I dropped the car into reverse, and backed into the small opening, leaving the passenger door of the Lexus no more than five inches from the Jag.

Walking around to the back of the restaurant I carefully scanned the patio until my eyes fell upon Jack. His back was to me, but there was no mistaking his sitting posture. It was him alright. He was dressed in a blue suit and had two beers standing in front of him.

As was typical with Jack, he was talking to a couple of guys at the next table and I could see they were totally absorbed in whatever he was telling them. I knew they wouldn't be discussing investment strategies, but as I watched them all break into laughter I was damn certain that while neither of these two gentlemen knew it, they would soon be clients of Flynn and Gunn Investments.

Two more for the king.

Though I had seen it done a thousand times I never understood how Jack did it. It was never exactly clear to me why people were so instantly impressed with him. On the surface there was nothing in his physical, intellectual or social background that would justify the level of adulation Jack routinely received. Yet there was something about him, some intangible quality that people instantly liked, and it made them almost seem eager to embrace his views and opinions.

Approaching our table, and studying Jack from behind, some of my worst fears began to emerge as a condescending view of him forced its way into my thoughts. All of a sudden he became someone I didn't really know. And I even felt like warning the two guys at the table beside him to watch out, the guy they were talking to was not what he appeared to be.

It was a terrible feeling. The man who had shaped my life more than all others was sitting less than twenty feet away and some perverse side of me seemed intent on looking down on him. If not for the fact that Jack had caught sight of me in his peripheral vision, I might have turned around to collect myself. But having been spotted, I reluctantly pulled out a chair and tried to smile, and as I nodded in acknowledgement of Jack's cheery hello, I did so wondering if it had been a mistake to have followed him so closely for all of these years.

"Hey, how ya doing? Sorry I'm late," I returned his greeting before sitting down and swigging on the beer he had ordered for me.

"No sweat, I just got here myself," he answered, before ending his other conversation with a simple, "I'll be in touch guys."

Turning back to me Jack continued, "I gotta get out of here fairly quickly, so I ordered us both the fish and chips. Is that okay? Because I'm sure we can still change it."

"No that's great, thanks," I answered, and once again reached for my beer.

"So, how you doing? Hell of a weekend, eh?"

"Hell of a weekend."

Looking across the table I noticed that Jack was wearing the same suit as the last time I saw him - right down to the shirt and tie.

"Yeah, but I think I'm going to have a good week, and if what they say about good things coming in threes is correct, I just might have myself a great week."

I was expecting Jack to be a little down after his trip to the Falls, so it surprised me when he started our conversation in such an upbeat mood. Seeing him this way helped lift my spirits a little bit, although it didn't stop me from noticing how tight his suit looked on him.

"Why, what do you mean?"

"First let me ask you something."

Before Jack posed his question, he picked up his beer and took a long sip. Watching him lift his glass I could see that one of the suit's sleeve buttons was dangling sadly by a single thread. Sipping on my own beer I shrugged and tried to look away.

Feeling a wave of disappointment come over me I struggled to bring my disparaging view of Jack into check. Thoughtlessly removing my sunglasses in order to wipe my brow, I was caught off guard by Jack's reaction.

"Holy shit, man! What happened to you? You look like Jerry Quarry… after Frazier was finished with him."

As it was with the garbagemen, it took a second to understand what Jack was talking about. But eventually it clicked in.

"What? Oh, the face. Sorry, I really didn't think it was that noticeable."

"Not that noticeable! Christ man, your face looks worse than this tie I'm wearing."

Seeing an opening to break some of the tension I was feeling, I responded to Jack's insult in kind.

"Jack, I may look a little beat up but there is nothing in this bar that looks worse than your tie."

"Oh yeah, what about her?" Jack answered, pointing at a large and unpleasant waitress whom he knew I had unsuccessfully made a play for several years ago.

Looking over at Marge I started laughing as I recalled the night she spurned my drunken advances.

"Okay, okay. You win. Several things in this bar look worse than your tie… Okay?"

"I don't know what you're laughing at. Marge turned you down."

"I know, I remember… Now, I said you win. Let it go."

Jack was a dangerous man to engage in a battle of wits. He remembered everything and always knew which soft spot to attack in order to claim victory.

Refusing to leave myself open to further ridicule I moved quickly to change the conversation.

"It's nothing really, I simply fell down. I'll tell you about it later. Now, wasn't there something you wanted to ask me?"

"What?"

"You said earlier there was something you wanted to ask me. What was it?" I reminded him as I slipped my sunglasses back on.

"Something I wanted to ask you... Oh yeah... Do you remember a girl named Karen Corrigan?"

The sound of her name brought my attention right back to the conversation.

"Karen Corrigan."

"Yeah."

"Sure, I remember Karen. In my grade everybody knew her. In fact many of my classmates claimed to know her better than they really did."

"What do you mean?"

"Nothing, it's just that in my age group, Karen was the prettiest and best built girl at the Abbey. So, of course everybody at St Ig's lied about her. Half my tenth grade class claimed to have felt her up at one time or another... and it was all bullshit. You know how little boys can be."

"Yeah, I suppose. How 'bout you?"

"No, never said it, never did it. Although I adored her all through high school. But with the exception of one New Year's Eve kiss she was never anything more than a secretly loved acquaintance."

I wasn't sure where Jack was going with his inquiry about Karen but I had a feeling there was no point in telling him about the nights of my youth I spent manually relieving myself while dreaming about her.

"That's funny, because she told me she always had a little thing for you too."

"She did?"

"Yeah, she did. She even mentioned the New Year's kiss. But she said you never asked her out or anything."

"Really? She did?"

"No, I'm just shitting you about the kiss."

"You prick."

"Oh come on now, let's not lose our sense of humour. Besides the rest of it is true. You should have made a move."

"Ah well, I'm sure I was over her by the time I turned thirty. Anyway why are you asking me about Karen?"

"I met her this weekend and you're going to love this. You know how you're always busting my ass about how the only reason people knew you in high school was because you were my cousin."

"Yeah."

"Well, here's one in your column. I was standing around yesterday, waiting for some word on Bruce. I'm just staring at those Falls, half trying to decide whether or not I should jump over myself - just kidding - but suffice to say I'm feeling pretty low, when all of a sudden I feel this little tap on my shoulder. And I turn around and see this woman standing in front of me - looking at me like we know each other, and before I have a chance to ask her what she wants, she said it. She looks me straight in the eye, and she says, 'Excuse me, aren't you Hannibal Rankin's cousin?'"

Having spent all of my youth being known as nothing more than Lucky Jack MacDonald's younger cousin, the irony in Jack's tale was instantly clear to me. I had ridden his coat tails to the top of everybody's party list all through high school and now twenty years later, he was finally catching a ride on mine.

"So how did it feel to be relegated to second party status?" I asked with a smile.

"It wasn't too bad. I thought you'd get a kick out it. Anyway she introduces herself, asks what I'm doing down there, asks how you're doing, rackety rack... and we get to talking. Eventually I tell her why I'm there, she's very sympathetic and supportive and all the rest of it and anyway, we end up going out to dinner at some little Italian joint on the American side."

"Really. So how was it? How's Karen doing?"

"Not bad. She wound up in some place called Queenston?"

"Queenston? What the hell is Queenston?"

"It's a little border town down in the Niagara area. She's divorced, no kids and is thinking about moving back here."

"She's divorced?"

"Yeah, she was married to some scumbag lawyer. Sorry about being redundant." Jack paused before carrying on. "He got himself mixed up in a real estate scam in St. Catharine's and as the walls started to close in on him he decided to ease the pressure by beating the shit out of her."

NOT

"You're kidding! Fuck, I hate guys like that."

"Yeah, me too, and after getting to know Karen a little bit I hope I get a chance to meet the gutless prick someday. Anyway, she said she put up with it for a while, but that it just got worse and worse, so finally she bailed."

"Wow. That's really something."

"Yeah well, she's okay. At least she says she is. Anyway you can ask her yourself this weekend. She's coming to town, staying at her parent's place. So I thought maybe the four of us could do dinner."

"Sure, if I'm around you got a deal. But we might be up at the cottage."

"Whatever. If you're here, we'll do it. If not, we'll do it another time."

I didn't want to dwell on his date with Karen, but Jack sure seemed happy when he spoke about her. And I couldn't blame him. In many ways the single New Year's kiss I had shared with her almost two decades earlier was still a major highlight of my high school years.

I was in grade eleven at the time, and was, as per usual, at the party without a date. Karen was also in grade eleven, and was, as per usual, at the party with Sean Grady. Grady was not only two years older than Karen and I, he was also the biggest and best looking kid at St Ignatius.

Anyway, after about ten minutes of post midnight celebrations I was able to position myself in front Karen. And that's when it happened. The kiss. After almost two years of being desperately in love with her, I was finally going to kiss Karen Corrigan.

As I leaned into her, all I was expecting was a pleasant little peck. And to that end, as well as not wanting to be disrespectful, I made sure that my lips were both tightly closed and bone dry. So much so, that Karen probably thought she was kissing a chicken when we first made contact.

But as we came together, her lips parted ever so slightly, and in an instant I could feel her soft, rum-and-coke-flavoured tongue gently pushing against my mouth. Caught off guard, I was too excited to worry about any punitive action Sean Grady might take, and opened my mouth just enough to allow for the longest, warmest, sweetest kiss I had ever known.

I have no idea how long it lasted, but I do know that its depth of feeling caused me to become so light headed that I almost fell down twice. And that somewhere during our single kiss, and perhaps it was just to steady me, Karen moved her arm around to pull me closer and as her hand pressed softly against the small of my back, it left an imprint I could feel for years.

Of all the memories I have of high school, there are few I recall as vividly as that kiss. And while I decided to keep the details of the moment to myself, when our waitress arrived with our lunch orders, I was unable to contain the urge to order a rum and coke.

"So you met Karen, that's great. Is she part of what you meant when you said that if good things come in threes you might have yourself a great week?"

"Yeah she was, meeting her was a very good thing. And when I arrived home this morning there was a message on my machine from Matt Bossio. You remember him?"

"No."

"No. Well, he'll be my direct boss at F & G, and he called to tell me that my license was in and I could start anytime."

"Hey! Super, maybe you're on a roll?"

"It's a small break, but I'll take it. And if my good luck continues, or comes in threes so to speak, maybe I can turn up $8500 before Friday. I have a meeting set for tomorrow morning that might solve everything."

"Oh yeah, with who?"

"A guy by the name of Terry Donnelly. Works for Peoples Bank, he called this morning as well. I've known him for years and now that I'm back in the business I'm hoping this guy might cut me a little slack."

"You think he will?"

"If he's smart he will. I've arranged for his bank to lend out a lot of money. Donnelly knows that, so I should be okay."

"Great, keep me informed. If it doesn't go well I've got a couple of ideas myself."

"Oh yeah, what have you got in mind?"

Knowing that Jack would veto any thoughts I had about selling personal property to raise the money I decided to lie.

"Let's just say it involves you impersonating a potential buyer for..."

"Hold it. Hold it. I see where you're going, but let's forget the larcenous plans until at least Wednesday. By then I'm sure I'll be ready to impersonate fucking Madonna if it'll help. But I think I might be okay with this guy Donnelly."

"Sure, Wednesday it is."

"Don't worry about it, Hannibal. We'll get the money."

"I know we will. There's always a way – right?" I answered, feeling gratified that Jack was still including me in his plan to raise capital.

"You bet," my cousin answered with a smile.

I had to admire Jack for the confidence he was showing in the face of his approaching deadline. He was four days away from losing all that he owned, yet even sitting here in that ragtag of a suit, and not having enough in the way of liquid assets to even pay for the meal he was eating, Jack MacDonald could still walk the walk.

Watching him signal Nicole to bring him another beer, I was pleased to once again recognize at least a small part of the Jack I had always known.

"So, that must have been one brutal trip to the Falls you had this weekend?"

"Yeah, it was pretty bad. Something like this really plays with your mind. I must have stood there, looking into the face of those Falls for hours trying to figure why all this had to happen. And of course there are no answers. So you get sad, and angry, and depressed, you get all of these different feelings, and then you go back to not knowing what to feel about it at all."

"Well at least they found him. I don't know if that counts for much, but I'm glad they'll be able to give him a proper burial," I offered as a small condolence.

"They found him all right. Typical Bruce, eh? Showing up on Monday morning."

"What do you mean, typical Bruce."

"Well you know how he was, we should have known he'd turn up on Monday morning. Poor bastard, even dead he was probably still trying to show up for work."

"Yeah, I guess," I stammered out nervously, uncertain as to whether or not Jack was trying to be funny. Until the solemn look on his face made me realize that he saw Bruce's Monday arrival as the final cruel irony of the whole episode.

Speaking quietly and deferentially, I decided to ask Jack what he knew about Bruce's suicide.

"You mentioned on the phone that there was some pretty difficult stuff going on. What gives?"

"Huh,… Jesus, Hannibal, where to begin?"

Jack paused to take a long swig of his beer and as he lifted his arm, all I could see was that damn button dangling from his sleeve. It was still driving me crazy, though not so much as before.

"I don't know when it all started, but it came to a head this past winter. He called me in April and told me he needed to see me ASAP. I hadn't seen him in a while, but there was nothing unusual about that, especially with him being a new Dad and everything. Anyway, I say fine, where and when? And he tells me the only place he can meet me is the Clarke Institute and the sooner the better."

"The Clarke! Bruce was in the bin?" I asked in disbelief.

"Yup, for almost a month."

"Why? I mean, what for?"

"Same reason as the rest of them, depression," Jack explained, lumping all forms of head problems into one easy-to-define category.

"Jesus, I had no idea."

"Yeah I know, but I did. It had been a while, but Bruce had been in before."

"He had?"

"Yeah." Jack's slightly admonishing tone politely suggested that I keep further questions on the matter to a minimum. "Anyway last Valentine's Day Bruce picked up an Eternity ring for his wife. He said she'd acted strangely throughout the pregnancy, and he wanted to reassure her, and help ease her into the last week of it, and well… while the poor bastard was hiding the gift somewhere in their closet he finds a picture of Jennifer and she's − she's ahh − well, she's in action so to speak."

"In action, what do…?"

"She's fucking some guy."

"Holy shit! You've got to be…" I started to hack out before Jack cut me off.

"Hold on to your hat, because it gets worse."

"Jack, I'm married. Believe me, I don't think anything could be worse than that."

"Well, I'll let you be the judge," Jack protested, before raising an eyebrow and adding. "It was Richard that was fucking her."

"His brother?"

"His brother."

"Whoa, shiiiit. That is worse," I answered quietly, my mind racing to process all that Jack was telling me.

"His brother? How could his brother?" I started to ask before my voice trailed off in stunned disbelief and anger.

"It's complicated. They'd been using Richard as a donor in order to conceive a child. Bruce couldn't have kids. His count was too low."

"So they used Richard? Richard was the sickest fuck..."

"Yeah, I know. But he was fucked up for a reason and there was a strange alliance between the two brothers," Jack responded calmly, before suggesting in the same admonishing tone he'd used earlier, "Now if you'll just sit still for a minute I'll tell you the rest of it."

Speaking quietly, and pulling his chair in tight, Jack leaned across the table until his face came to within inches of my own. And after locking his eyes directly on mine, he carried on.

"Like I said, they'd been using Richard as a donor, and after three or four tries, at a cost of about five grand a pop – still nothing – and money was getting tight - so Bruce figures – in all the frustration... Richard and Jennifer just decided to cut out the middle man."

As Jack was telling me all of this, he was doing so without even a trace of anger in his voice. If anything there was almost a hint of sympathy in his words. And that was something I couldn't understand at all.

"Jesus Christ, Jack! You almost sound like Richard and Jennifer were trying to do Bruce a favour," I finally spat out.

"Yeah, well if you're ready for the full creep show Hannibal, I'll lay it out for you."

The full creep show – fuck, isn't that what I've been listening to?

"When I met Bruce in April we sat in this small, sterile room... Bruce was in an old wooden rocking chair, dressed in his pajamas. He looked terrible. Anyway, like I said, I knew he'd been in for treatment before, although I never knew why. But after he told me about Richard and Jennifer he informed me of a couple of other things as well."

I could tell Jack was feeling quite nervous with what he was about to tell me. He was speaking at a very fast pace, and at an almost inaudible level, very uncharacteristic of his normal pattern of speech.

"After telling me about his wife and brother, Bruce closes his eyes, leans back in his chair, and says, 'Poor Richard, did you know about him?' When he asks me if I know about Richard, I'm thinking he wants to know if I knew about Richard and Jennifer. But before I answer I realize he's talking about something else. And then he says 'You knew didn't you?'… almost like he's accusing me. So I say, 'No, Bruce I didn't know.' And he says, 'Are you sure? Because I thought I didn't know either, but I remember everything now.'"

He wasn't doing it on purpose, but every time Jack assumed the role of Bruce Thatcher in order to relay Bruce's story, he looked and sounded so much like him that it almost felt like Bruce was sitting there with us. And it was very disconcerting to watch him subconsciously capture every Thatcher characteristic as he spoke in turn for our fallen friend.

"So then Bruce closes his eyes, and says 'Jack, could you ever hate me? I mean if you knew something about me, something really bad, do you think you could hate me for it?' And as he's asking me this there's a wounded quality in his voice that has me ready to jump out of my skin. And then tears start pouring down his face and he asks me again if I could ever hate him?" Well at this point I'm getting a little freaked out, but I'm trying to stay calm, and I say 'No, Bruce, of course not. We've been friends for almost thirty years. I could never hate you.'"

"And he says 'Good, good, because he did it to me too, you know. I just thought I should tell you. He did it to me too.'"

As Jack continued on with the story I was feeling more and more uncomfortable with each passing moment. And the sight of him leaning back and imitating Bruce had me squirming around so much in my chair I just couldn't hold my tongue any longer.

"Jack, I'm not getting what you're telling me. Who did what to Bruce? Was it Richard? What did that fucking asshole do?"

"It wasn't Richard. It was their Uncle Fog, and he did it to both of them."

"Uncle Fog? What the hell did Uncle Fog do?"

"Bruce told me that when he was eight or nine years old he heard some noises up in his room, and when he went up there he saw Richard lying on his back, being held down by their uncle. Richard was crying, just above a whimper, begging Fog to leave him alone. Fog had pulled Richard's pants down and… and ah, well, he was sucking his cock."

"Oh, fuck… no. No, no, no.

I felt dizzy as the meaning of Jack's words began to register. *Uncle Fog, a fucking gear box. And to his own nephews… Oh God no, that can't be right.*

It felt like I had just been horse-kicked in the face.

"Holy shit, Jack, you've got to be kidding me. How could anybody do such a thing?"

I had a lot more to say than to simply offer an inane and rhetorical question. But as the reality of what Jack had just told me continued to sink in, I felt too crushed to say much of anything.

Dropping my head into my hands I listened quietly as Jack tried to pick up my thoughts for me.

"I don't know how anybody could act like that. It's been driving me nuts for a couple of months now. I don't know what to make of it. I mean, you look around and you know that people are getting off in every manner possible. Boys with girls, boys with boys, girls with girls, you name it, they're doing it. And they're using whips, chains, midgets, vibrators, and God fucking knows what else to help them. And to most of it all you can say is, 'Hey, to each his own.' But these pricks who hurt little kids? It's too sick to comprehend. And do you know what the worst part is? Bruce blamed himself. He hated himself for not helping Richard that first day he saw his uncle on top of him."

"That's crazy, what's a little kid suppose to do against a full grown man?"

"I know. I know it's crazy, you know it's crazy. And looking back on it I think that even Bruce knew there was nothing he could do. But the mind is a funny thing, and I don't think he ever got over the feeling that he should have helped his brother."

Hearing of the unspeakable acts that had been carried out in the Thatcher home, a home I had played in hundreds of times myself, I couldn't believe I had grown up so close to such deviance and such danger. And when Jack added, almost inanely, "I guess the uncle molesting Richard eventually gave way to the uncle molesting Bruce," I became so consumed by rage I could feel myself shaking.

"Hey, Hannibal, I know it's tough to hear all this. It's sad, it's shocking, it's everything that's bad, but you will get a handle on it," Jack advised, perhaps sensing the level of my anger.

"Are you sure? I mean, this all happened right under our noses and I didn't have a clue. What are you supposed to believe in? It makes me wonder if there isn't some pervert at the school lining up one of my boys? Or is some pervert on the street… how in the fuck are you suppose to raise kids with this kind of…?"

My thoughts were out of control as my hostility continued to grow.

"God Almighty, if someone ever did something like that to one of my kids I'd kill him with my bare hands. Honest to Christ I would. And I wouldn't give a shit if it meant spending the rest of my life in…"

"Hannibal, give it a little time, you will get a…"

"I don't want to get a handle on it. I don't want to…"

"Yeah, well if you don't, you just might wind up jumping over the Falls one day yourself. There's no way to understand why this happened. Some people out there are just plain sick. It's not everybody, it's just some people."

"Yeah, maybe, but… I ahh… you know, you see this kind of shit on Oprah everyday, and it really doesn't mean that much to you. Then you find it in your own backyard and it's just so… I can't tell you how bad I feel right now."

Looking over at Jack I had the impression his mind had drifted back to the day he met Bruce at the Clarke. The expression on his face was the same look he'd worn when he first told the story. Yet as he spoke he tried to remain calm. As it was in his nature to do, Jack was taking control of the situation.

"Well, now you know what I meant when I told you Bruce was dealing with stuff that make your problems and mine look awfully simple. He had a pretty tough life. I guess he just couldn't come to terms with what happened. It's such a shame, because I keep thinking that maybe if he'd given himself a bit more time, maybe… maybe… Ah well, either way, it's all a terrible mess. Bruce is dead and nothing's going to bring him back. Andrew doesn't have a father. Richard, well as bad as I now feel for Richard, even if he does try to assume the role of father, I can't see how he'd be a terribly good influence. And Jennifer, well I don't know what her story is, but in light of everything else, I'd hate to guess how stable a person she's going to be. What a fucking disaster."

As I reflected on Jack's summation the anger this news had evoked began to subside, giving way to a sense of despair. I started thinking only of Richard and Bruce, and the betrayal each must have felt as their own uncle destroyed the innocence of their childhood. How terrible it must have been to have grown-up in the midst of such evil.

After a lengthy break in the conversation, Jack caught me a little off guard when he abruptly changed the subject and inquired about the status of my upcoming date with Barb.

"Speaking of big messes, did you cancel your date with Barb?"

Confused by Jack's change of direction, I couldn't decide what to tell him.

"What?" I answered, obviously stalling for time.

"Did you cancel your date with Barb?"

"No, not yet. I haven't been able to reach her."

I was hoping this lie would be the end of Jack's intrusive search for information. It wasn't like him to really push an issue. However the words "reach her", had barely escaped my mouth when Jack followed up.

"When?"

Still looking at him I could see that Jack had discovered the button that had been dangling from his jacket sleeve, and while he nonchalantly tried to finger it back into place, he followed up on his unanswered question.

"I mean... you said you were going to cancel. So, why haven't you?"

"I will, as soon as I get a chance. I tried to get hold of her yesterday and couldn't."

"Listen Hannibal, I know it's not the same thing, and maybe it's none of my business, but this situation with Bruce and Uncle Fog and Richard and Jennifer... I dunno... following impulses is a dangerous thing to do."

It was plain to see from the look on his face that Jack's sole motivation in questioning me about Barb was strictly out of concern for me. All the same, I did not like being compared to a child molester and had to struggle to hide my irritation at his meddlesome observation.

"Jack, I'm going to cancel. Nothing is going to happen! Believe me!"

"Well, I know that's what you're thinking. Or maybe you're thinking that you can go over to her place and just give her an honest opinion on the apartment and that's it. But let me tell you – Don't Go! Because the whole time you're there, you're gonna want her, and if she wants you, once you're in her apartment, it'll happen. Believe me! She'll be right there in front of you, live and in person. You'll be able to see her, smell her, and touch her. And at some point you will. And then, before you know it, you'll be screwing the hell out of each other on the kitchen table. You can count on it. You won't be able to help yourself."

In the whole time I had known Jack, for all the advice he had given, he had seldom preached to me. And now here he was, for the second time in two days, once again standing high atop the pulpit. And it was starting to piss me off. How did he know how I would act once inside Barb's apartment? What made him think I couldn't control my urges and impulses? Who had died and made him God? It felt very uncomfortable to have Jack talk to me this way, a situation made even more uncomfortable by the excitement I felt at the thought of screwing Barb on her kitchen table.

Still, I knew he was only trying to help. So I decided to allay his fears without further protest.

"Jack, under no circumstances will I be going to Barb's place. Okay? You have my word on it. Now ease up please, before the people around us start mistaking you for my mother."

"Okay, okay, I'm off the case."

What irritated me most about Jack's unsolicited advice was the fact that he might well be right. His mind worked in such a logical way he was often able to accurately project outcomes based on personal or historical data. He knew things about people that were not readily obvious to the rest of us. It was the natural head start he had in regards to making friends and influencing people, and even if I was a little pissed off at the outcome he had forecast for me, part of me was pleased to once again see most of Jack's personal magnetism shining through. Bankrupt or not, Jack Mac-Donald was still a pretty sharp guy.

Taking my promise not to visit Barb's apartment as a cue that our business at Shantys was finished, Jack raised his hand and signalled Nicole to bring us our bill. Sitting quietly as she approached, I reached for my wallet while Jack once again started fingering the button that had caused us both such trouble during lunch.

Without turning his attention away from the button, Jack noticed me going for my wallet and immediately stopped me.

"No, this one's on me. Let me put it on the Visa card you lent me, and I'll take care of this and my Niagara Falls expenses next week." Then without waiting for a response he said, "Ahhh, fuck it," and yanked the small button from the sleeve of his jacket. Smiling as he turned to me, Jack continued, "I couldn't fix this thing with a needle and thread, so I don't know how I think I'm going to fix it with my finger." Then, placing it on to his thumbnail, he flicked the unfastened button into the bushes behind me. "This suit looks like shit anyway. One of the many pitfalls of having no money."

After watching the button sail over my head and out of sight, I turned my attention back to Jack. I wanted to tell him about the difficult time I was having dealing with his current predicament, but that I would be there for him right to the bitter end. However before I had the chance, Jack again carried on talking.

"Hey Hannibal, sorry if I came across like an asshole with that little speech, but I'd hate to see you mess things up at home. I know that under normal circumstances you'd never fool around on Caroline, but honestly, sometimes you can find yourself in a situation where it's impossible to resist. So what you've gotta do is avoid those situations. You know what I mean? Anyway, I've said enough about that. Let's get out of here. I've got a job I can go to, Karen's coming to town this weekend, and I have to get my hands on about ten grand before Friday."

"Sure, let's go. And don't worry about the money, we'll get it."

"Damn right we will... Oh, and by the way, you never did say. How was it?" Jack asked as he handed Nicole the Visa card.

While I could see he was kidding around, I didn't have the slightest idea what he was talking about.

"How was what?"

"The kiss," he said, winking at Nicole. "Your New Year's kiss with Karen. How was it?"

The easy charm of Jack's rhetorical question seemed to wash away any remaining doubt I felt about him. Yeah, he may have run out of gold. And he may have felt a little lost and beaten up the last time I saw him. But now, with crunch time fast approaching, I could plainly see that Jack MacDonald was still Mister Cool. He wasn't sweating about any deadline. Jack was back in charge. He'd handle Friday with or without my help.

Acknowledging his question, I stood up and held my position near the table while I pretended to think back. Making him wait, I picked up my glass, and slowly finished my drink. Savouring each drop, it wasn't until my mouth had absorbed the final rum and coke flavoured ice cube that I gave my patiently waiting cousin his answer.

"Oh, the kiss? Well that was a long time ago Jack, and to tell you the truth, I don't really remember."

Chapter Twenty-three

CHAPTER TWENTY-THREE

DRIVING HOME FROM SHANTYS, I tried to force the horrible circumstances of Bruce Thatcher's childhood from my thoughts and concentrate only on what remained to be done before I could leave for the cottage. My desire to get away was now bordering on obsession and as I raced home I was already planning out how best to tackle the obstacles that stood in my way.

I don't know why I wouldn't allow myself to think about Bruce. It certainly wasn't that I "had a handle" on what had happened to him. I only knew that once the rage his story provoked in me had subsided, it was too troublesome to think about Bruce any more. I just wanted to see my family.

Of the three small pieces of business to be looked after prior to my departure, the one that mattered most was making sure Jack would have access to $8500 by Friday. This was essential, and would have to be taken care of before I would feel free to leave.

The item that mattered least was contacting Bill Ferguson. Far from being essential, informing my lawyer that I would not be accompanying him to court was really nothing more than a question of manners. I wasn't going to debate the issue with him, and there was nothing he could say that would make me change my mind.

The third item I had to take care of was the most puzzling. What to do about Barb? I hadn't yet really figured out how I was going to extricate myself from this particular mess, but I did know that whether I met with her or not, I would be leaving for the cottage on schedule.

Arriving home I was considering the optimistic spin that Jack had put on his prospects of getting the $8500 he needed from The Peoples Bank. I was relieved to hear that he had a plausible plan to get the money on his own, even if his plan did strike me as being a little naive. It had been my personal experience that pinning one's hopes on the possible benevolence of a bank was not the smartest of bets. Having made this determination, I planned to follow up on my proposed art sale to Sean Masse, even if it now served only as a backup plan.

Once inside the house, I immediately moved upstairs to check my business line for messages. As I had hoped, Sean Masse had called, and while his message only asked that I get back to him as soon as possible, I knew that he was ready to barter for the six prints.

Resetting the answering machine, I felt no great temptation to return Masse's call right away. As much as I needed to secure a good deal with him, there was no need to hurry. Over an hour remained before the artificial deadline I had created for him was set to pass. I could afford to wait. His calling early only meant that he had an offer he was anxious for me to accept. So fuck him, let him sweat a little bit.

Picking up the phone, I called the offices of Marshall Kellog and Christie, in search of Bill Ferguson. Unable to reach him once again, I decided to end my personal participation in the matter of Commercial Credit Bank vs. Hannibal Investments Inc. *et al*, by leaving my instructions with his secretary.

"Yes, could you tell Bill that John Rankin called, and let him know that I will not, I'll repeat that, I will not be joining him at the Courthouse tomorrow morning and if he needs to talk to me he can reach me at the cottage any time after eight."

"Is there anything else?"

"Sure, wish him good luck for me."

One down, two to go.

Throwing my feet up on my desk, I began loosening my tie

and studying one of the prints I had offered to Sean Masse. It was the *High Kingdom Snow Leopard*, and the artist's snow-flecked rendering of this rare and endangered cat was classic Bateman. The serenity and menace of nature, captured perfectly in a single instant. A lone predator, masterfully coloured to blend into the picture's bleak terrain, sits undisturbed, her bushy, upturned tail the only hint that a moment of murderous ambush is near.

It was the first picture Caroline and I had bought together, and was still my personal favourite. Yet as I pondered selling it, I once again felt no sorrow, or self-pity over its possible liquidation. In fact, far from being depressed, as I pulled my unfastened tie from around my neck, I did so gratefully reflecting on what a lucky man I had been all of my life.

It was a realization I had started to see glimpses of over the past couple of days. But now, like a blind man whose sight had returned, everything was so clear to me. I had lived a remarkably problem-free life.

I was almost thirty-six years old, and in all of that time, nothing truly bad had ever happened to me. Not once. I've seen, and I have read about, bad things happening to good people, on countless occasions. From people like Bruce and Richard Thatcher, to my old classmate Ed Flanagan, to strangers in the newspaper, good honest people who undeservedly fall victim to some cruel twist of fate. It happens every day. But to me, never, or at the very least, not yet.

I'm alive, and I still have everything - wife, kids, health, home - everything. I have it all, and I always have. For all that I had come to believe I had lost over the past few years, I could now see that the only thing I had really lost during this period was the wisdom to recognize my own unending good fortune.

And now maybe that was back.

Sensing the moment to strike was right, I picked up the phone and dialed the number for Masse Art Gallery. I felt a rush of adrenaline as I pressed each number, and had to consciously calm myself as I prepared for the battle that was about to take place. The interests of buyer and seller were about to collide, and while, as a cash-strapped vendor, I would begin this economic clash as a heavy underdog, I also knew that there were ways to level the playing field.

"Mr Rankin, so good of you to return my call. How are you today?"

"Oh, that's no problem," I answered, taking Sean Masse's over-politeness as a signal that he was intent on screwing the hell out of me. "And I'm just fine thanks. Yourself?"

"Busy, busy, busy. You know how it is."

"I sure do Sean, some days it never stops eh, big guy?" *Come on asshole, let's hear the offer.*

"Isn't that just so? Anyway, I think I have good news on those pieces that you wanted to sell. I'm just not sure if the price will be what you were hoping for."

You have good news for me, but you don't think I'm going to like the price. What freaking turnip truck does this guy think I just fell off?

"Oh yeah? Great – how'd we do?"

"Well I was hoping it would be for so much more but honestly things are just so tough out there. I'm sorry I couldn't have gotten…"

Come on you pitiful little prick, don't be afraid - just say the number.

"Sean, Sean," *You fucking creep* "please don't worry about it. You and I have been doing business for such a long time that we're practically friends, right? I trust you completely and I know you'd always do your best for me. So, just tell me how we did."

"Well, the only firm offer I have right now is for $4400, and that's for all six pieces. I know it's not the money we discussed but honestly, it's the best I could do on such short notice."

Masse's voice had softened as he tried to close the deal, but the way he said "firm offer" and "right now" was a sure tip-off.

He was feeling me out, trying to gauge my level of desperation, while leaving himself room to back-pedal. If I were to balk at the "firm offer" he had "right now", he would quickly retreat, before alluding to some potential future offers that he expected would be much higher. All of which was fine and good, but I was working with a deadline here.

"Forty-four hundred! Holy smokes! Things really are tough out there," I blurted out, as if truly astonished by his offer.

This guy was even more slippery than I first thought. Well, if that's the way you want to play it Sean it's about time you learned a short lesson in the art of negotiation.

"That's okay." *Nice and comfortable now, keep him relaxed.* "I appreciate your efforts. It was so good of you to try and help me out. I really mean that…" *Now, let's see if this dumb shit can handle a curve ball.* "But I think I have them sold elsewhere anyway."

"Oooohhh,… geez,… you have them sold elsewhere?"

The shock in Masse's voice was also marked with a noticeable twinge of disappointment, and his reaction to my sudden shifting of gears was exactly what I wanted to hear. Poor old Sean had tipped his hand. He had my pieces sold already, and for good money.

"Yeah, yeah, after we spoke I gave Jack a call. Well you know Jack, ever the cash cow, and he said he'd take the whole load off my hands for the eighty-five hundred you and I figured them to be worth."

"Oh,… I see… well, ahhhhh…"

This guy was pathetic. He sounded like he was about to cry. A deal he figured was in the bag was beginning to slip away, and the silly bastard didn't know what to do about it. What a fool. Now, if he was only smart enough to grab the lifeline I was about to throw him.

"Well you know, I don't think Jack really wants the stuff. I'm sure he's just buying them to help me out."

Now, listen carefully you little turd.

"But I wanted to talk to you first, because I was afraid that you, as a favour to me, might have offered these prints to some of your more preferred clients at the price we discussed and were now committed to deliver."

Come on, Sean - understand what I'm trying to tell you. It's not that complicated.

"Oh, well, ahhhhh…"

"But, if you HAVEN'T committed the pieces, and aren't waiting on any other offers, then it's not messing you up, if I sell them to Jack, right?"

"Ahhhhh, well actually…"

I could almost hear a light bulb click on as Masse slowly clued into the strategy I had set up for him.

"Yeah… Yeah… I was waiting to hear back from one more guy… I told him he had until four to let me know, just like you instructed me. So, I don't know,… could you wait for me to give him a call? Just to make sure he doesn't want them. He's a big customer and I'd…"

Grovel, grovel, grovel… you miserable prick.

"Oh, hey Sean, listen bud, you know I'd never screw you up with a customer. But don't call him, okay? I'd rather sell these things to Jack, you know, so maybe I can buy them back one day. But if your customer does call by four, and he accepts your offer… then I'll honour our agreement. Like I said big guy, we're practically friends."

As our conversation ended, I wished I were as confident about getting into heaven, as I was that Sean Masse would be calling back, and soon. He had no choice really. He probably had the prints pre-sold for at least ten thousand dollars. What was he going to do, turn his back on an easy couple of grand just to screw some of his own customers. I don't think so. Jack's money was a lock.

The only decision I had left to make in regards to my dealings with Masse Art Gallery was whether or not I would actually sell the prints if Jack were able to come up with $8500 on his own. I didn't want to move these items unless it was necessary. But on the other hand, I could also use the money.

Stepping out from my desk, I allowed the sweet moment of victory to fade into memory, before bouncing down the hall to my bedroom.

Disappearing into the walk-in closet, I emerged moments later carrying a small gym bag and wearing a purple golf shirt with a pair of black jeans. Laying the bag on the bed I then began searching for the bare essentials I would need to enjoy two or three days at the cottage.

It was three-forty-five by the time I started shoving the few pairs of shorts, socks and underwear I would be taking with me into the bag. Time was running out. If I was to make it to the cottage on schedule, I had just forty-five minutes to hit the bank machine, buy some wine, and appraise Barb's apartment.

Looking into the mirror, trying to flatten my shirt's badly rolled collar, I couldn't really figure out what made me decide to keep my appointment with Barb. I didn't really want to go. I didn't really have time to go. And I was even past the notion that I was under any obligation to go. Yet in spite of all of this and even factoring in Jack's pessimistic forecast of what was likely to take place, I was going anyway. I had to. I couldn't afford to be afraid of what might happen.

Over the past couple of days I had felt a noticeable amount of control returning to my life, and I wasn't going to give any of it up by running away from a predicament of my own making.

If somewhere behind Barb's front door I was forced to answer a question about who I really am, then so be it. Because whether I liked the answer I got or not, the thing I had become most certain of was that I couldn't run from the question. Over the past few years I had done enough running. I would run no longer.

Moving from the mirror to the bed, I grabbed the gym bag and began heading downstairs. Tossing the bag by the front door, I turned towards the kitchen just as the phone started to ring.

"Hello, hello?... Mr Rankin? Sean Masse here. You're not going to believe this, but my customer called, and well, what can I say? This must be your lucky day..."

Chapter Twenty-four

CHAPTER TWENTY-FOUR

DRIVING NORTH ALONG Leslie Street, I looked across Highway 401 and was relieved to see westbound traffic moving briskly. I figured it would be. After all it was only Monday. There was no reason to expect Friday-type congestion when an endless stream of commuters and cottagers would clog all city exits.

My journey to the Muskokas would start as an easy one, and with the realization that it was set to begin in less than half an hour, I impatiently pressed down on the accelerator.

Turning right onto Finch Avenue, The Who's 'Won't Get Fooled Again' was pounding through the speakers and feeling like I was on top of the world I opened the Lexus up completely and blew by a slow-moving Chrysler. Looking ahead at the tall grey buildings standing out on the horizon, I kept the car perfectly under control as I sped past a badly lagging Camaro, before easing up on the gas, and sliding over to the outside lane.

My confidence was soaring as I moved up the hilly terrain towards Barb's apartment. Gone was all of the fear and anxiety I had felt in facing her again, as was most of the embarrassment. Also gone was any perception of danger. I could handle being alone with her, and handle it with ease. Setting her straight about what had happened between us and appraising her condo would be a piece of cake. I could do it graciously, and be on my way in less than twenty minutes, even supposing she answered the door in her birthday suit.

Far from being uptight about my situation with Barb, I was now seeing the entire episode as quite trivial. It all seemed so silly. A thirty-six-year-old man getting carried away with a teenage girl. It was absurd, too absurd to be taken seriously. Just another case of a man getting drunk and making an ass out of himself. It could have happened to anyone.

It had been a long time since I had played the fool around a pretty girl, but Friday night was certainly not a first. Making an ass out of myself over a woman was something that started happening to me shortly after I discovered them, and it became a pattern that carried on into my mid-twenties.

The first time it happened was in grade two, when my total infatuation with Paula Dundee caused me to tear up her homework on the way to school one day. Not the smartest of strategies when trying to endear oneself to another party, but what could I do? I was in love.

I don't really know what I was thinking when I decided to destroy the tiny model volcano Paula had prepared for science class. But I did know that as she raced forward to the schoolyard, crying hysterically, it was going to be difficult to explain to Principal McDonough how this act of vandalism was meant to be an expression of affection.

I think it was my inability to explain my actions that caused the strapping I received for the incident to be so severe. The large, autocratic principal of Corpus Christi Separate School, who dished out justice with a zealousness that could only have come from the belief he was acting in the name of God, removed almost all the skin from both my hands as he pounded away in search of a reasonable explanation.

Yet no matter how hard or how often he struck me, I remained defiantly silent. I had no choice really. How could I explain to him what I couldn't understand myself? I had no idea why I broke Paula's volcano. Though I had a feeling it had something to do with Miss Ellie May Clampett.

A couple of nights before, a bunch of us were over at Paul

Hillman's watching the Beverly Hillbillies. There was nothing unusual about this, in fact in 1964 such an evening would have been a fairly routine event. Routine until around half way through the show, when some of the older boys started talking about Ellie May's "body".

It wasn't clear to me what the fuss was over Ellie's body. I had been watching her for over a year, and had never noticed anything unusual about her build. To me, she looked no different than Jethro, and no one was passing comment on him. But after listening to the other boys laugh and giggle about wanting to kiss Ellie, and about wanting to touch something they called her tits, I did start to notice that there was something different about the shapely Miss Clampett.

All of a sudden I could tell that she was completely different than Jethro. She was so curved and so rounded, and so beautiful. In the span of a heartbeat I became so captivated with Ellie that it was difficult to even notice the other characters in the show. From that point onward, whenever Ellie appeared on the screen, all I could do was stare at her in amazement.

Of course, even at this early age I knew that girls and boys had different parts. But this was the first time I had any inkling that there was a purpose for our anatomical differences. And while still not knowing what this purpose was, as I watched Ellie, I couldn't stop myself from quietly grinding my pelvis into the floor beneath me. Though I had no idea why.

Welcome to the world of women.

Crossing Don Mills Road, I scanned a nearby mini-mall hoping I might see a cash machine. Spotting a bank, as well as a grocery store that dispensed wine, I roared on by, my final escape route to the northland now clear. And happily tapping down on the car's turn indicator, I pulled up to a red light signalling left.

There was a small cobblestone road that led directly to Barb's building, and presenting myself to the security guard at the gatehouse, I patiently waited for permission to proceed.

The middle-aged guard studied me carefully, before even bothering to call up to Barb. But after he finished his conversation with her, his demeanour became more friendly and he waved me past the gate with a pleasant nod.

Reminding myself that I was there to estimate the value of the apartment, I took note of the guard's manner as I pulled into a nearby parking area, and stepped out of the car. Once out of the car I took a final look at myself in the side-view mirror and, for aesthetic reasons, decided to keep my sunglasses on for the duration of my visit.

Studying the grounds as I walked up to the building, it was plain to see that the condo Barb was thinking about investing in definitely offered an upscale lifestyle. Aside from the professional security, the recreation centre had two pools, four tennis courts, squash courts, sauna, showers, weight room, billiard room, and lots more.

The grounds were well planted and immaculately kept, while the lobby looked like something out of a grand hotel. A twenty-year-old girl could do a lot worse than end up in a place like this.

After stepping into the elevator, I pressed nine and calmly began to review my objectives and rules for the meeting that was about to take place. *Minimize the friendly banter, avoid even casual contact, do not accept any offered refreshments, and above all else, just tell the truth. Follow these rules and you'll be out and on your way in fifteen minutes.*

A quiet ding signalled my arrival at the ninth floor and moving into the hallway I decided to remove my sunglasses and leave my damaged eye uncovered. Fuck it, I wasn't there to look good.

Once out in the hall, I wasn't really sure which way to turn, but after moving left, I could hear a voice behind me calling out.

"Yoohooo... Hannibal! Hello... I'm down this way," said the spider to the fly.

Looking around I could see Barb standing beside her open doorway, smiling happily as she waved me onward.

"Oh, hi... yeah, I knew where you were, this going the wrong way bit, is just an old army trick."

Shut up you big jerk, you're not here to be funny either. Just take care of your business and get the fuck out.

As I started down the hall I was relieved to see that Barb was properly dressed. By the way our last conversation had ended I was afraid she might greet me in some obscene, teddy-bear negligee, or something like that. Which I was prepared to handle of course, but all the same I was glad I didn't have to.

Contrary to my earlier fears, Barb was dressed quite conservatively. She had on a white silk blouse, buttoned almost to the top, a long, blue, pleated skirt, and a pair of high-heeled shoes. Her look was much more formal than I was expecting, and it made Barb appear a bit strange to me. She seemed more like a young businesswoman than the California beach-girl I knew from the Genuine Deli.

Extending her hand as I arrived at her door, Barb greeted me warmly.

"Hiiii… come on in."

Keeping the damaged side of my face turned away, I ignored Barb's hand, and without touching her, playfully stepped around and presented her with the door - as if she were the guest.

"After you Barb. You know what they say, age before beauty."

"Huh?"

"Nothing, you go first," I said, gently ushering her inside and closing the door behind us.

Hearing the door click shut, I made sure the conversation moved along, and that it remained focused on the task at hand. I didn't want any awkward moments of silence to allow Barb, or myself, to start thinking about anything other than the apartment.

"This is a great looking building. I checked out the grounds and the rec centre on my way up, and I must say the builder did a very nice job on the place. It's very impressive - really."

Slow down, you're babbling a little bit.

"Oh, thanks. I hope you didn't have any trouble finding it?… Yeah, they just remodelled the entire – Geez, what happened to your eye?"

Ah, the eye. Shit. Well, I guess I knew it was going to come up sometime. Okay, one little lie.

"Oh, nothing really… I, ahhh, was playing squash yesterday and got clipped with a racquet. That's all, no big deal."

"Wow, it sure looks like a big deal. Does it hurt?"

"No, it's nothing, honestly," I said, somewhat touched by the look of concern on Barb's face. "So don't worry about it, it looks a lot worse than it feels."

"It doesn't look all that bad. In fact it looks kind of cool."

"Well, that's very kind of you to say, little buddy. Now, what does a guy have to do to get a tour of this place?"

*Knock off the bullshit. What's with the "little buddy" krapola –
where do you think you are, Gilligan's Island? Come on, keep moving.*

"Oh, I'm sorry. Right this way," Barb answered, before skip-
ping ahead of me and playfully twirling around as she entered the
living room.

The living room was the long part of a large L-shaped area,
which also served as the dining room. Having completed her
twirl Barb then threw her arms out beside herself as far as they
could reach, and enthusiastically shouted, "Tadaaaa! So what do
you think?"

So what did I think? Looking into Barb's face as she waited
for my response it was impossible not to notice how truly beautiful she was. And watching her hold the outstretched pose she had
assumed it became equally difficult not to notice how her large
breasts heaved against the delicate fabric of her blouse. She really
was some kind of specimen.

It wasn't that I was getting all horned up or anything like that. I
was still okay with being alone with her. It's just that she was a mar-
vel to behold, and so long as I kept this observation to myself, there
could be no danger in privately acknowledging such an obvious fact.

However, slightly more troublesome than quietly observing
Barb's physical beauty, was trying to rationalize why I noticed that
her long skirt would unzip down the side.

Easy, stupid – eyes on the road.

Thinking that Barb had spun around to model her clothes for
me, I answered accordingly.

"You look great."

Walking towards me as I responded, Barb furrowed her brow
and began to giggle.

"No, not me silly… the apartment. What do you think of the
apartment?"

Nice start, Hannibal. Get a grip you idiot.

"It looks great. I thought I just said that," I answered, pretending to be surprised that she hadn't heard me right the first
time. "How big is it?" I added casually.

"Oh, I thought you said that I looked… ummmm. Almost
fourteen hundred square feet, I think. I don't know if that
includes the balcony or not," Barb answered, obviously puzzled by
the trick her ears had played on her.

Nice recovery, Hannibal. Now, keep your eye on the ball.

"Fourteen hundred, that's a nice size... let's have a look around," I suggested, noticing for the first time the sweet presence of Barb's familiar aroma. "Where shall we begin?"

"Well, let's start on the balcony," Barb answered. And with that she slipped her arm through mine and began leading me towards a sliding glass door on the far side of the room.

"So you didn't have any problem finding the place?"

"No, not at all... as a matter of fact, I used to own this building."

"Really! Wow!"

"No, I'm just kidding."

Walking arm in arm with my tour guide, I once again admonished myself for keeping up the silly banter – *Stop it, it serves no purpose.*

Moving through the living room I thought about complimenting Barb on the furniture, but decided to forget it. The smell of her perfume, as well as the memory of that graceful spin in the living room, had squashed my desire to carry on a continuous conversation. Besides I wasn't there to talk about the furniture.

As we approached the balcony doorway I was quite relieved to be going outside. Barb's silk-covered breast was pressing into my forearm as she led me along, and I was looking for an opportunity to break the surprise arm lock in which I was trapped. On top of that, for some reason I was also starting to feel quite warm, and a blast of cool air would certainly be nice.

Stepping outside, Barb let go of my arm as she turned towards a table situated to our left, and from behind her I could see a bottle of wine and two glasses resting on a small serving tray. Reading the obvious signs, I immediately knew that the balcony was where Barb intended to make her move.

Watching her fill a glass to capacity, I started to tell her that I wouldn't be having any but then decided to hell with it. The sudden hot flash that had started inside had left me so bloody parched I'd have accepted a glass of anything right about then. And if this was where Barb was planning to make her move, well, having a glass of wine in my hand was hardly going to prevent me from setting her straight.

"Here, I thought the least I could do was offer you some refreshments."

As she turned towards me, I studied Barb carefully to see if she would interpret my accepting the wine as a sign that the intimacy level of this meeting was escalating. But as she handed it to me, there wasn't even a hint of change in atmosphere.

Apparently, this was not a Harvey's Bristol Cream moment, and it passed without so much as a clinking of glasses.

After handing me the wine Barb nonchalantly turned away and pointed over the balcony.

"The place has a pretty nice view, and it's even nicer at night. I wish it was on a higher floor, but when Gram moved in, this was the only southern exposure available, and from what I understand that's the preferred view from this part of town."

Southern exposure? Oh, the apartment, right.

"Definitely. A view of the downtown is what you want. It adds value to the place. No question about it," I stammered out, caught off guard by Barb's astute observation. "So what kind of taxes and maintenance are they taking on this place?" I continued on, trying to refocus my thoughts.

In the back of my head, I could hear Barb rhyming off some numbers, and I knew she was answering my question. But none of it was registering with me. As cool as Barb was acting, I was certain that she had led me out to the balcony to find out what was going to happen between us, and I was too much on the defensive to follow what she was saying. But before I even had my first sip of wine, she once again put her arm around mine and whisked me back into the apartment.

"Yeah well, the money to carry the place is not really an issue. My grandfather left us all pretty well off. That's why the others don't mind giving me a deal on the place. The estate will hold the mortgage and my trust fund can easily handle the payments, and the taxes, and whatever else might come up."

"So what's the problem then?" I asked, trying to catch up in the conversation.

"Well, the problem is that I don't think I really want to live here. But if I can get in at such a good price should I buy it anyway, and rent it out till the market picks up again. That's why I thought you might be able to help. I was wondering if being a landlord was a real pain."

Taken aback by Barb's entrepreneurial aspirations, I tossed

back some wine, and thought for a minute. So that's what this was all about. All she really wanted the whole time was my opinion on being a landlord.

"No, not at all, in fact it's quite easy, especially with a place like this. You'd have no trouble getting a good tenant in here."

"Really? So you think I should go for it?"

"Well, you've gotta put your money somewhere, and if you can afford to play, real estate is as good a bet as any. So if you think the price is right, I'd say do it."

"You do, just like that? Wow! Well the price is definitely right. At least I think it is. Come on, I'll show you the rest of the place and you can tell me what you think."

Walking with her towards a small room just off the kitchen, I was trying to bend my arm in order to sneak a peek at my watch.

"This is the den. You'll have to excuse the mess."

I don't know why women always say that. "You'll have to excuse the mess." Aside from a CD case resting on the couch the den's appearance was pristine.

"Oh, hold on a sec, let me put on some music - any requests?"

The den was beautiful. Not overly large but very well decorated. The built-in bookcases and entertainment unit must have been worth a few thousand dollars alone.

Watching Barb reach into the shelves above the TV, I quickly glanced down at my watch. In all I had been there for about fifteen minutes and, tossing back the remainder of my wine, I started to plan my exit.

"No, whatever you want. Anything but Madonna."

"Madonna!" Barb protested, "Get real."

Looking at Barb as she stretched up to reach the CD player, I felt glad I had decided to keep our appointment. No harm had come of it. Regardless of what happened between us the other night, she was a nice person, and I was happy that she found my opinion on her investment decision helpful. Yeah, coming over was the right thing to do. But as the first note of R.E.M.'s 'Drive' began filling the room, and I realized that I hadn't taken my eyes off Miss Sutherland's shapely rear end for almost a full minute, I knew that it was time for me to get the hell out of there.

Barb was clearly excited as she glided back across the room and once again took me by the arm. She looked like a kid on

Christmas morning as she pulled me into the living room.

"You know what?… I think I'm going to do it. I'm going to call my uncle first thing in the morning and tell him to start the paperwork. Isn't that great?"

"Hey, good for you, but listen, I really gotta get…"

Ignoring me, Barb threw her arms around my neck and pulled herself in real tight.

"Thanks Hannibal. I know it doesn't seem like much, but it feels great knowing that a man as successful as you are agrees with my plan. You're a great guy."

While first resisting her hug I did eventually decide that I could indulge her a little bit. It was just a hug. Pulling her in even closer I moved my nose over her long scented hair and inhaled deeply. Swaying to the music, I knew that I should have pulled away, but I just didn't want to. I kept thinking that holding her for one more second wasn't going to make any difference. And it wasn't until Barb pulled back from me, that we actually broke away from one another.

Once parted, Barb didn't miss a beat in continuing on with the tour.

"Here, you're not going to believe the job they did on the kitchen. Everything is brand new - cupboards, floor, lighting, the appliances, everything. And it was all done just last year."

Stepping through the doorway, Barb began to point out the room's many features but again I was having trouble following her. The wine was hitting me much harder than I thought it would. All of a sudden I felt another hot flash, and as Barb started to explain about California Lighting, and convection ovens, and whatever else, my head began spinning so badly that in trying to lean against the doorway I almost fell down.

"Hannibal, are you okay?… Are you feeling alright?"

After steadying myself against the doorway, I tried to cover for my embarrassing misstep by reaching up to my damaged eye and pretending to be in pain.

"Yeah, I think so. Sorry, I've been having a little trouble ever since I got that whack in the head yesterday. Dizziness, headaches, that kind of thing."

"Oh, I had no idea. Please sit down. Can I get you some water, or an aspirin, or something?"

"No, I'm okay. Don't worry, the dizziness comes and goes. But, maybe I will sit down for a second."

Walking over to a chair, I began to realize that the heat, and my sudden loss of composure, had more to do with how good it felt hugging Barb than with any amount of wine I might have had. I was losing control here, and looking at the table on which Jack had forecasted Barb and I might end up fucking our brains out wasn't really helping.

Sitting down while I tried to regain a measure of control, I tried unsuccessfully to drive the graphic image of Jack's prediction from my thoughts. In need of distraction I looked up at Barb. Her back was turned to me as she drew a glass of water from the sink and I fought to clear my head by resuming our conversation.

"Please carry on with what you were telling me. I am interested, really. The cupboards are made of what?"

Come on... stay cool.

But even as I tried to concentrate on her answer, I once again caught myself staring at her well-rounded backside. Except this time I was imagining how easily the untapered blue skirt would slide up around her waist. Holy shit, I was getting into some trouble here. And with that realization I quickly decided that after a brief respite I would inform my lovely young hostess that as much as I liked the apartment, I really did have to go.

Unaware of the crisis I was dealing with, Barb handed me a glass of water and, as requested, continued chirping along about the kitchen.

"The cupboards aren't really new, they're only refaced. But you can't really tell the difference. And even though the final decision was Gram's, it was actually me that picked out this bleached oak look."

"So, you'll be getting the kitchen exactly the way you would have done it yourself," I chimed in enthusiastically, my head beginning to clear.

"Yep, even the way they built the microwave in over here."

"Well that's just great. This whole place is really super, and I think buying it might turn out to be one of the wisest investments you'll ever make."

"You do?"

"Yes, I certainly do." Now, time for my getaway. "But I gotta tell ya, it's getting…"

"Really? You think it's that good a deal? And wait you haven't seen the best part yet. Come on."

This time, instead of taking my arm, Barb grabbed me by the hand and started leading me down a short hallway. Moving towards an unopened door, I was feeling self-conscious about the heat my hand was generating as Barb towed me along. She must have felt it. She would have to have been dead not to.

Hesitating as we reached the door, Barb drew my eyes to hers as she pushed it open.

"Hey Hannibal,… can I ask you a question?"

"Sure."

Pausing as she led us a few feet into the room, Barb then lifted my hand to her face and stepped squarely in front of me.

"Why haven't you kissed me?… I've been waiting for you to kiss me ever since you walked in the door."

From the second I had arrived at the apartment I was aware this moment of truth so to speak, was likely to come. And while I had spent large parts of the past two days getting ready for it, when the moment arrived, it still caught me off-guard.

I had assumed Barb's question was going to have something to do with real estate, and when it didn't, I was lost. The well-rehearsed "family man" speech, that I thought would start on reflex, just wouldn't come out.

All I did was look down at Barb, and watch in silence as she guided my hand across the softness of her face, slowly kissing each fingertip as it passed over her mouth.

In the awkward silence that followed, Barb never took her eyes off me as she let my hand go, and stepped backwards, before sitting down at the foot of the bed.

Turning my eyes from the weight of her patient stare, I began looking around, still hoping I could find the words to explain myself.

In surveying the bedroom it was plain to see that Barb was expecting a lot more than a kiss to come out of our late afternoon rendezvous. And why wouldn't she? The last time I saw her, I told her how much I wanted her, and the last time I talked to her, I gave her no indication that my outlook had changed.

In anticipation of what she believed was the true purpose of our meeting, Barb had set her room up like it was part of an ad campaign for Victoria's Secret.

Surrounding her on the oversized bed was a carefully laid out assortment of naughty silks and satins. There were two pairs of stockings, a couple of garter belts, three pairs of designer-cut panties with co-ordinating bras, a purple bustier, two short very short night-gowns, and a pair of white cowboy boots. All of which I'm sure was there at my request, except maybe the cowboy boots.

On the headboard sat another bottle of chilled wine and a tidy little arrangement of snack foods. Alongside of which stood an unopened box of Trojan condoms. A twelve pack, no less - apparently I had led her to believe that I was moving in.

How did I let things go so far?

Looking down at Barb, bobbing hypnotically before me as she rode the crest of the bed's silent waves, I knew that my only hope of getting out of there was to run. Just turn around, and without explanation, run. I was in over my head. But now there was even a problem with simply running away.

Ever since Barb finished kissing my fingertips, I had been feeling a kind of primitive desire I hadn't known in years - or maybe ever. Running at this point no longer seemed like an option.

Jesus Christ, I wanted her. More than anything I could ever remember wanting, I wanted Barb - right then and right there. What I didn't want was to make Caroline the butt-end of an adulterous affair. Yet each moment that I stood there it became easier and easier to convince myself that what was going to happen between Barb and me, had nothing to do with my wife.

Oh fuck... why couldn't I have her... and not have to hate myself for it. Even just once?

The next thing I heard was the sound of Barb's shoes hitting floor. She had slipped them off and started moving further back onto the bed. As she moved, her skirt began riding up her legs, and by the time she had edged her way to the middle of the bed, the skirt had become wrapped around the base of her hips, leaving her lacy red underwear fully exposed.

Run dummy... you can't let this happen.

I couldn't be sure if Barb had wriggled her skirt in such a

provocative way intentionally or not but once it happened two things became perfectly clear. The first was that she was well aware of the explicit view she was offering me. The second was that no matter how hard I tried, I couldn't look away.

Realizing that the sight of her underwear had gained my undivided attention, Barb knew that the deal was done, and decided there was no reason to carry on with even the slightest pretence of modesty. Lying back into her pillows, she casually allowed her legs to fall further apart so that I might enjoy an even less obstructed view of her French cut panties. And now, mostly brain dead, I responded to this move with all the willpower of Pavlov's dog.

The dinner bell had rung, and the mere sight of Barb had transformed me into a drooling prisoner of anticipation. My entire existence held captive by the prickly delicacy she was tempting me with.

I couldn't believe what was happening. Just a few minutes earlier, I had been prepared to make my stand at the first sign of danger. And now here I was falling to pieces simply because Barb had shown me her underwear.

It was so frustrating, not only was I being seduced, I was going down without putting up much of a fight.

Fuck… what are you doing? Just turn around and leave! Please, you're not this big an idiot… RUN!

But how could I run, when I could barely even breathe?

It wasn't until Barb spoke that I was finally able to raise my eyes from the bewitching view of her inner thighs and while I didn't hear her the first time she spoke, when she reposed her question, I heard it quite clearly.

"So… What do you think?"

Lifting my head and looking straight into her lovely green eyes, I found myself unable to answer, but as I stepped forward to join Barb on the bed, I did so, cursing everything that thirty-six years of living had brought to me.

Chapter Twenty-five

CHAPTER TWENTY-FIVE

INDIAN SUMMER. You could feel the warmth even before you stepped out the door. Though still a full ninety minutes before noon, the mercury had already topped seventy on the old Fahrenheit scale, and seemed poised to move even higher.

Such conditions are rare in Toronto at this time of year and if not for the debris of autumn that blew so carelessly about in the day's high winds, it would seem to be more like mid-August than the final week of October.

This unexpected return to summer conditions was not only a pleasant surprise for my daughter and I as we marched towards a small hill located at the side of the house. It was also a well-timed blessing for the rest of the city's residents, many of whom had spent the previous night partying in the streets.

Arriving at the top of the gentle slope on the yard's east side, I knelt down in front of Whitney and teasingly started to put our regular Saturday morning game in motion.

"All right. Do you want me to roll down the hill first?"

"Nooo, me go fus."

"Okay sure, then I'll go right after you."

"Noooo."

For the past couple of months my Saturdays have begun goofing around in the backyard with my youngest child. We usually start with a prolonged rolling (or "wolwing" as Whitney calls it) session, before engaging in an even longer, and more chaotic, game of something more or less resembles soccer.

It's all stuff we used to do quite frequently throughout the course of a week, but now, due to current circumstances these yard-games have become a strictly weekend activity.

Whitney is almost two now, and while she can't quite talk yet, that doesn't stop her from continually trying to set the household agenda. Every Saturday morning, as if she interprets my appearing downstairs in a sweatshirt as a signal that her personal dupe is on duty, she starts firing instructions at me like I'm someone who owes her money.

Usually starting with "Woll, woll. Daddy. Otay, woll."

And my day is under way. A short walk to the yard with her favourite ball tucked under my arm, and her little hand pressing gently into one of my own. Not a bad way to start a day.

The playfulness of my suggestions as to how we should start the game, had, as intended, caused Whitney to think I was somehow trying to trick her. Usually "wolwing" starts without any care as to who goes down the hill first, but if I was adding some new wrinkle to the game's beginning, there had to be an angle.

I could see her trying to figure out what I was up to. She had obviously concluded that there was an advantage to be had in going either first, or second, but had no idea which one.

Seeing that she was a little bit stumped as to what her next move should be, I decided to offer a third option.

"Do you want to go down together?"

"Nooooo."

Apparently Whitney was going to veto all suggestions until my wolwing strategy became clear to her.

As I waited for my daughter to find a solution to the problem I had planted in her head, I lay back in the grass. I was in no hurry to get the game started. I have all the time in the world on Saturdays. At least I like to think I do.

I took a job in early August as General Manager of Patriot Leasing's newly formed Canadian division. The Free Trade

Agreement will eventually allow American financial companies to operate without restriction in Canada, and Patriot, in trying to get a head start on the competition, contacted me about setting up an office in Toronto.

I don't know if the position pays very well. Having not held a job since my days as a courier, I had no way of gauging the fairness of Patriot's $60,000 opening offer. My first reaction after hearing the number was that it sounded pretty low. When you've had years in which $60,000 might be a month's income, it's tough to get excited when such an amount becomes your annual salary. However, after Patriot agreed to throw in a company car, and a bonus structure that could bring my annual income up to about $95,000, I refused to be blinded by past glories, and grabbed the lifeline with both hands.

The job itself isn't bad. It's the same stuff I used to do, except now I'm doing it for somebody else. It's been a busy time, but with some of my old customers starting to do business again, I was able to earn my first bonus cheque after only a couple of months on the job. And I felt pretty good about that.

The hours I have to spend at the office make it impossible to see my family as much as I once did but, this drawback aside, I find I'm enjoying my new career a lot more than I thought I would. In fact, if not for the embarrassment of having to tell people that I no longer work for myself, most days it feels pretty good to be back in the saddle again. Even if it is somebody else's saddle.

I don't know if I'll be able to hit my full bonus numbers or not, but with Caroline now working part-time for our former interior decorator, we are generating enough income to maintain a comfortable, albeit low-frill, lifestyle.

This will be the third month in a row in which we haven't had to crack an RSP in order to cover our basic expenses. And so long as Caroline and I are able to confine our tastes in fine dining to the delicate cuisine offered at chez Red Lobster, this pattern is unlikely to change.

The sale of the cottage went through as planned. I still have a few regrets about letting it go, but it's nice not having to sweat out the $2300 mortgage payment each month. And the extra cash this leaves me has allowed us to hold on to a couple of investment

condominiums left over from my days as a real estate mogul.
Although I had to give up the Lexus in order to get both of these
properties remortgaged.

The Lexus is gone, and gone without regret. I let it go the
week after I started my new job. It was time to move on, and since
I had negotiated the use of a Volvo 850 as part of my remunera-
tion package with Patriot, I took some of the money we saved on
the Lexus, and bought Caroline a….. aaaa… well…. aaaa, I guess
I bought her a minivan. Okay, so part of my new life still sucks.

No, actually the minivan is fine, even if it is a little used. It's
not what I ever expected our next family vehicle to be, but what
the hell, life is full of surprises. And if exercising my right as a
father of three to proudly park a minivan where a Lexus used to
stand is the biggest thing I have to complain about then life can't
be treating me too badly.

And it isn't.

In fact, life has been pretty good these last few months. Not
only has all the hard work setting up my new career paid a couple
of early dividends but I've even caught a few breaks I'm not really
sure I deserved.

I won my lawsuit with the bank.

I wasn't in attendance when the judge handed down the
order, but in the matter of Commercial Credit Bank vs Hannibal
Investments, Judge Louise Hoffman agreed that the bank was
indeed owed every cent outstanding on the loan. However, after
determining that the bank was owed all that it had claimed, she
further ruled that the bank should have protected its own interests in this matter by seizing any deposits made to this account as
soon as the first partner of the original loan bailed from the project. By not doing so, the bank had allowed more than enough
money to cover the debt to flow into, and ultimately back out of
the account. And since it hadn't grabbed the money when it had
the chance, it was now "estopped", from collecting the debt from
the loan's guarantor. Me.

The judge decided the only avenue through which the bank
could properly recover any portion of the $160,000 it was owed
was by taking possession of and liquidating, any and all assets still
owned by the corporate entity that had borrowed the money.

In short, she awarded the bank nothing. The corporate entity that was now duty bound to surrender its remaining assets to the bank had been shut down for over two years. All that remained of it was a couple of boxes of envelopes, and a stapler.

I'm not sure, had I been in attendance on judgement day, whether I would have offered the bank's lawyer the "remaining assets" he had won for his client or not. But I like to think I would have. It's always best to be fair when dealing with a lawyer. And while a couple of hundred envelopes and a stapler weren't going to help him recoup much of his client's $160,000, if the judge felt the bank was entitled to it, I would have complied.

If for no other reason than it would have given me the opportunity to remind the portly barrister that the judge's decision did not, in any way, "estopp" him from stepping out in front of the courthouse and kissing my ass.

Well, what's the point of winning if you can't crow about it a little bit.

"Daddy, daddy... me go, otay?"

"Sure, you can go if you want to. I just thought you'd want me to go first...."

"Noooo!"

"Are you sure?"

I could tell by the sly grin on Whitney's face that it was beginning to dawn on her that it didn't really matter who went down the hill first. And as this realization took hold of her she charged past me like I was yesterday's news.

"Hey, I'm gonna get you."

Immediately pursuing Whitney, I rolled cautiously behind her while continuing to protest her surprise dash down the hill.

"Hey, no fair - you cheated. I was supposed to go first this time."

Convinced that she had really put one over on her old man, Whitney howled in triumph as I rolled up beside her at the bottom of the hill.

The day after Bill Ferguson informed me of the judge's decision, I received another piece of welcome news. Jack called to let me know that he had secured the money he needed to save his home. His buddy at The Peoples Bank had come through for him in spades. The king had done it again, and while the $10,000 line of credit he received from the bank was victory enough on its own, it also provided me with a little bonus as well.

Less than a minute after Jack finished telling me about his success with the bank, I was dialing the number for Masse Art Gallery. Over the previous two days I had decided to sell the Bateman prints regardless of how Jack made out at the bank. And since my cousin no longer needed the money, it was I that would be banking the $8500 these pieces had garnered.

For the first time in almost two years, I was going to have a little financial breathing room, and I used it to pull myself together, and put some feelers out in the job market.

Three weeks later, the Patriot offer came in.

I haven't seen that much of Jack lately. We still speak by phone a couple of times a week, but ever since we both started working again it's been difficult to get together.

He's going full tilt down at Flynn & Gunn, and he says things are really hopping down there. The mutual fund business is enjoying an unprecedented growth spurt, and judging by the suit Jack was wearing the last time we did hook up, I'd say he's catching his fair share of the action. He looked like he was right off the cover of *GQ* magazine.

The new suit aside, Jack still has a long way to go before his financial condition can be taken off the critical list, but at least he's moving in the right direction. Joe Friedman has filed something called an ABIL on his behalf, which should eliminate his debt with the creditor he fears the most, Revenue Canada. This ABIL (Allowable Business Investment Loss) will make the $100,000 he invested into Good Word Printing completely deductible against an equal amount of past or future income. According to Joe, once the ABIL is processed, Revenue Canada will probably owe Jack a few thousand dollars.

When he's not tied up at work, my cousin seems to spend the rest of his time with Karen Corrigan. I don't really know how serious they are about one another. She's coming off a divorce, and he's been a bachelor for a long time, so it's tough to tell where the whole thing might lead. But they do seem to get along well.

It's amazing how life can sometimes turn around on a dime.

I don't know if it's the fact he's making money again, or if it's the time he spends with Karen, but Jack sure does seem like a different person of late. He was always an upbeat and confident guy, but now he seems awfully relaxed as well. I guess he's happy. Maybe even a little bit too happy.

He called me earlier this week and told me that he was moving. He said he had put in an unconditional offer on a four bedroom house in Rosedale, and would be closing the deal within the next few days.

Listening to his surprising news, I began to congratulate him, but after hearing the word Rosedale, I started thinking - *Rosedale, how in the hell are you going to move into Rosedale? You can't buy an outhouse in that neighbourhood for less than half a million dollars.*

Jack ignored my lack of response and went on to tell me that the only way he was going to get the new place was if he acted right away. His condo would have to be put on the market immediately and he had a real estate agent coming over that night to give him an appraisal on the place.

As soon as Jack used the word appraisal I should have known something was up. But it wasn't until he asked me if I thought he might get a more favourable assessment on his apartment if he served the agent some wine, and maybe spread a little lingerie around his bed, that I realized the true purpose of his call was to give my chain a little pull.

He's a funny man my cousin, and because I know he'd never bring the matter up in front of anybody else, I laughed at Jack's story almost as hard as he did.

I didn't mind Jack kidding me about Barb. I had told him about my rendezvous with her a couple of weeks after it happened. And I knew from that moment on I was exposing myself to some future good-natured ridicule. But since we both knew that I did eventually manage to haul my ass out of Barb's apartment without completely breaking my wedding vows, it was a given that sticking it to me privately on this matter fell within the boundaries of fair play.

It has been almost four months now since I weaseled my way out of Barb's bedroom, and while I recall each detail of our near miss encounter with perfect clarity, I still don't understand how I let things get so far out of hand in the first place.

I knew the whole time I was in Barb's company that sleeping with her would be wrong, and I honestly felt, prior to my visit, that I wouldn't have any trouble keeping my hormones in check while alone with her. Yet in spite of my best efforts to resist her, at the moment I stepped forward to join Barb on the bed I had become so wired for sex that I don't think I could have stopped myself supposing Caroline was in the next room.

Christ, I was turned on. And it wasn't just Barb and her red underwear that had done it.

It was everything in the room that day. It was the lingerie and the cowboy boots, and the thought of this beautiful young girl taking the time to display them for me the way she did. It was the movement of the waterbed and the music coming from the den. It was the bottle of wine on the headboard, and the box of condoms resting so casually against it.

Nothing was turning me on more than the sight of those goddamn condoms, and I don't think I've even used one in the last fifteen years. Jesus, she'd gone out and bought a twelve pack.

I remember looking at Barb, lying so suggestively in the middle of all that lingerie, and thinking to myself that this was not a simple afternoon romp I had been invited to. It was a once in a lifetime banquet, and each of those condoms was another ticket to the food line.

I had twelve free passes to a fantasy. A fantasy I just couldn't resist. And as I crawled up beside Barb, I could feel a pressure just under my belt line that practically doubled me over in pain. Something was growing down there that belonged in some kind of Hall of Fame. It was like after going through my whole life as a size six or seven, I had suddenly become size twelve triple E.

Sexually speaking, all I could ever have wanted was right there. And it was wrapped in the most beautiful and youthful package I could ever have imagined.

But it was almost right from the moment I first kissed Barb that the fantasy started to fade, and I began to feel the vast difference between a fantasy and the reality of living it. It was as if the act of touching her had caused the clock to strike twelve. And I knew almost immediately that the awkward pecking going on between us was going to lead nowhere.

There was no longer any sense of excitement, or dreamlike

abandon in what we were doing. There was only reality, and the inescapable knowledge that what was happening between us was going to do me a hell of a lot more harm than good.

If not for the fact that I really didn't know how to stop it, this "affair" would have ended after one kiss. It was only the time I felt I would need to concoct an escape plan that necessitated a second kiss. And while kiss number two ended with no plausible excuse for leaving in sight, by the time kisses three and four had passed, whatever reason I was going to use to end this liaison had become moot.

The size twelve Hall of Famer that had led me to Barb like some short of rogue divining rod had already begun to dwindle, and was quickly heading towards the Hall of Shame.

The moment had been lost. I was experiencing full blown equipment failure, and neither my ego, nor any other power on earth was going to be able to revive him. Elvis had left the building.

"Daddy, know wha.... ?"
"No. What?"
"Know wha...?"
"No. What?"
"I yuv you"
"I love you too sweatheart. Does that mean I get to go next?"
" Nooooo."

Tumbling over backwards as Whitney pushed away from me, I remained flat on my back in order to allow her to think that she had tricked me yet again. Lifting my head I began shouting some thinly veiled protests as I watched her race back up to the top of the hill.

"Hey, no fair. You're cheating again. I'm going to get you."

Whitney's high-pitched screams were her only response, as she reached the top unescorted for the third time in a row.

She's a pretty sharp little girl and having lived all of her life with two older brothers, she's become fiercely competitive. It was now her belief that our Saturday morning game had an objective. And that the whole purpose of the exercise was to roll down the hill without allowing me to do the same.

Eager to claim victory, Whitney barely reached the crest of the hill before she dropped to her stomach and started back down again. Howling, laughing and screaming like she had just captured a new continent.

I remember leaving Barb's apartment feeling more like a cockroach than a human being, but if God did grant me one inexhaustible talent it would be the ability to justify my own actions. And in as short a time as it took to reach the cottage I had already managed to convince myself that maybe I wasn't such a bad guy after all. In fact, maybe I was an extraordinary man, a man of such high moral standards that there could easily be a sainthood in my future.

Yeah, I might have been a rat for getting so carried away with Barb in the first place, but once the situation progressed as far as it did, only a saint, like me, could have walked away from it.

Saint Hannibal. A patron who saves all men on the verge of adulterous sin, by rendering them impotent. Or something like that.

Of course in hindsight, I realize there was nothing saintly about my visit to or departure from Barb's apartment. In fact not only was there nothing saintly in my actions that day, there wasn't anything moral either. Morality had nothing to do with my decision to pull away from Barb. If it did, I don't think I'd look back on it with the odd pang of regret.

No, it was only guilt that saved me from myself that day. And while I take no satisfaction in having acted honourably out of conscience as opposed to character, I do find it comforting to realize that for once my parochial upbringing had served me well.

Guilt, the enduring burden of the middle class, and the fundamental tenet of a religion I thought I had abandoned many years ago, had reared its head to save me. Who'da figured?

Three days after my bumbling departure from Barb's apartment I returned to the city to attend Bruce Thatcher's funeral. The service was held on Thursday morning and I drove back from the cottage to say my final goodbye to Bruce fully confident that I had come to terms with his death. I was still sad about it, but after hearing the circumstances of his childhood I had been able to rationalize why the whole thing had happened.

Arriving at the church I still felt more or less at peace and it wasn't until I stepped inside and saw his coffin that I realized there was a lot more to grieving a friend than simply rationalizing why he died.

Just the sight of the brown box that would house Bruce's

remains for eternity left me feeling numb all over. It was like for the first time since I heard about his death a real sense of loss was setting in. I was finally starting to understand that Bruce was gone, and he wasn't coming back.

I don't remember hearing a single word offered at the service. I was too lost in my own thoughts to follow what anyone else was saying. But I do remember standing at the grave, still so numb I purposely refused to say a private goodbye to Bruce as he was lowered into the ground. I guess after having denied myself any real emotional response to his death, when it came time to bury him, I wasn't ready to bid him farewell.

I spent the next day taking care of a few small business matters that had to be addressed before I could head back to the cottage. There was some paperwork to sign at Bill Ferguson's office, and I had to pick up a cheque from Sean Masse, as well as tend to some other small banking matters. All of which was handled without incident. But while on the outside I was carrying out the functions of a perfectly normal day, inside I was becoming morbidly preoccupied not only with Bruce, but also with the whole concept of time, and how quickly it passes.

I was becoming afraid again, not so much of death, but of the uncertainty of life. And I almost slipped back into the same funk that had been smothering me for the previous three years.

After wasting so much time worrying about cars and condos and office buildings, and a whole lot of other bullshit that never should have mattered to me, now that I had put all that behind me, I suddenly felt I needed to know that I was going to have enough time to put everything else back together.

I needed to know that I was going to be given the time that people like Ed Flanagan were never granted and that Bruce Thatcher didn't think he needed. I had to know that my own time was not going to expire before it was supposed to. I felt like I needed some sort of divine guarantee in order to carry on.

Three days after the funeral, and after twice postponing my return to the cottage, I took a drive down to the city's Beaches district. It had been several years since I'd stopped by the old neighbourhood, and for some reason I just wanted to see it again.

It took about twenty minutes to arrive on the street that I had thought would turn the clock back three decades, but as soon as I arrived, I was immediately struck by how different everything looked. I'm not sure why its dramatic change in appearance surprised me so. It's not like I was expecting to see Paul and Neil Hillman standing on the road organizing a hockey game, or anything like that. It's just that I wasn't expecting to see such a ghost town either.

There was nothing going on, and this lack of activity made the street seem so different from the one I had once known so well. It was Sunday morning, and there was no hockey game, no baseball game, nor any other sign of street activity. The only evidence of life was some gardening activities being carried on by a number of the street's middle-aged occupants. And it was being done on the front lawns of houses I no longer even recognized.

The neighbourhood had become much more affluent than it was when I was a child, and most of the houses had gone through extensive renovations. The entire block looked like it had been sand blasted, flagstoned, and interlocked.

Jim Scott's old house now appeared to be some sort of a space-age palace. The old Hillman place had taken on the look of a museum. And the Thatcher home, being the most obvious victim of 1980's architectural mischief, was now twice its original size, and looked like it had been rebuilt to withstand a nuclear assault.

Stepping out of the car, I didn't feel overly connected to this strange setting, and as I passed unaffected by the many homes in which I had once been a welcomed visitor, I realized that this feeling was unlikely to change.

Even as I walked up to old number fifty-four, I felt no great attachment to my former home. It wasn't that the place had changed all that much. Aside from a new paint job, and the fact that it seemed much smaller, my old home looked very much like I remembered it. It's just that the nondescript front door I had pushed through so many thousands of times as a kid was now somebody else's door, and had been for almost twenty-five years.

Too much time had passed, and it wasn't long after I started walking through my former neighbourhood that I began to feel a little bit like an intruder. This wasn't my space anymore and I could tell by their subtle glances that my survey of the area was making some of the local homeowners a little nervous.

Stopping in front of Jack's old place it was becoming clear to me that whatever I was trying to find in my old stomping grounds no longer existed. Whatever it was the last couple of days had caused me to feel I needed in my life, I wasn't going to find it in my past.

It wasn't until I took one final look around before heading back to the Lexus that my eyes came upon a sight that struck a familiar chord in me.

It was the old Watson home, and it hadn't changed a bit. I didn't know if Phil Watson still lived there but I could see a small man sitting up on the front porch, and just out of curiosity I started to walk towards him.

Approaching the house, just out of habit, I kept a very watchful eye on the front lawn. The wily Oggy would have to be forty to still be alive, but I was taking no chances. However, just as I started to cross the street, any fear of Oggy Watson instantly faded away. The small man sitting on the front porch turned out to be an old Chinese woman.

Damn, not only could I not find a happy memory on my old street, I couldn't even find a bad one.

But just around the time I turned away from the Watson home, I was overtaken by an unmistakable sense of deja vu. Standing in the middle of the intersection, I was surprised to find that there was a small crack in the mask of time and I had stepped through it when I arrived at what had been "centre ice" in this neighbourhood a generation ago.

In the span of a heartbeat it was 1965 again, and wave after wave of the most vivid memories began rolling through my mind. All of a sudden I was eight years old again, and not long into this surprising return to my past, I thought of "the goal".

Walking over to where Bruce Thatcher had scored the only ball hockey goal of his career, I stood in the middle of the street and relived the moment. I could see it all so clearly - Jack taking the original shot - Blair Malone making the save - the collision - and the green ball sitting all by itself in front of the open net.

It seemed like it was happening all over again. And as my mind celebrated the vision of a ten-year-old tapping a ball into an empty net, I found myself wondering if Bruce remembered the goal he scored that day as well as I did. Or if it was something he had forgotten many years ago?

In all the time that had passed since it happened we had

never really discussed it. But because I suspected Bruce would recall the moment with perfect clarity, I suddenly felt as though I had found a proper place from which to say goodbye to him.

I'm sure that to the neighbours who saw me standing quietly in the middle of the road with my head bowed I must have looked like a poster child for the chemically imbalanced. It's not often you see a man offer a moment of prayer to a piece of asphalt, and I'm sure that the old Chinese woman was wishing that I would get the hell out of her neighbourhood. But as I asked whoever it is that watches over us to take care of my friend Bruce, I could hear the sounds of our childhood whistling through the trees above me, and for that moment I couldn't have felt more at home.

"Daddy, cashh me. Otay? Daddy, cashh me."
"What? No. I can't catch you. You're too big."
"Daddeee…"

As per usual, our morning rolling activities were ending with Whitney doing a number of kamikaze runs down the hill, which end with a death-defying leap into my arms.

It's a natural evolution of our original game. Once the thrill goes out of rolling, my daughter gets more adventurous and starts charging down the hill at breakneck speed.

Whitney knew that my protests were not to be taken seriously. She was perfectly aware that I was able to catch her and without giving my warning a second thought she lowered her head and started barrelling towards me.

Looking back at it, I'm glad I dropped by the old neighbourhood, and found a comfortable spot to say goodbye to Bruce. It didn't help me find any of the guarantees I'd been searching for, and it certainly didn't provide me with any clues as to what it is I'm suppose to be doing here on this earth. But I do know that after being there, I felt a lot better as I drove up to the cottage.

I guess it helped bring closure to all of the things that had happened that week. And within hours of being reunited with my family, everything seemed to be returning to normal.

Ten days later we packed up the cottage for the last time, and turned the keys over to its new owner. It wasn't an easy thing to do, but as I took Caroline and the kids for one final cruise around the lake, I didn't feel as though I was losing anything important.

In the time that has passed since we packed up the cottage, life has been pretty good to me and my family. It isn't a fairy tale or anything like that. I still have my moments when I can't believe I have to work twelve hours day in order to put bread on the table, just so I can wake up the next morning and start all over again.

There are definitely times when the endless grind of commuting, and meetings, and seminars, as well as the constant selling can make me feel like my life isn't going anywhere.

Yet more often than not, I realize that these daily frustrations are only a footnote to my existence.

Over time I have come to realize that, in most ways, my life can be as easy or as difficult as I want to make it. And on the days when I choose to make it easy, I can see that my true fortune was never to be found in the material wealth I acquired in the eighties.

The true source of my abundant wealth has always been that I have forever been blessed with all of the things that give life meaning. And never was this more evident than it was last night.

A number of years ago I started buying season tickets for the Toronto Blue Jays and while I now have to sell most of them as soon as they come in, I keep the playoff tickets for myself.

About a month ago I approached my sons and promised them that if the Blue Jays made the play-offs, I'd take each of them to a game. One game, and they could pick which one it would be.

Shane, the younger of the two, decided instantly that he would take the first available ticket. He was leaving nothing to chance. He wanted to see a play-off game, and he wanted to see one before his brother did.

Michael, being a year older, and a bit more astute in gauging the significance of each game, decided that he would pass on the playoff round, and wait to see if the Jays made the World Series. And when they did, he pressed his luck even further and decided to pass on game one and two in the hopes that the Series would make it back to Toronto, where he would attend Game Six.

So that's where we were last night, the ballpark. Where my son witnessed one of the truly great moments in the history of baseball, and I witnessed something that, to me, will always be a miracle.

It happened at about 11:40 p.m., when a true gentleman from the American mid-west stepped up to the plate and with one swing of the bat carved out a place in history for himself and sent fifty thousand electrified fans into the sporting equivalent of a twenty minute orgasm.

We had won it again. This tragically image-conscious city, which so desperately yearns for US acceptance as a "world class" metropolis, had claimed America's game for the second year in a row. And the party was on.

It was a thrilling moment, even for one such as I, who doesn't really care that much for the grand old game. Baseball is a game of such tradition that its supporters see a mythology in it that holds it apart from other sports. But while I think I understand the game more than most of my fellow season-ticket holders, (most of whom would believe that a Baltimore chop is a style of pork) I can't help but feel I'm missing something every time I watch it. Because mostly, it bores me.

I suppose you'd have to be an American to really love the game. Maybe it has to be in your blood, like hockey is in mine, before you can fully appreciate what it's all about. However, my general ambivalence to the sport notwithstanding, after the moment it brought to my life last night I shall be forever in its debt.

The Blue Jay's dramatic come-from-behind victory will stay with my son forever. And in years to come he will tell countless people, including his children and his children's children, that he was there, live and in person, the night Joe Carter hit the shot of the century. And when he tells the story, the most important part of it will not be the home run itself, but who took him to the ballpark so that he could see it.

I know this to be true, because I saw it in his face.

As Mr Carter and the rest of the players danced triumphantly around the bases, my son saw none of it. He was too busy looking at me, trying to fully understand what he had just seen.

"Did you see it, Dad? Did you? I think that means we won. Dad, did we? Did we win?"

Pulling my son up into my arms, a simple nod was all Michael needed as confirmation of victory, and when I delivered it, he threw his arms around me like I'd hit the home run myself.

He clung to me for several seconds, before pulling his head back, and through star filled eyes, gushed,

"Ahhh Dad!... Can you believe it?... Can you?"

And as the euphoria in his words filled the slight space between our faces, I could see that Michael was living a moment he would never forget, and that he was experiencing a happiness, the likes of which it may never again be in my power to grant him.

It was just a moment between a father and his son, but it taught me as much about what I'm doing on this planet as I had learned in the past twenty years. And it helped me realize something.

As I've gotten older I've had to accept the fact that my life is not going to be many of the things I might have once hoped for.

I'm never going to host the Tonight Show. I'm never going to win the Stanley Cup, or be the heavyweight champion of the world. And that $50,000,000 I once dreamed about is sure starting to look like a long shot.

But as I sit peacefully in the long grass of a miraculous autumn day, watching my two-year-old daughter come charging down the hill at me one more time, all I can hear is the sweet sound of her innocent laughter as she throws her arms out to embrace me. And it fills my head with only one thought.

It's something I've been thinking about a lot lately... What a great day to be alive.